KING'S TREASURE

LARGE PRINT

MARIE JOHNSTON

LE PUBLISHING

 Created with Vellum

Broke, jobless, and stranded in Las Vegas on Valentine's Day, I am forced to call my parents for a bailout. Again. A pampered princess and wannabe environmentalist, I know I'm a cliché and would do anything to change it. So when I meet Xander, a struggling photojournalist with absolutely nothing in common with my domineering, millionaire parents, I know just where to go next:

A wedding chapel.

But when I wake up the next day, my matrimonial rebellion comes with an unpleasant surprise. My husband is no penniless globetrotter—Xander King is the son of a billionaire oil tycoon, and my parents couldn't approve of the match more. Now the only thing that could shock them would be a quickie divorce…except my new husband has a proposition for me.

I take one look at Savvy and know I could spend the rest of my life with her. The feeling is mutual…until she figures out who I am. I didn't mean to hide my identity, and I thought a desire to get out from under the weight of familial baggage was something we had in common. But with Savvy just moments from proposing divorce, I offer her the one thing I'd been ready to walk away from:

A hundred million dollars.

All Savvy has to do is stay married to me for a year and then she'll get half of my trust fund—except I have no intention of letting her go after 365 days. I've spent a decade running from my father's disapproval and my brothers' successes. Now I'm willing to spend a lifetime convincing the woman I love to stay put by my side.

For all the latest news, sneak peeks, quarterly short stories, and free material sign up for my newsletter.

CHAPTER 1

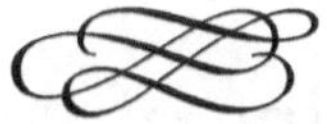

avvy

ENERGY-SUCKING neon lights lit the night sky around me. Our destination was ahead. The Venetian towered in front of us in all its refined glory. Walls of glass windows. A fake canal. Oodles of water that were both decoration and recreation, making tourists forget they were in the middle of the desert.

My environmentalist brain wanted to calculate the sheer waste displayed along the Strip, but I stopped before I could summon actual numbers. My career goal was to bridge the divide between extreme change and *please, just do anything to help the earth.*

Others in my line of work were quickly dismissed by big companies like those that filled this desert oasis. They wanted consultants with reputations as large as theirs who charged more than anyone in my entry-level position would make in a lifetime. But my last name, Abbot, could at least make some corporations stop and listen. Between my father's security consulting agency and the obnoxious wealth of my mother's side of the family, I was a foot in the door.

Which explained the last-minute work trip to Las Vegas with my coworker and best friend, Brady. I'd wedge us in and keep the door open long enough for him to charm the execs with our nonprofit's spiel: *Saving Sunsets is the bridge between the bottom line and the world outside. With our expertise, we can save the environment and save you money.*

Simple. Generic. But it was meant to get us a place at the conference table. Our knowledge and revolutionary ideas were supposed to take it from there. But since I'd started working for them shortly after they opened their doors, we hadn't had much opportunity to consult. Brady and I were in our mid-twenties and a lot of CEOs doubted we had experience in anything but beer pong. Most days, my job resembled an annoying telemarketer's. *Hello, we haven't had a chance to talk to you about your car warranty.*

One more block. Tourists meandered past us, mostly couples in some form of foreplay. Hearts in their eyes, hands down each other's pants. I didn't expect to find anything different in Vegas on Valentine's Day, but their footwear looked more comfortable than mine. I hadn't packed my humanely manufactured heels and instead grabbed a cheap pair that imitated something Mother would wear, along with one of her silk blouses. The shirt was comfortable, but my toes were pinched and throbbing. Too bad we didn't have the same shoe size. What I wouldn't give to wear my Toms.

Can you maybe. . . not?

Bernard's hesitant hand-wringing when he approached me about what I wore to these meetings ran through my mind. My boss was all about environmentalism, unless he thought it'd cost our fledgling and perpetually struggling nonprofit potential business. I wore my eco-friendly slip-ons, fair-labor cotton shirts, and secondhand skirts around the office; a hole-in-the-wall space in a strip mall on the outskirts of Washington, DC. But, away from the office when I met clients, I was the girl I was raised to be. I wore designer labels I hoped no one noticed were several seasons out of style.

My family was in the one percent, but I was expected to make my own way, aside from the room and board they were helping me with. And I needed their help. They'd made that perfectly clear.

When Bernard hired me, he nearly fainted when he'd learned I didn't come with my family's wallet.

I guess we'll have to do some fundraising. . . or something.

Brady was in charge of the 'or something.' I was the affluent face of the company and Bernard was supposed to be the brains, but with each passing month, I wondered how our doors stayed open. The guy couldn't sort his own recycling.

This trip was a prime example. Instead of doing a virtual meeting with the owner and CEO of King Oil, Bernard had flown me and Brady in coach to Las Vegas. Gentry King didn't live or work in Las Vegas. The oil tycoon was from Montana. He'd raised his four boys there and he still worked there with his new wife, who also happened to be his assistant.

I knew all this because I'd researched his

company. I'd uncovered everything I could about King Oil and the portfolio of environmental issues they championed, encouraging their investors to dive deep into their pockets.

Bernard wanted Saving Sunsets to be part of that portfolio. Badly. As soon as he'd found out Mr. King was in Las Vegas, he'd begged for an interview and booked our room and tickets. To be fair to Bernard, if we could land an account like King Oil and earn some credibility, the nonprofit would live to see another sunrise. But my carbon footprint for the year was growing at an alarming rate, thanks to the cross-country trip.

"These shoes are killing me."

"You should've just worn your vegan shoes." Brady strolled next to me with his tie loose and his suit jacket hanging open. Like me, he came from money, but unlike me, his parents had cut him off as soon as he'd veered off the politics path. In contrast, my parents had opened their doors when I'd come limping back home after four years of college, during which I had struggled to do my own laundry and feed myself. Brady, however, had found some roommates and supported himself.

The guy joked around like he didn't take this job seriously, but he did. It was a stepping stone for both of us. Bigger and better things were ahead. The only problem was that neither of us knew where to step next, and sticking with Saving Sunsets was starting to feel like clinging to the side of a capsizing ship.

Brady glanced down at my feet. "Something tells me a guy born and raised in Montana isn't going to know Jimmy Choos from Famous Footwear."

"Tell Bernard that," I muttered, wishing I'd stayed true to myself, or that these were really Jimmy Choos. "We should get there early and have time to practice our pitch."

Mr. King was here for pleasure, but since it was easier for people to get to Vegas, he stayed longer to do business. As much as I wanted to dislike someone who spearheaded an oil company that fracked and drilled all over the earth, Mr. King seemed to keep the environment in mind. King Oil funded two wind energy projects and at least one solar energy farm. Turning his trip to Vegas into business was something Saving Sunsets would recommend: streamline travel and save all parties involved more time and money. It was more than I'd expected out of someone in his position, but exactly what I'd hoped to find.

Bernard was beside himself with excitement. Which wasn't unusual. My boss was kind of flighty. I didn't know how he got away with being the CEO, but I guess since the board was made up of his brother-in-law and his childhood dentist, he got to make decisions that would otherwise be questionable. Like the pricey electric car with Saving Sunsets' logo painted on the sides. *It's a write-off.*

I could think of several better ways to

use that money, including a raise. It was kind of my job.

Despite Bernard's questionable example, we tried to keep the environment in mind. Walking between hotels was a better idea than an Uber.

I'd kill for an Uber right now.

My phone buzzed. Since we were early, I stopped and pulled it out of my Saving Sunsets canvas tote. "Hold on. It's Bernard." I slid to the edge of the sidewalk to answer. A tongue-tangling couple with shirts that read *Just Married* almost ran into Brady, but he sidestepped them to stand by me. "Hey."

"Sapphire." Bernard's harried voice filtered through the line. He was usually worked up about something, but this had me shooting a concerned look at Brady.

"Is everything okay?"

"No. *Ohmigosh.* No. I had no idea. I mean, he married my sister, you'd think he'd be more compassionate. I'm *so* sorry."

"For what?" Like most conversations

with Bernard, I wanted to scream, *Get to the point!*

"The board just met and shut us down."

"Excuse me?"

"Shut. Us. Down."

I struggled to follow what Bernard said on a good day, but this was startlingly clear. "But. . . but. . .how?"

"Money, Sapphire Jewel. The meeting with King Oil was my Hail Mary, but the board won't give me another chance."

"The president is your brother-in-law." I put it on speaker for Brady to hear. Our heads tipped close to hear our doom.

"He said, and I quote, 'Too many damn chances for a flake like you.' I should've never trusted him. My sister never had good taste. I'm sorry. The meeting is canceled."

I exchanged a look with Brady. We'd studied our asses off for this meeting. We'd figured out a way to pitch Saving Sunsets and how we could help King Oil provide education to its investors. We had ideas that could cut twenty years off King Oil's pledge to be carbon neutral by 2050. All for nothing?

"So we're going home? Can you send the flight information?" Brady asked. He hated being in suits and bitched about big cities like Vegas. Yet he and I both still lived in DC. Saving money from Saving Sunsets' paychecks was difficult at best, but job hunting for two rich kids with no experience in the environmental field had been harder than each of us had anticipated. We'd chosen to build our resumes, but it didn't look like Saving Sunsets was going to help with that.

"*Brady*," Bernard keened. "They cut off the money. I can't get you tickets."

My eyes flared and I stared at my friend. "The hotel?" Bernard had gotten a suite with two rooms—an expensive one, as an apology for the last-minute late nights we'd spent cramming before flying out.

"Sapphire Jewel, I'm so sorry, my hands

are tied." His breath hitched dramatically and I could picture his hands flailing.

"Bernard, money doesn't just run out," Brady said evenly. "How long has the company been in trouble?"

All Bernard's last-minute meetings and travel, his new car, and the eco-friendly suit he'd boasted was locally crafted and hand-tailored flashed through my mind. Why hadn't I seen it before?

"Wha— I can't—" Fake static came through the line.

Brady leaned closer. "What about our last paychecks—"

"Bad connect—" The line went dead.

I blinked at the phone.

"I can't believe he did that." Brady spun around, hands on his hips. "Slimy bastard. How am I going to make rent this month?"

"I'll never be able to move out of my parents' house." I shouldn't be worried about that when I was stranded in Las-freaking-Vegas. "How are we going to get home?"

He shoved a hand through his dark hair. "I don't have any cash and my card is at the limit." He blew out a breath and leveled his knowing gaze on me.

"No." I scowled, shaking my head. "No. He already thinks I'm helpless and he'll do nothing but say I told you so."

"Savvy. It's our only option. You know my parents won't help."

"Brady." We were at an impasse. It was either call my father or walk home. We couldn't afford a bus ticket across town, much less across the country. I'd gladly pay for the bus fare if I could. It'd cost less than whatever life lesson my father would teach me. "Fine."

I could call Mother, but she had less compassion when I was in a tough spot than my father. She wouldn't have let me move home if Father hadn't talked her into giving me a chance to job hunt and save money. *You don't want the girl to end up like that poor friend of hers, living in a fetid box with others who have God knows what morals.*

Brady's roommates were nice enough and his apartment wasn't fetid. It had. . . a *smell*, but with five guys and three bedrooms, it could be worse. It wasn't the other guys, or the tiny space they resided in, it was that they lived one unexpected bill away from being homeless.

I didn't want to be in that position again. I'd had my own little rebellions over the years and they'd all failed miserably. I'd made it through college with massive debt, using my last name to accrue too many loans, and it was nothing less than anyone expected. I was impulsive, a pampered little Sapphire.

"Sapphire," Chief answered, his gruff tone not the comfort I wanted in the moment.

"Hey, Chief." My oldest sister, Emerald, had coined the term and I think he liked it. Instead of Dad, he was Chief. "I, um. . ."

"Confidence, Sapphire. If you don't speak with it, everyone will know you don't have it." Said as if I didn't have any.

He was right, but only because I had been raised by a family who questioned every decision I made. I hated proving them right. I sucked in a breath and let the story pour out, every humiliating detail. The lack of transportation funds, the hotel room, and that Brady was stuck with me.

My family didn't hate Brady. Once it'd become clear he and I didn't have the chemistry needed to date, they tolerated him, and they helped us if we needed it. Like when Bernard had been two weeks late with our paychecks and Brady was going to get kicked out. I'd asked Chief for a cash advance—for both of us. And I'd paid it back—with interest.

It's an important life lesson, Sapphire. Money isn't free. You have to contribute. That usually meant a weekend or two helping Chief out in his office, on top of my regular job.

"Savvy," he said, exasperation gusting my name out. "What if you couldn't call me? What would you do?" He didn't wait for my answer. I didn't have one and I was fighting anxiety. Was this when I'd get cut off again? Left stranded? "It just so happens that I'm heading to Vegas."

"You are?" I looked up at Brady and he cocked his head.

"King Oil was able to rearrange their schedule for a last-minute meeting." Chief chuckled, and it was full of all the derision I'd known was coming. "Now, I know why."

I closed my eyes. Would the humiliation ever end? Bernard's epic fuckup was Chief's gain. He'd never let me forget this.

"He's agreed to meet me for lunch tomorrow. I've been trying to get his account for years. I'd like you to be there."

My eyes flew open. "Why?"

Mr. King had no idea who I was, and Chief wouldn't want to explain that I was the account that had dropped out last minute because the owner was too flighty to run a business.

"You need a job, don't you? You still

have school loans, or do you have a plan to pay those off? You can start tomorrow."

I hated working in his security consulting company. The place sucked the life out of me. Chief was old school and had refused my insights on ways to go paperless. Instead, I had been given a yellow legal pad and a box of Bics. Then, he'd scowled at me when I'd dropped the box of pens in the middle of a meeting with a new client. Everyone had stared over their laptop screens at me while I'd picked up every pen and put them back in the box. "Chief—"

"And Lexington will be there."

"Lex?"

"You remember him, of course."

Chief tried to throw me in Lex's path like I was the rare sapphire that Lex couldn't live without. It didn't help that Lex was interested and constantly flirted with me. A man like Chief was the last guy I wanted to marry. Brady and I had joked about getting married to throw Chief off his game, but Chief had left me alone the last few months.

I should've known. He loved Lex. *A wonderful addition to the firm. He was in military intelligence, you know. He comes from a good family.* In Chief speak, that meant Lex's family had money. Unlike me, Lex probably had his own money.

And he had all the arrogance to show for it. I didn't want a husband like my sister Em's. Chief had set her up with another guy just like Lex, who happened to be just like Chief. He thought lightning could strike twice, but the last thing I wanted was a stilted marriage like Em's, one that paralleled my parents' way too close for comfort.

Em was a housewife, like Mother. She spent her days managing the house staff, planning soirees, and volunteering at any prestigious event that'd make her and her husband, Carter, look good. Mother had her own money, but Chief was in charge of the finances. Em was dependent on the allowance Carter gave her.

Was it wrong to try for more than that? As often as I got smacked down, it seemed like it.

"I remember Lex, but—"

"Sapphire. I'm flying to Vegas to bail you and your friend out—again. It's time you grow up. You'll be at lunch tomorrow and you'll talk to Lex, and when we return home, you'll work for me."

"Only until I get on my feet," I said sullenly.

"Sure."

My teeth ground together. He didn't think I could do it. The call ended and I filled Brady in on what Chief had said.

He whistled. "Tough blow." His grin spread wide. "Until then, I'm partying in Vegas on Abbot money."

I rolled my eyes. As tempting as that was, I had to prove Chief wrong. I was one more screwup away from being kicked out.

I couldn't waste time. "I think I might look for a job or something."

"We're in Vegas, baby. It's Valentine's Day. Let's party."

Brady was an opportunistic playboy. I avoided men like Chief but somehow ended up with guys like Brady. Somewhere between Peter Pan syndrome and commitment-phobe. That was the spectrum of men in my life.

But I wasn't here to date. I had the rest of the afternoon and the evening to prove Chief wrong. He thought I'd give up, marry Lex, and have little babies with buzz cuts who'd grow up and work at Abbot Security.

I wasn't that girl.

The Venetian dominated this block and spelled out *love* with its windows, as if the whole city was on the Chief's side. While I waited for him to transfer money to my account, I would have to do something drastic to show him who I really was.

IT WAS a good thing I hadn't told Chief what I was trying to do. Finding a career-advancing job in one afternoon in a city I didn't live in and hadn't planned on job hunting in wasn't my best idea. But there I was, wandering down the Strip back to my hotel.

Brady had messaged me and told me not to disturb his room because he had a guest. The guy worked fast. Good thing I had my own room in the suite. I'd have to fire up my laptop and keep searching.

My feet hurt. My head ached. And I was desperate.

A group of people dancing behind a woman holding a sign blocked my path. I slowed. I was close to my hotel. Which also meant I was close to the hotel I was supposed to have had the meeting of my career in. How awesome to get stalled at the scene of my latest failure in life.

Instead of pitching a project I was passionate about, I was going to meet Gentry King and impress him with my ability to take notes for Chief. I'd done so much research, dammit! When I learned that oil companies hired environmentalists, I'd been over the moon. Finally, I could work with a company where I did more than make a slide show telling their employees to recycle and turn their lights off.

King Oil didn't just talk about pro-climate business practices, they modeled them. King Oil headquarters was LEED certified. They hired companies that captured natural gas instead of flaring it into the atmosphere. They invested in alternative energy projects, and they adopted energy-efficient practices. I could be part of major change instead of saving a few square feet in the landfill by using a refillable water bottle, all in an industry that had a reputation for resisting any green practices. It would be a huge ego boost after the way my parents had tried to talk me out of my environmental science degree.

But I'd be sitting on the sidelines taking notes. On paper. Then, Chief would want a copy typed up. And more copies made and distributed.

I watched the group ahead of me. It was a walking tour of the Strip. The gaggle of women had stepped out of a '60s catalog, with gauzy shirts that revealed more than they covered, and bell bottoms more up to date than their vintage counterparts. Beneath their flower crowns, some of the women had long, frizzy hair that resembled mine. I'd finally let mine out of its tight bun, and if I hadn't flat ironed it this morning, it'd frizz just like that.

They danced and twirled, their arms held to the sky as they laughed and giggled. It was like a Valley Girl's reenactment of Woodstock. A little too much peace and love, not enough knowledge about the whys.

One had her flip-flops in her hand, braver than I was to walk barefoot on the concrete. Two others were hanging on each other, nuzzling necks and sneaking kisses. Of the two guys in the group, one had his mouth smashed on another flower girl's throat, but they somehow managed to keep up with the group.

The barefoot one waved to a passing man, who gave them a wide arc and shoved his hands in his pockets like he was afraid they'd grab him and incorporate him. "Your energy is bright, my friend."

He shot her an incredulous look and rushed past.

That was how my family saw me. Naively idealistic. Young and innocent and incapable, like a floppy-eared puppy. At home, I dressed like them. My family looked at me like that tourist had responded to news that his energy was bright.

Movement on the outer edges of the group only fueled my irritation. I was stranded in Vegas unemployed and struggling to be independent of my parents' money. It was bad enough my father would arrive shortly to witness me at my worst. And there were these tourists being followed by a photographer, no doubt capturing their most cringeworthy moments too. Like Chief, this photographer would make an example of how their best intentions weren't enough for the "real world."

He crouched, his camera aimed at the group blessing their way down the Strip. He brushed shaggy, dark brown hair off his forehead as he shoved a large camera to his eye. His folded legs were long and his biceps flexed through his hemp hoodie. His wide chest was on display, thanks to the camera bag slung low over his torso. Faded blue jeans hugged his thighs and broke over cowboy boots.

Just some dude taking pictures of beautiful women? No. I didn't know much about camera equipment, but the one he held looked serious. The lens was as big as a pomelo. He crouched, twisting himself into a pretzel to get the right angle. He was no amateur.

His half smile and the way his eyes narrowed on the group resembled the cynical grins of the older tourists passing by.

Protectiveness rose. Was he going to do some puff-piece making fun of the people here? That was how everyone in my life saw me, how they rolled their eyes when I inquired about the free-range status of the eggs I ate, or the pesticides used to grow the fruits and vegetables in the juice I drank. This man was going to immortalize that derision in photographs for others to make fun of.

My heart raced. No one from the group had noticed him, and if they did, they wouldn't care. *I* cared. I cared way too deeply and that had always gotten me in trouble. I didn't know how this would play out, but I had to stop it. I was in danger of acting before thinking, a crime my parents too often accused me of, but I'd run him out of Vegas before I let him make this crowd feel small.

~

Xander

I REFOCUSED and took another shot, the neon lights around us filtering down onto the men and women dancing their way down the Strip. I caught two with their hands in the air, one in a skirt that twirled around her ankles, her flip-flops held high in the air like an offering to the gods of Vegas. Highlights in her hair caught the reds and yellows of the glowing signs lining the sidewalk, giving her an ethereal quality.

"Praise Mother Earth," one of the women called over the tour guide's fact-dispensing speech.

Those people stood out among the other tourists roaming the night. Valentine's Day in Vegas. For a day all about spreading love, people here were surprisingly isolated. Couples walked hand in hand, or somehow even closer, absorbed in each other and oblivious to the spectacle around them. Some singles walked by too, hands tucked into their pockets, gazes never meeting. But everyone, coupled up or single or giggling in a group, kept firmly in their bubbles. Maybe they were avoiding their family like me. Maybe they had a birthday in two days that was a milestone for all the wrong reasons. Maybe they'd made excuses like I had to get out of a family dinner and sink into some blissful anonymity.

I didn't know what they were thinking, but those hippie tourists felt different. They didn't ignore the people around them. They weren't oblivious. They were ignored or ridiculed in return, but they persevered, their self-confidence winning every time.

Their free love for the world made me forget about the questions Dad had peppered me with and the way I'd avoided answering them. He asked about Grams's persistent hounding, about what my twenty-ninth birthday meant, and about my much more successful siblings.

I'd ditched my brother's anniversary dinner, changed clothes, and grabbed my camera. The city was full of inspiration. I should be able to get a few pictures that reaffirmed my life's decision. Then this group had danced by and I'd wanted some of their unfettered happiness. I wanted to capture it in my lens and somehow take some for myself, to forget that I was two days away from being noncompliant with my trust fund.

I clenched my jaw and snapped a few more shots. There was a couple making out like they were going to meld into the same person. I didn't focus on them—it seemed too intrusive, but I could include their desire in my pictures. My mind worked over various angles and how to utilize the shadows from the man-made lighting. My pulse thrummed. I hadn't had the drive to take pictures for years. A big issue for a photojournalist. Well, a *wannabe* photojournalist no one wanted to buy stories from.

What had Mama always said? *Don't assume a hobby makes good business. You have to be good at business first, and be damn sure that half the appeal of your hobby isn't that it makes you forget about business.*

When I was a kid, I had no clue what Mama meant, but I got it now. The hustle of trying to make money from my photos had sucked a lot of the joy out of taking them.

But something about this wild and free group that gave zero shits about what everyone thought of them prancing down the Strip made me want to focus that energy through my lens and see if I could absorb it.

My phone was going crazy but I left it tucked into my pocket. If it were my brothers, I couldn't trust that they weren't trying to lure me into Grams's web just to be dicks. If it was my dad, I'd rather continue avoiding him and the insinuations that I'd been freeloading all over the world for the last ten years.

It didn't help that Dad was kinda right, but I was also trying to make my mark. As it was, people only listened to me when they realized who my father was. Even then, they didn't listen for long. Big Oil meant evil in most of the circles I tried to sell my work.

I'd started using a pseudonym, but that was like starting over. My middle name and Mama's maiden name didn't open doors like my real name, but it didn't get those doors slammed in my face as often as my real name did.

My phone finally went silent. My family should be used to my voicemail. I changed the aperture on my camera and refocused.

"You think that's funny?" A voice as smooth as warm brandy washed over me. I didn't look at the speaker. I didn't have to—my mind filled in the pieces. A strong woman. Formidable. Determined and gorgeous. Dad had always said I was half in a fantasy world, and I was willing to stay there a little longer and listen to the mystery woman talk.

I lowered my camera and scanned the group. They were moving farther away and taking my inspiration with them. Would I ever get it back? "What do I think is funny?"

"Young people trying to make the world a better place. Take your hack fluff piece and go find a real story."

Hack fluff piece. She thought I was a journalist? The irony was, I hadn't made the jump to legitimate professional, but she was upset thinking I was someone I tried hard to be. Mystery Woman took me more seriously than my own family did.

I kept my gaze forward, my camera loose in my hands, and remained squatting, enjoying the hostility in her tone. I shouldn't egg her on, but I couldn't help it. "I'd have to figure out how they were helping the world before I had any material for an article."

"They obviously care about the earth."

"Doesn't mean they're helping it."

She sputtered and I chuckled.

"Relax. My camera is a judgment-free zone. They made me want to take a picture, so here I am, taking a picture."

"You aren't a journalist?"

"Photojournalist."

"But you aren't doing a piece on them?"

"If I were, I'd have to interview them first. They could be a bachelorette party for all I know. I'm mostly interested in how their energy makes me feel, not how much alcohol they've had." I released my camera to hang from its strap around my neck and finally looked up.

Damn. The voice hadn't prepared me for the face. Glittering, deep blue eyes flared wide when our gazes met. Her golden-blond hair hung over one shoulder, catching the glow of the neon light, giving her a soft halo that was at odds with her sharp suit and heels.

I rose, using the movement to look her over. She was too fine to look away. Her posture went from rigid to unsure. She kept her arms crossed but stepped back. I tensed with the desire to close the distance. Something about this woman told me that I wouldn't come across another like her, and I wanted to make the moment last. But I towered over her a few inches. I refused to intimidate her by crowding her.

She glanced at the tourists. One of them was blowing kisses to everyone who passed and telling them to treat the earth as if it were as precious as their iPhone. "So, you're not making fun of them?"

"No. I happened to be in the area and had my camera. Do you know who they are?" I'd ask if she was with them, but her outfit was the opposite of theirs. I could picture it though. This woman with bare feet, traipsing in and around people, her long hair free and streaming behind her.

I had a good imagination. Besides her hair, she was dressed for power, not saving the environment.

"No. But I like their vibe and I know it's one a lot of people make fun of." Her gaze flicked around. Other than the tourists wandering farther away, she and I were alone on the sidewalk.

I took the camera from around my neck and flicked a few buttons, pulling one of my photos up on the display. It was okay for an on-the-go picture, but not one of my best. I didn't know what my best was anymore.

If I'd finished my degree, maybe I'd have more insight instead of just guessing.

If I'd finished college, maybe I'd have a job that'd allow me to upgrade my equipment.

The woman's stunning blue eyes turned molten when she viewed the picture. The way I adjusted the shutter speed made the lights twinkle, casting a surreal glow onto the crowd. They looked like wood nymphs trying to heal Sin City.

Those lush pink lips of hers parted. "That's really good."

"Glad you think so." I'd like to be more enthused, but all I could see was how much the final image fell short of my vision. I needed a better camera, but that wouldn't happen for a long time.

She looked up from the display. "Who do you work for?"

"I freelance, but not a lot of people are looking to do features on the denizens of Las Vegas."

Her lips curved into a smile. "Maybe they'd find Hollywood tourists more interesting?"

I chuckled. How unexpected. She'd been ready to rip me a new one, but she'd taken the change of tone in stride. "I could try it the next time I swing through California."

Except I was itching to leave the country again. I'd used some of my dwindling funds to come back for my brother's anniversary celebration. I had enough to leave again, but it was exhausting. Ten years of roaming the world to make a name for myself and I was just . . . tired.

Maybe that was what made me keep talking. "I like to do articles that link different communities around the world. How we're alike, and how we're different in our similarities."

She tilted her head, her expression prompting me to say more. Not just a *we're going to humor the middle kid for a minute before we brush him off* look, but valid curiosity. No one had been interested in my photography since Mama had died.

I flicked through the pictures to shots of Red Rock Canyon I'd taken earlier. "These aren't exotic, but it gives you a taste of what I do. For instance, I was in Sri Lanka not too long ago. They have rock formations, like Sigiriya Fortress and Dambulla's caves, that are tourist attractions, similar to Red Rock Canyon. So, maybe I'd do a story on how rock formations make up the backbone of some important tourist stuff."

So that had sounded better at the beginning. Then I'd run out of steam and blown it toward the end. Riveting shit right there. I waited for the same dubious expression I usually got after telling people my story ideas.

But she just nodded, her eyes losing focus as she thought about it. "I mean, when you think about it, geography often plays a key role in tourism. When I was in college, we studied the tradeoffs between preserving the land and bringing in money to support it."

The longer she talked, the higher my brows went. Who was this goddess?

She peeked at the pictures, reluctantly edging closer. "Those are beautiful. The colors are so vibrant."

I hung on the awe in her voice. "It's at sunrise." I had been too jet-lagged to sleep and stressing about the dinner with my family and my inevitable encounter with Grams. I'd figured a place like Red Rock Canyon was a give-me for nice pictures.

"Do you have the photos from Sri Lanka?"

"I have some of the countryside." They were nothing I'd put in a calendar. The trip had turned out to be fruitless as far as pictures went. Anyone with a phone could take the equivalent of what I'd captured. Unwilling to explain that I took menial jobs to pay for room and board while I traveled the world and failed to make a name for myself, I steered the conversation toward her. "What do you do? Are you from around here?"

Her smile lit up the night better than any of the casinos. "Is anyone really from Vegas?"

I laughed, her quick humor still a surprise after the way she'd confronted me. She was also smart. I was just some guy in a big city asking her a semi-personal question. "Fair."

"I, um . . . I'm kind of a consultant. On environmental issues."

"That's respectable work." And it

explained her defensiveness when she'd thought I was making light of the earth, air, wind, and fire brigade.

"Right. Yes." Her gaze flickered, hiding an emotion I couldn't identify. "I'm between jobs at the moment. I was here on business and now I'm not."

"Long story?"

"Tragically short and predictable, I'm afraid." She glanced around. "If I'd been paying attention."

"As a freelancer, I'm almost always between jobs."

Her grateful smile cut right through my chest. I swept my eyes over the curve of her full cheeks and pointed chin. Her heart-shaped face made her look youthful and innocent. But the keen look in her eyes told me that she wasn't much younger than me.

"So I take it you're not from Vegas either?" she asked.

"I grew up around more cattle than people."

"Space to roam."

I didn't miss the wistful note in her voice. She must've grown up in a city. I wanted to ask more questions, know everything about her, but I didn't even know the most basic detail. "What's your name?"

A faint blush stained her cheeks. "Savvy."

"Savvy." The name rolled off my tongue too easily. Her skin glowed, soft and inviting, but she wasn't mine to touch. "Is it short for something?"

"Yes. How about you?"

Again, fair. She'd given me her name, but I'd given her nothing. My real name was normally innocuous enough, except in certain circles. When I was back in the States, I used it less. I was in Vegas, just some normal guy taking pictures, and for some reason, I didn't want that image to change in Savvy's eyes.

I gave her my pseudonym. "Tate. Want to go grab a drink? I have a whole SD card of pictures I could show you."

CHAPTER 2

avvy

"I . . ." I broke into a fit of giggles. The five dollar bouquet of white carnations drooped in my hands as I doubled over. "Ohmigosh. Wait. Wait. I, Sapphire—"

Tate's adorable brow crinkled and I realized why.

"Didn't I tell you that my real name is Sapphire?" I leaned forward like it was just him and me, no strangers watching us and waiting for me to finish. "Sapphire Jewel."

My giggle was too loud, but I was buzzing pretty hard. I wasn't *drunk* drunk, but it was a good thing we could walk wherever we needed. Or that he could give me a piggyback ride because my feet hurt.

Maybe I was a little drunk.

To be fair, he would've known my full name, but he'd gone to pick out the rings while I'd given the chapel assistant my information. Then, I'd been choosing my flowers when he'd filled out his part of the paperwork. I had to hand it to Las Vegas, getting married here was efficient.

Chief was going to lose his shit.

Tate laughed, and the deep sound rumbled through my belly. Oh God, this man made me hotter as the night went on, and it had nothing to do with the alcohol. His eyes were only a little glassy. How many beers had he drank?

We'd had so much fun talking that I'd kept

ordering drinks as an excuse to stay with him longer. He was a humble guy, shy about his photography, but he had no qualms telling me about his travels. He roamed the world, working his way through each country. His jeans were faded because he worked in them.

That was hot.

Lex wore tailored suits like Chief. Like Em's husband. I wanted something different, but as the night had been drawing to a close, the eventuality of a marriage to Lex and being firmly under Chief's thumb had loomed large.

Then I had a killer idea.

And the wedding chapel in the casino had a no-show. It was fate. I'd found a real working man I was attracted to.

My parents thought I was impulsive. They thought I couldn't make big decisions on my own. Chief thought I needed to be taken care of, that I needed a man.

Oh, I got me a man.

I refocused on my soon-to-be husband, then focused again when it took too long.

Tate's brown eyes twinkled as he looked at me, like I was a dripping ice cream cone he wanted to lick from bottom to top. He'd been doing it all night until my insides swirled like the room around me would do if I had another local cider. "Tate is my middle name."

I let out a theatrical gasp, and then dissolved into laughter. This night kept getting better. Who needed names anyway? "What should I call you?"

"Xander."

"Xander." I tested it out. I liked Tate, but Xander was cool too. Simple. Common. Not a name you'd find on a guy on the rowing team at an Ivy League school. Em's husband rowed. Wait—his name was Carter. Also simple and common. Whatever. Xander was a simple guy and he didn't know my family was rich. I won. "Okay. Okay. I, Sapphire Jewel, do take Xander Tate to be my lawfully wedded husband." I'd said it. Oh. My. God. I said it.

I was getting married. And I'd just learned his first name.

Mother was going to faint. *Is this one of those responsible decisions you lecture me about, Mother?*

I broke into giggles and Xander's grin widened. Calm down. I took steadying breaths, gazing deep into his warm brown eyes. They centered me. His kind, accepting eyes and his *I live life on my own terms* attitude were why this was such a good idea an hour ago.

Xander's everyday life sounded like the one I'd been dreaming of but was too afraid to pursue. I wouldn't have to be scared with him.

A flush spread through my body. The last thing I felt around him was fear.

"I, Xander Tate, do take Sapphire Jewel" —the way he growled my name made my legs quiver—"to be my lawfully wedded wife."

The guy at my left—John? Jacob? Jingleheimer Schmidt?—said a few more things I didn't pay attention to before he pronounced us man and wife. I whooped and flipped the bouquet in the air. The assistant—our witness—didn't bat an eye.

Vegas, baby.

Tate—*Xander* captured me in his arms and planted his hot mouth on mine.

That was the first time we'd kissed. To say we'd waited until marriage was the absolute truth.

Take that, Chief. I had a husband. I didn't have to play nice with Lex tomorrow.

Xander lifted me up, the movement made me dizzy, and it had nothing to do with the drinks we'd had at the casino bar. My thoughts vanished as I pressed against his hard body. I didn't take after Opal Abbot, my porcelain doll mother. I was five ten. Most guys didn't try to pick me up.

I opened for him, my husband. He lazily swept his tongue against mine but managed to do it with such authority that I moaned. He claimed me so easily. The theme of the night. Everything around Xander was easy. Talking. Laughing. Telling him my dreams of the future. His encouragement for me to follow them.

Wait until I told Brady. I got married in Vegas!

A throat cleared next to us and I peeled myself off Xander. My feet touched the ground but he didn't let me go.

I smiled at him, biting my lower lip, and held my left hand out. A ring. It was a factory-produced diamond and not a blood diamond, that was all I cared about. And that Xander had thought to ask? A sign that my impulsive decisions weren't all terrible.

A niggling thought arose. How could such a simple guy buy a diamond ring, even an engineered one, on a moment's notice? I brushed it away. He traveled. He had to keep some money in reserve.

My exes had never felt right. They were more Chief's speed and that meant they were wrong for me. I wasn't going to be my mother in thirty years.

This fire between Xander and I would only grow. It had to.

"We have another ceremony in ten minutes," the wedding officiant said. "Stop at the desk and pick up your marriage license. Thank you for trusting us with your happiest day." He sounded like he'd said it a million times, but I didn't care.

Xander clamped his big hand around mine and led me out. The license was in a pretty envelope that smelled like my grandmother's perfume. He folded it and tucked it into his back pocket.

"Your place or mine?"

Brady's message. He'd be the first to know, and while he was my best friend, he was in our suite with a random hookup. Xander wasn't random. He couldn't be. He was the bold decision, the major upheaval in my life. Brady relied on my parents' support as much as I did. Xander risked all of that. I wasn't ready to tell my friend. "Yours."

He tucked me into his side as we left the

little chapel hidden in the casino and found a bank of elevators. He pushed the button.

He was in this hotel? Right. Yes, he'd mentioned that. We'd talked about so much other stuff, I'd forgotten. He was from Montana and had grown up ranching. He traveled the world taking pictures and writing pieces on everything from deforestation to sex trafficking. But he was having a hard time breaking into serious photojournalism because that wasn't what his background was in and he had no network yet. He was in town for his brother's anniversary party and his dear sweet Grams was riding him hard about getting married.

When he'd said that, it had clicked. Getting married would solve my problems *and* his. The most pressing was Lex. Chief would be livid. He might not want me working for him.

What would I do?

Job hunt with my wandering photographer? How would that work?

My buzz threatened to flatline, but I'd had *a day*. I'd figure it out later.

The elevator doors opened and we spilled inside. I giggled and buried my face in his shirt. He smelled fresh, like detergent and soap—not the perfumy stuff. Natural soap. Citrus and cedar. Addicting.

The door closed and he crowded me against the wall. We were the only two on board. I stared into his dark eyes, not believing that I was going home with him.

"Mrs. Sapphire Jewel," he whispered as he brushed a few strands of hair out of my eyes.

I inhaled. Should I change my name? To what? Who cared? It wasn't Abbot. "I thought I was Mrs. Xander."

The corner of his mouth kicked up. "I am a king and you are my jewel."

A shiver raced down my spine. He made me feel special, delicate, and I liked it. The guys I'd dated in high school had wanted to impress Chief more than me. The guys I'd dated in college had known how wealthy my family was, but they'd run when they'd learned I'd been severed from all that wealth until I learned some sort of lesson.

What would Xander do when he found out?

"My room's close to the elevators," he growled, sending a shiver down my spine and erasing all doubts. "I've been wanting those long legs wrapped around me since I first laid eyes on you. Too much too soon?"

I spread my hands across his broad chest. I couldn't recall a guy ever telling me that I drove him crazy. "Just right and not nearly soon enough."

He palmed my ass with both hands, holding me so tight that I wrapped my arms around his neck and hitched my legs up. "Is that what you want?" he murmured.

"Yes," I breathed. So much. Fire whipped down my body. This was it. We were *married*. It was our wedding night.

Heat bloomed through me, igniting nerve endings that hadn't been tended to well enough for more than a few years. Our first kiss had beat out any I'd ever had, wiped their memory from my mind.

What would sleeping with him be like?

I yanked his head down before I could lose my nerve. His lips landed on mine and I was lost in him until the slight jerk of the elevator alerted us that the doors were about to open.

His hands remained on my ass as he spun. I clutched him and giggled. A middle-aged couple passed us and the woman sighed wistfully. "Remember when we used to do that?"

The doors closed and I buried my head in Xander's neck as his strong, assured strides carried us down the hall.

"We're never going to quit doing this," he said in my ear.

"As long as your back can take it."

"My body will take anything you have to offer." He stopped at a door in the middle of the hall and wrestled the door open. Inside was nothing like the two-bedroom suite Bernard had booked for me and Brady. Too extravagant for one night for a company that couldn't afford it. Xander's room was simple, like him. One room besides the bathroom and one bed. He hadn't gotten more than he needed.

We spilled into the room, but he stopped to pin me against the wall.

The kiss he gave me was long and deep, melting me more with each second. He released his hands to cup my face, his hips anchoring me so I didn't slide down. "I'm going to spread you out on the bed and open my wedding present."

I kicked my heels off. Somehow, I knew the relief paled against the pleasure that was yet to come. Which one of us was getting the present? The marriage fairy had dropped the perfect man on my doorstep. He was everything I'd been looking for. I had the rest of my life to learn about him, starting with tonight.

Xander

I WAS HOLDING my wife in my arms. My *wife*. She gazed at me with those deep blue eyes full of wonder. Like I was some sort of dream come true. I'd always been the annoying middle brother, the needy one who'd finally gone off to do his own thing and stopped bothering everyone. I'd traveled the world and there was never anyone waiting for me in all the places I'd been. Any relationships I'd been in hadn't stood the test of time. Either they hadn't wanted to travel with me, or I hadn't been enough of a reason to uproot themselves and leave.

Meeting Savvy while we were both on a trip seemed fitting. We could go anywhere. Together.

I had no attachments, not even to my family. I didn't even have an address. What I couldn't do electronically went to the ranch and Dawson let me know if something looked important.

But I had a place now—with Savvy. The woman who'd kept me from failing my family yet again. When she'd announced that we should get married, my brain had hung on the offer. I shouldn't have married a woman I'd just met, but I didn't react to her like she was just any woman. And that she'd wanted to get married only two days before I lost something that had been weighing on me for the last year?

Fate. I wasn't going to question it and I couldn't wait to learn everything that made my wife tick, starting with her body.

I carried her to the bed. Housekeeping had left the blinds parted, giving us enough light without having to turn one on. I wouldn't care if we were under floodlights, but I wanted her comfortable.

I set her on the bed and she untangled her legs. She bit her plump lower lip as her gaze traveled over me. I was usually dressed casually, to the point of looking aimless, but she'd seen through me. Instead of the loser with no job my dad saw, Savvy saw me as a photographer. She was more excited about my career than anyone in my family.

I took my wallet out, pulled out a condom and set it on the bed. Her gaze followed my every move. We'd have the I'm-clean-are-you-clean-what-about-birth-control talk soon, but tonight was about us exploring and learning each other and I didn't want to delay. From the way she wiggled her ass, she agreed.

Next, I unbuttoned my shirt. She moved to do the same with her cream blouse.

"No."

My low command made her stop, uncertainty flickering in her eyes.

"I want to unwrap you myself."

She rolled up to her knees, putting her at the edge of the bed. "I want to do the same with you." She stroked her hands over my shoulders, then worked one button at a time. By the time she reached the last one, my dick was throbbing so bad that I was afraid the act of unzipping my pants would make me come.

She pushed the garment off my shoulders and down my arms. The shirt fluttered to the floor. Her lips parted. "Oh my."

I kept in shape, doing manual labor in exchange for food and lodging on my travels. But growing up hauling hay bales, riding horses, and working cattle hadn't hurt either.

She spread her hands over my chest, her nails scraping over the chest hair I'd never thought twice about until now. It was enough to cover my pecs with a trail disappearing below my waistband. Was she used to manicured men? I'd never taken a razor to anywhere on my body other than my face, and sometimes even that didn't get a shave for months.

"You're so … manly," she breathed, like I was some rare specimen she'd thought was a myth. She poked my biceps. "Those are real muscles."

"As opposed to . . ."

A laugh erupted, but it choked off as she brushed her hands down to my waistband. "Manufactured. Manscaped."

When she fumbled with the button and zipper, I groaned. The touch of innocence in the move was erotic. I didn't care if she'd done this a couple hundred times or once, I was enough to make her stumble. "You're killing me, woman."

Her gaze jerked up. "I feel like I should be insulted when you refer to me as 'woman,' but it's sexy as hell."

I cupped her cheek. "Because you are. I'll say *woman* a thousand times if it makes you feel good."

Her eyes were luminous in the transient light. She didn't look at what she was doing, but she lowered my zipper and pushed my pants down, my boxer briefs with them. My dick bounced free. That got her attention.

"Oh. That's . . . that's big."

"Thanks."

She didn't even know how well I could

use it. I might be a failure at a lot, but pleasing a woman had never been on the list.

"You must hear that all the time." Her question wasn't sarcastic. Real curiosity laced her voice. She wanted to know how experienced I was. I'd been sexually active since I was sixteen and Jenna Baker had let me trade her virginity for my own in the back forty after homecoming. I'd had dry spells and I'd had periods where I was with someone new every weekend. If Savvy asked for details, I wouldn't be able to tell her much. Size didn't matter. Frequency didn't matter. The only thing that mattered was how it was between my wife and me.

So all I said was, "I only care about you saying it." That was the truth.

A sultry smile curved her lips and she wrapped her hand around my erection. My moan couldn't be helped. She was the perfect mix of firm and unsure.

She pumped once, twice, her expression full of desire and curiosity, but I couldn't wait. I lifted her top off and she had to release me so I could get it off. Pale blue lace cupped creamy, full breasts. I thumbed the dusky pink nipples poking through and a shiver wracked her body. Somehow, I got her bra unhooked without fumbling. I watched her as I worked her jeans open, waiting for any sign of hesitation. We'd met hours ago, but this was no one-night stand.

I pushed all of the material down her hips as far as they'd go with the way she kneeled on the bed. Unlike me, she was neatly trimmed but I wouldn't care if she didn't do a damn thing or waxed herself bare. She was beautiful. I palmed her, her slickness coating my fingers.

"Xander," she breathed.

My resistance was shot. I wanted to see every part of her, but I needed to feel her now. I needed to be buried inside her.

Claiming her mouth, I wrapped one arm around her and used my other hand to pleasure her, to get her ready for me. I slid a finger through her soaked seam, then reversed the move until I hit her clit. Her whole body jerked in my arms and she let out a ragged moan, as if only my touch could get her off.

I circled her nub until she undulated against my hand, urging me to go faster and harder. I inserted a finger, using my thumb on her clit. When her walls clenched around my finger and she arched, I released her mouth to watch her climax spill over her. She dropped her head back, her mouth open, moaning my name. My real name spilling out of those pretty lips was the best start to this marriage.

I removed my hand and instantly missed her heat. I laid her back and finished removing her pants. Multitasking, I stepped out of my shoes and kicked out of my pants as I tore open the condom and rolled it on. Savvy was boneless on the bed, gloriously naked. A rare jewel.

I kissed my way up her body, and she twined her limbs around me. Since I knew nothing about her sexual history, I placed myself at her entrance but didn't shove inside. I went slow, letting her body tell me how fast and how hard. She was tight but accommodated my size, thanks to her recent orgasm. It wasn't long before she was demanding all of me, thrusting up, needing more.

Seated fully inside, I had to pause, overwhelmed. The way her body gripped mine, how she stroked my back, her legs hooked around my hips, it was all I could do to hold my orgasm back.

"You feel so fucking good." I nibbled along her chin, holding myself in place over her with my elbows.

She rocked her hips up, but I had to revel in everything her for a little longer. "Xander." Her hands swept across my shoulders. "I can't believe . . ." Her smile was soft, shy. "I can't believe you're real."

I withdrew and thrust back in. Her eyelids fluttered. "I'll show you how real I am. And that I'm all yours."

I claimed her with hard, powerful

strokes. I didn't think I had enough patience to get her off again, but I forced myself to see to her pleasure as I took my own.

She tightened around me, her back coming off the bed, her round, perfect breasts shoved in my face. "Xander. Oh God, more."

In. *Grunt.* Out. I was reduced to the most basic form of myself, but this was still about more than me getting off.

Heat exploded around my dick as her cry echoed off the walls. Finally, I let myself go, filling the condom, buried as deep as I could go.

Gritting my teeth, I grunted like a fucking caveman through my orgasm and collapsed on top of her. My face pressed to the mattress next to her head. "I'm crushing you." But I was too drained to move.

"No," she murmured. "I like it. I . . . like you."

My lips twitched. She liked me and the sex was explosive. This marriage could've started off worse. "I like you a whole damn lot too."

I pulled out and rolled next to her. She curled into my arms. This was only the beginning.

CHAPTER 3

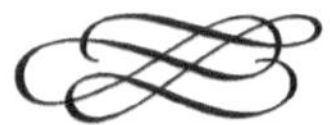

*S*avvy

I BLINKED my eyes open and my gaze landed on a broad back. I held up my hand. The diamond sparkled in the light creeping through the blinds.

Married.

I sat up. Daylight spilled through the curtains and I saw the room for the first time. Really saw it. I mean, I'd seen enough when we'd first had sex on the bed. Then we'd had sex in the shower. And when dawn had approached, he'd woken me to do it again. So, yeah. I hadn't seen much detail beyond the off-white ceiling, the white blankets, and the tiled walls of the bathroom.

The curtains were a thick brown and matched the chair that held a backpack. A beat-up suitcase and a camera bag rested on the desk. Did he really travel that light?

My husband.

We hadn't gotten any pictures of our wedding. We didn't have any pictures together. I only had a ring as proof that I'd done the most impulsive thing of my life mere hours ago.

Xander rolled over. My heart clambered into my throat. I'd met him when it was dark out. The bar lighting hadn't been the brightest, and the wedding chapel had been suspiciously dim as well. Ah, Vegas.

But in the harsh, unforgiving light of day, Xander was even better looking. His skin was bronzed—all over. He barely had tan lines around his waist. Did he just wander outside naked?

Dark hair flopped over his forehead and brushed his nape. Eyes the color of dark rum pinned me in place and I struggled to draw in air. He was so—so—*much*.

God, I was married. To this guy.

"What's wrong?" His low rumble cut through me, reminding my body of how good he could make me feel. I'd never orgasmed that hard before. Never that often. And it happened with a damn stranger.

I clutched the pristine sheet to my chest. My hair had to look like an eagle's nest and I didn't have a lick of makeup on. Not after water had sprayed down on me while he'd licked me until I'd sobbed his name. He'd asked what was wrong. I started with the most obvious. The most important—that I'd married a stranger to piss Chief off—would have to wait. "I don't have any clothes."

He lifted a dark brow, and his gaze

dipped to where I'd plastered the sheet against my chest. "I don't mind."

If he kept looking at me like that, I wouldn't either. But I'd made a whopper of a decision last night and I had to endure the consequences. This would all be for nothing if I didn't follow through. "I'm supposed to meet Chief and I'm sure the place is no less than business casual. My clothes from yesterday are . . ." I looked at where they were crumpled on the floor. "No longer viable."

"We can go back to your hotel so you can change."

I glanced at the clock on the end table. Horror propelled me off the bed. The sheet stayed in place and I was standing naked in the middle of the room. He propped himself on his shoulder, a ridiculous set of washboard abs flexing in the morning light, and with that scattering of chest hair— I dragged my gaze to his face only to find desire darkening his eyes.

No one looked at me like he did. I was

grateful the harsh light of day and my hungover panic didn't diminish it.

"We're going to be late." On time was late in Chief's world.

Xander rolled off the bed. My breath whooshed out of me. His heavy manhood was half erect and he really was as tall and broad as I'd remembered. "Then I'll wear what I wore yesterday. We'll be a united wrinkled front."

The restaurant Chief chose for the meeting wasn't a jeans and hoodie type of place. I gulped. I could do this. It was present Xander as my husband, or get set up with Lex in front of an oil CEO I respected.

Xander lifted his pants off the ground. I watched every ripple and flex of his muscles, enjoying the distraction. Digging his phone out, he frowned at the screen.

"Is everything okay?" I forced myself to quit staring at him and grab my clothes.

"No, it's all working out. My dad had to cancel lunch today. He ended up having a business meeting. So I'm not missing anything."

I got my bra on and stepped into my organic cotton underwear. We were going to show up like we'd never slept last night and I'd tell Chief that I was married. Butterflies exploded in my stomach. Chief was going to lose his ever-loving shit.

His reaction would be worse than when I'd told him I didn't want to go to Georgetown. He'd withheld my college fund, and now I lived with my own debt and was stuck under their roof so I could make my monthly student loan payments.

So, yeah. Maybe I'd enjoy today and think about what the rest of being married meant later.

I yanked my silk shirt over my shoulders and scurried to the bathroom. I cleaned up the best I could. Xander's toiletry bag was on the counter. He took the minimalist approach. Toothbrush, toothpaste, comb, razor, shaving cream, deodorant, and not much else. I used the toothpaste and did what I could with the comb, eventually giving up and twisting my long hair into a messy bun secured by my own hair.

I rushed out of the bathroom and dove for my pants. Xander had a half smile when he disappeared into the bathroom. Less than five minutes later, he was out. I doubted it ever took him longer than that in the morning.

"Ready?" he asked. His hair was combed off his face, but it was already falling over his forehead. I wanted to run my hand through it. I loved the way it slid through my fingers. I also loved that it was exactly the style that annoyed the crap out of my father.

"Let me see where we're going." When I pulled up the place in Chief's message on my phone, I was dismayed to see it wasn't far. "We can walk."

My poor feet. I'm never wearing heels again.

We could catch a cab, but I tried to walk whenever possible, which in DC wasn't always a valid option. Then there was my mother's insistence on having me use our driver. Public transportation wasn't something I'd grown up with and had yet to learn to navigate. I was free to walk here, so that was what I'd do.

Xander faced me, looking like an urban cowboy, utterly relaxed and unconcerned. "Whenever you're ready."

My stomach fluttered and I pressed my hand to my belly. This was going to be ugly, but I could get through it. That didn't stop the impending conflict from dominating my thoughts.

Xander attempted small talk on the way to the restaurant, about the weather, how many people were on the Strip, and how hungry he was, but eventually he grasped my hand in his and gave it a squeeze. "It's going to be fine."

My smile was hesitant. It wasn't going to be fine. At best, it'd be tense. At worst, explosive.

How would Xander's family take the

news? He'd said he wasn't as close to them as he used to be. There was the brother in Montana. Then another whose anniversary he was in town celebrating, but I couldn't remember where that brother lived, or why they'd been in Vegas for the anniversary. And he had another successful brother who worked for a large company.

I knew a lot about Xander, but I came up short on specifics. The butterflies in my belly gained in momentum.

How bad of an idea was this?

As we approached the place, my body vibrated with tension. On top of my major announcement was the fact that we were late. Chief abhorred tardiness—and I was perpetually time challenged.

Xander ushered me into the casino first. A sign pointed us to the restaurant. Chief roamed outside the entrance. Tight shoulders, a scowl that could clear a room, and ruddy skin growing more red. He was livid.

Then he glanced up and his hard gaze

jumped from me to Xander and then to our linked hands.

"Sapphire Jewel Abbot. What do you have to say for yourself?"

Xander gripped my hand tighter as humiliation crashed over me. Chief spoke to me as if I were fifteen, not twenty-five.

Did fifteen-year-olds get married whenever the hell they wanted?

"Chief," I said lightly. "Sorry I'm late."

Irritation flashed across his face. "For once, I'd like for that not to be your greeting." He spared Xander a glance. "What's this?"

"I, um . . ."

"For God's sake, Sapphire," he hissed and leaned closer, acting like Xander didn't exist. "This is an important business meeting, and you show up looking like you haven't been to bed yet."

Oh, I'd been to bed. I'd been to bed hard. "Actually, Chief. I want to introduce you to Xander. My husband."

The silence that fell between us was

glacial. I was surprised the ground and walls didn't crystallize with frost.

"What?" His voice was barely loud enough to reach me. My late arrival had made him angry, but this announcement morphed him into a nuclear warhead. No doubt his mind was working on all the ways to mitigate the damage.

"Xander and I got married last night. Xander. This is my dad. Walter Abbot."

Xander released my hand to hold his out. "Nice to meet you." He was so steady, not at all intimidated.

Chief continued to pretend Xander didn't exist. "I would've thought you were smarter than being taken by a guy who's after your money."

"Like you often tell me, *I* have no money, and I never told him that my family is wealthy." I chanced a glance at Xander. His brows were only slightly lifted. He was surprised, but the news otherwise had no bearing on his demeanor. But he didn't know how wealthy my family was.

"People like him *know*. Just like you should know better. If it's not the money, it's the . . ." He waved his hand, his face deepening from red to purple.

Xander stepped in. "Savvy has a lot more to offer than her wallet or her looks." He took my hand again and it was all I could do not to hide behind him. His words probably made things worse, but I appreciated the effort. It was already more than any previous date had done.

Chief zeroed in on Xander, like my new husband was an enemy sniper hiding in the backyard. "And what is it, exactly, that you do?"

One of the men hanging out in the entry of the restaurant wandered out, his gaze drifting over me.

Gentry King. The man I'd worked so hard to impress yesterday was about to witness Chief humiliating me. I hoped he was too busy and disengaged from the daily details of his work to realize the professional Sapphire Abbot he was supposed to have met with yesterday had shown up today married to a guy her dad hated.

Mr. King wasn't any different than his pictures, but his presence packed a punch. He was almost as tall as Xander, his shoulders just as broad, but his expression was much less hostile than Chief's. No doubt he was putting two and two together and figuring out I was Chief's daughter. I wouldn't have believed the power he held over Chief if my father didn't visibly calm down the instant Mr. King stepped closer to us. This account was extremely important to Chief. My mini-crisis was averted. He'd hold himself together through the meal, but I'd get another berating afterward.

Mr. King's gaze left me and landed on Xander. His brows rose, his eyes filling with curiosity, but also brightening, like he was happy to see my husband. "Xander? What are you doing here?"

Before I could muddle through how

Gentry King knew my new husband, Xander said, "Hi, Dad."

Xander

WHAT THE HELL was Dad doing with this trumped-up jackass?

But as I answered Dad, Savvy's hand went limp. I let it fall away—it was either that or tighten my grip and crush her bones to hold on to her—but when I glanced at her, I froze.

Her eyes were full of dismay when she turned to me. "You're a King?"

"And you're my treasure," I said automatically. Hadn't she caught my play on words earlier?

Did she not know my last name? I struggled to recall when we'd each shared that detail. The ceremony wasn't as clear as it should have been. We'd both had a lot to drink but we hadn't been stupid drunk.

"You . . ." Walter Abbot blinked back and forth between me and his daughter. The next time his gaze landed on me, it was like he saw a whole new person. He was seeing Xander King now, a kid from a family that owned an oil empire. He switched his lighter blue gaze to Savvy, a smile playing over his lips, his eyes shining. "You married a King?"

"Married?" Dad echoed.

Fuck.

I didn't want to break the news to my family like this. "I haven't had a chance to call you yet. To call any of you." Dammit. Were all my brothers still in town? I was torn between triumph that I wasn't the one to fuck up the trust fund, and desperation to show them that I was serious about this girl. She wasn't a means to an end. I wasn't using her.

Dad's wife, Kendall, exited the restaurant and another man I didn't recognize wandered out after her. Were we making a spectacle or were we just that late?

Kendall's keen gaze evaluated the group as she stopped at Dad's side. She flashed me a kind smile. "Xander, I didn't think we'd see you again before we left."

Dad's smile was tight, only as polite as necessary. The smile I was used to when he discussed me and my lack of accomplishments with others. It was a mix of perpetual disbelief and disappointment that I hadn't done more with my life coming from the family that I had. "Xander was just going to introduce us to his new wife."

"Oh." Kendall blinked, her eyes going round. "*Oh.*" I hated how she said it with frank understanding. Kendall and Dad thought I'd only married Savvy to meet the terms of my trust. Maybe it was a little true. It *was* a shitload of money. But the thought denigrated Savvy more than the Chief did.

I put my hand on Savvy's back and she

jerked straight. It was a tense situation, but she seemed unhappier with me than with her father. "Savvy, this is my father, Gentry King, and his wife, Kendall. She works for King Oil as well."

Kendall grinned, leeching some tension out of the air. "So nice to meet you, Savvy." My stepmother was only a couple years older than me, but she was a good fit for Dad. Aside from running the company, he'd been as aimless as me before he met her. "Have you had a chance to introduce her to the others?"

"Others?" Savvy squeaked.

"My brothers." I had told her all about them. Mostly stories about us growing up and the death of my mother when I was eleven.

"Right." She nodded stiffly, clasping her hands in front of herself. I briefly met Dad's eyes. It was enough to see the simmering disappointment. He was a romantic and while he didn't want to see the money from my trust go to someone else, he also didn't like the idea that I was using someone.

I didn't either. I was determined to make this a real marriage. I'd never met anyone like Savvy. I'd never been with someone I couldn't get enough of physically. With others, walking away had been easy, and I never needed to nurse my wounds for long if the breakup hadn't been my idea. But with Savvy? Any parting would be brutal.

The man on the other side of Chief was closer to my age and I didn't like the proprietary way he glared at Savvy. That must be Lex, the guy Chief wanted her with. He fit the stereotype. A tight haircut. A pinstripe suit tailored within an inch of its life. A stick up his ass.

"Well," Chief clapped his hands and Savvy flinched, "this just turned into a celebration. My dear daughter beat me to forming a partnership between our families."

Dad laughed good-naturedly, but I

could tell when he was humoring someone. "Good thing weddings and business negotiations are usually mutually exclusive."

We came from a small town where we did business with people sometimes just because we knew them and that they were good people. Dad wasn't making any promises just because Savvy was my wife.

Lex's lip lifted, like he was disgusted with Savvy. He mimicked Chief when we'd first walked up and pretended I didn't exist.

"Let me inform the staff." Chief rushed into the restaurant and ordered several bottles of champagne. Dad and Kendall murmured together as they walked after him. Dad threw me a careful glance over his shoulder before they disappeared inside.

Lex lingered, blocking our path. I wasn't a violent guy, but I wanted to beat off the arrogant, condescending look he gave Savvy. "How is that going to affect your career? Aspiring conservationist marries into oil tycoon's family."

Savvy stiffened and her response after meeting Dad finally made sense. Either she hadn't seen my last name last night, or she hadn't put the two together. Why would she? My last name was generic in most circles, and we'd only talked half the night. We'd described what made us, what formed us, not what our family names said we should be. Our marriage was impulsive and beautiful and I wouldn't change it.

Lex didn't give up. "In fact, didn't you fly here to teach King Oil about how bad they're being to the world?"

Okay, that detail was unexpected. "You were here to meet with my dad?" We'd gotten around to a lot of specifics about our life, but all she'd said about her work was that it had gone out of business at the most inopportune time.

"Where's *Brady*?" Lex's tone dripped with glee. Like I didn't know about Brady. "You two are so close."

I should've waited to ask her about the meeting when we were out of earshot of this jackass. Would Lex be shocked that I knew about Brady? I didn't know a lot. He was her coworker and her best friend. If she'd wanted to be with him, she would've been. I wouldn't dictate who her friends could be. I bet this guy would forbid her from talking to Brady ever again if he could.

"He's at the hotel," she answered even though that asshole didn't deserve it.

Lex turned his arrogant gaze to me. "Does Daddy support you like Mr. Abbot supports Sapphire?"

"I'm a photographer. Also an environmentalist. I might be from an oil family, but the two partner together more than you'd think. I'm surprised you don't know of King Oil's effort to reduce their carbon footprint. If you're interested in doing business with the company, you should also know what's important to them."

Savvy's luminous gaze swiveled to me. An invisible ripple ran through her body.

Her eyes narrowed and it was like her mind was restarting from whatever had stalled it earlier. "Right, Lex. I'm sure Chief would appreciate learning everything you know about King Oil's progress in that area."

Lex's lips pressed together. "It's not critical for security. If you're so well informed, why didn't you know who Xander was?"

Her lips formed a troubled line. "I researched the company, not the CEO's personal life."

She wouldn't have found much. I didn't have anything to do with the company, yet I knew more about it than Lex. I hated to act like a dick, but the situation called for it. "Actually, the environment is quite important to King Oil and its security." I recalled Dad's conversation from the anniversary dinner. "Security consultants, right? Tampering with oil equipment can lead to severe environmental impacts, and there's always someone less concerned about the environment willing to take over."

Finally, Savvy relaxed under my touch. "We'd better get in. Chief's starting the celebration."

Lex spun on his heel. For not being related, he acted a lot like Walter Abbot.

"I'm sorry," I breathed to Savvy, not knowing if I was apologizing for being a King or for our impromptu marriage.

She sighed and her eyes filled with the weariness of someone much older. "Me too."

CHAPTER 4

avvy

CHIEF DID the cringeworthy toast and proceeded to chew Mr. King's ear off about how well their companies could work together.

What a mega fucking coincidence. A perfect storm of connected events. My ultimate rebellion had turned out to be the best thing I'd ever done in Chief's eyes.

I'd come to town to meet with King Oil.

Xander had come for his brother's anniversary dinner, and so had his father. And I'd happened to meet and fall for Xander and fuck up my own stab at independence while making Chief prouder of me than he'd ever been. All because I'd opened my legs for the right guy.

Go me.

The craziness of my sudden marriage finally sank in. What had I been thinking? I shouldn't need a guy to be independent. Just like I shouldn't have to live with my parents at twenty-five. But there I was.

Xander King.

How had I missed his last name? Even if I hadn't, would I have connected him to King Oil? Would I have cared? I'd wanted to work with the company, not marry into it.

Big Oil.

Good one, Savvy. The voice in my head sounded just like Brady. *You hit the jackpot of husbands. Now you won't need Chief to foot the bill.*

Since no one chatted to me or Xander

while waiting for appetizers, I peeked at my phone. As if sensing juicy drama, Brady had texted. *Where you at?*

I sent back *Long and tragically ironic story. Call you in a bit.*

I put the phone face down on the table and looked around. Chief was working Gentry King hard. He was even talking with Kendall, and since Chief was very old school when it came to women, I could only assume Kendall had a shit load of power within the company. That left Lex, who oozed *I'll cartwheel while I kiss your ass* as he tried to work what he thought was magic as Chief's wingman.

I had to admit, Gentry King wasn't what I'd expected. Congenial and not falling for my dad's smoke and mirrors, he wanted cold, hard facts and clear declarations about what the security consulting company could do for his business. Kendall held her own too, firing off questions that made it obvious she was more than just a side piece.

They were a couple, huh? So he'd not only fucked around with his assistant, he'd married her. Xander had said his mother died when he was young, so at least Gentry had been single when he'd met Kendall.

I suppressed a maniacal giggle. My middle sister, Pearl, wasn't going to believe how this had gone down. I thought I'd been brave to get married in Vegas. She'd flexed her independence by running off and joining the military after telling Chief and Mother she was studying abroad. I looked like a child playing at being a grownup next to what she'd done.

Xander leaned close and murmured, "I feel obligated to point out that Dad met Kendall before she was his assistant."

Dad. God, this was surreal. I whispered back, "But did he sleep with her before or after she started working for him?"

It wasn't my business. If I could find fault in King Oil, then the way I'd ruined my chances of ever working with them wouldn't sting so much.

The corner of his mouth hitched up. "While I try not to think about my dad sleeping with anyone, they met when she was flying to interview with my brother. But they got stranded. Then he offered her a job at the company and after seeing how invested she was, he asked her to work in the inner office."

"Inner office. Is that what they call it nowadays?" A company rife with nepotism. And I'd married into it. Real fierce and independent, Savvy.

His expression flickered, but his faint smile remained in place. "Well, my brother works there too, so it's not like that."

Gentry King employed his wife and son. If he recognized my name from the canceled meeting, would he think I'd married Xander because of who he was? I was here as Chief's assistant, but I wasn't taking notes, because he was thrilled that I'd married Xander.

I would never be taken seriously. I couldn't take myself seriously. "I came here to meet with him professionally and now I'm his daughter-in-law."

"You can still talk to him professionally. When it comes to business, he'll listen."

I could pitch him right now. Maybe he'd listen to my spiel on new technologies for harnessing wind power other than the massive turbines that many landowners balked at. He backed a research and development project into wind-powered micro-generators. Part of my position at Saving Sunsets was to do the footwork on these up-and-coming technologies and compile data for companies like King Oil.

How would it look if I launched into my pitch? Chief had retired from the military and started his own successful business. Mr. King ran an oil company. They'd both had a healthy resume by the time they were my age. In contrast, after I'd lost my first job, I'd married the first man I'd met. "How old is your dad anyway?"

"He'll be fifty-one soon. My oldest brother was born when he was nineteen and then it was pretty much a baby a year after that."

And he'd accomplished everything with small children. Super. "And Kendall?"

He ran his thumb over his lower lip. How was this guy single? He was the first guy I'd dated whose family was probably wealthier than mine. "She's the same age as my oldest brother."

I cocked a brow. It wasn't like I didn't see age gaps in marriages. Many of Chief's friends were on their second or third spouse, and each one got younger. What I hadn't seen before was the equality in the relationship that Kendall and Gentry displayed. If the woman in the relationship gained power and success in her own right, the marriage soon dissolved. It's why Em didn't work—and why Pearl wasn't married or serious about anyone. She had big plans and no one would stop her.

Was I going to be Em or Pearl?

"What do I even call them?" I hadn't meant to snap, but it came out bitchy. This day had twisted in a way I hadn't seen coming. "Gentry and Kendall? Mr. and Mrs. King?"

"Gentry and Kendall are fine. We're just poor country folk," he drawled. "We don't stand on formality."

I scowled at him but when he broke into a grin, I couldn't help but return it. "I think Chief won't care what you call him." I shook my head. "He's so happy."

Xander's lips thinned. "He wasn't before he learned who I am."

I didn't bother to deny it. Chief thought I should be with a guy like Lex, but it's Lex who wished he was more like Xander.

Our food arrived and the talk of business died down.

"So, Xander," Chief said. "What do you do?"

"I'm a freelance photojournalist."

Chief covered his ripple of displeasure. That wasn't what he'd wanted to hear. "And what is that exactly?"

"I use pictures to tell the news of the world."

Chief's interest perked up. "You go to war zones and take pictures of the front lines?"

Chief liked to talk like he'd been big shit in his day. Maybe he had been and I didn't understand. What I did understand was that his "front line" had been a desk, and any immediate danger to himself had been minimal. We hadn't been the normal military family, getting uprooted every few years. Chief had spent most of his career in or around Washington, DC. Not that his service wasn't important, but he judged everyone else on how much action they'd seen, or how many troops they were in charge of.

"No," Xander answered and Chief's hopefulness faded. "I prefer to travel to more remote regions, less popular if you will, and capture what life is really like."

"Where have you been published?" Lex

asked like a shark scenting the first drops of blood spilling into Chief's seas.

"A few local news outlets have picked up some of my photos over the years."

"In the States?" Lex prodded.

Xander's eyes flicked to his dad before he answered. "I'm working on getting my foot in the door."

That's what he'd been talking about when he admitted to not measuring up to his dad. He thought he should be further ahead in his career, and his dad did too. Notoriety, maybe an award or two, and at least one major publication or news source under his belt.

We had more in common than our family's wealth. "I've seen his work. It's good."

Chief barely spared me a glance. "What did you go to school for?" He adopted a charming grin he used in meetings to attract clients. "I have to ask. It's my job as a dad."

I resisted rolling my eyes. Chief hadn't

attended school plays or any ceremony other than graduation. But I sat close enough to Xander to feel him tense.

"I, uh, majored in business media design and I . . . quickly became more interested in the media and design side."

That was the only moment I'd ever seen Xander ill at ease. I was sure I'd learn the story eventually, but since we'd known each other less than twenty-four hours . . .

"And that was where?" There was that hopeful tone in Chief's voice again.

"University of Montana."

Chief's mouth worked. It killed him not to make a statement about the lack of an Ivy League education. It was the same look I'd gotten when I'd told him I didn't want to go to Georgetown. "Staying close to home. There's nothing wrong with that."

Good thing Chief wasn't Pinocchio. His nose would have hit the wall and kept going.

Gentry jumped in. "Missoula is in the

same state, but in Montana that still means he was six hours away from home."

Lex chuckled and I bristled, bracing myself for an attack. "That's where those private planes come in handy. Though now that you're married to Savvy, you won't be able to use them anymore. She'll quote the statistics about how much worse for the environment they are."

Well . . . they were.

All eyes turned to me. Xander pushed his mashed potatoes around on his plate. "I don't usually use the private plane unless I have to rush home for some reason. Then I can't deny the convenience."

"It certainly makes doing business around the country much more expedient." Gentry's smile was professional, and I couldn't tell what he was thinking, unlike Chief, whose hand was clenched around his fork. Lex had mis-stepped in front of the client and Chief couldn't say anything. "But I agree, it comes at a great cost that isn't always monetary."

I wanted to laugh and point at Lex. *The private plane is Gentry's, idiot.*

Chief relaxed, but it was only a show—his blood pressure would likely worry his doctor. "Sapphire is a bit of an environmental enthusiast."

Leave it to him to minimize my biggest passion in the world, the thing I'd dedicated my life to.

To Gentry's credit, his expression was pleasantly curious as his gaze met mine. "Good. We need more people like that." He chuckled and glanced at Chief and Lex. "You don't grow up working the land with your bare hands and not develop an avid appreciation for the earth we live on."

I sat straighter.

Kendall's smile was equally as friendly and enthusiastic. "We'll have to get together sometime. I've done several reports for our investors regarding wind energy and what we can do to support it."

"What about solar energy?" I didn't add that I'd looked into the ways they incorporated new solar techniques into their headquarters to reduce the cost of heating. If Gentry wasn't going to ask me if I had been the one to cancel on him today, I wasn't bringing attention to it.

She grinned. "That's a great question. We've been looking to incorporate it into our energy solutions plan, and we've looked at both active and passive technologies." She chuckled, but her eyes were bright. I wasn't the only one passionate about the topic. "Some of the bigger oil companies prefer to concentrate on oil and natural gas, but ultimately, it's a finite resource. Gentry's goal is to keep King Oil relevant for centuries to come."

For the rest of the meal, I geeked out with her. She was a wealth of knowledge and my respect for Gentry grew along with my appreciation for how Xander had defended Kendall against my initial stereotype.

I didn't know how the rest of my

marriage would go, but at least we'd make it through lunch.

Xander

AFTER THE COLLEGE QUESTION, my steak tasted like sawdust. I'd managed to answer it without lying, but not telling the truth was just as sour.

Chief wasn't done asking the blunt questions Dad had been needling me about for years. "Where do you live, Xander? Where's my daughter getting whisked away to?"

There was no sugarcoating my answer. "I use my brother's place for a physical address, but otherwise my home is wherever I land and can find work while I take pictures."

Silence descended around the table. Dad bypassed doing that awkward thing where he made excuses for me, and I had to give him some credit. He didn't belittle me in front of Chief and Lex. He let me answer for my own damn life, which at the moment seemed worse.

"You're homeless?" Lex asked in a flat tone. Chief shot him a disapproving glare, but it was probably for the sake of my dad. If I weren't a King, this would be a slaughter.

"In the literal sense? I guess. I saw a chance to learn about the world firsthand and not from behind some desk and I took it. Could I go buy a house? Sure." No. I couldn't, not unless I asked Dad to loan me some money and then I'd have to tell him why I didn't have any and what I'd been living off of since I'd left home. "I choose not to."

That was a laugh. I couldn't even afford to rent an apartment.

"Well, then," Chief's voice boomed. "You're more than welcome to come out to our place for a while. Meet Sapphire's mother and my other two daughters. They're all named after jewels because they're so precious."

Savvy had said it was so he could leverage them for top dollar to be worn on some man's arm. "Savvy's told me a lot about them."

"Just call your mother first." Chief speared his steak. "She's going to be surprised."

He might be giddy that I connected him to King Oil, but he was having a hard time giving away his daughter to a stranger. If the arrogant bastard across the table weren't his preferred option, I'd respect Chief a little more.

Then it sank in. I had to meet her mother. And her sisters, Em and Pearl. Were they anything like Chief or Lex? Were they going to ask the same questions so I could fail the son-in-law test with the same answers?

"I'll be interested to see how your travels are affected." Dad held his glass of brandy loosely, his other arm around Kendall. A fleeting moment of gratefulness hit me for having Chief around, even Lex. Without either of them, I'd be getting interrogated, and with Savvy, I couldn't just leave on the first international flight out of Vegas.

"Time will tell. It's early yet and we have to meet each other's families."

I looked at Savvy but I couldn't read her expression. I hadn't known her long, but I knew her well enough that if she didn't want to bring me home, or meet my brothers, she wouldn't say so around Chief, and definitely not Lex.

"Good to know you'll be in the States for a while." Dad's smile was faint, hesitant. "Maybe we'll actually get a chance to visit."

"Maybe." My chest burned. I'd love to sit around and shoot the shit with Dad, but I'd gotten really good at making sure we were never alone together, that there was always someone else so I could redirect the conversation if I needed to. And with Dad, I needed to.

A guy could have a lot less than a dad who gave a crap about him. But my dad had been married with a kid by nineteen. He'd gone to work for Mama's parents. Grams and Grandpa DB had founded the oil company and built it from the ground up. When Mama had died, then DB, Dad had been made CEO, and Grams had been satisfied with controlling shares. That had been when Dad was only a few years older than I was now.

Talking with Dad made me feel like a useless fuck. A fraud. Lazy. Add in that he thought I'd only married for the trust fund money and not because I found Savvy enchanting and irresistible, and it was like dumping napalm on my inner fire of shame.

Kendall dove in for the save. I hadn't been around her a lot, but she seemed to sense when Dad's fatherliness was tapping me out. She peppered Chief with more questions about what he did and his time in the military.

I finished my food only because it'd look weird if I didn't when Savvy was pushing her salad around and rearranging her croutons.

Before the rest of us were done eating, Dad set his napkin on the table. "I apologize for cutting out early, but I have more meetings in Billings." He met my gaze. "I need to let the pilot know if you're joining us."

Savvy jerked her attention off her Caesar and met my questioning gaze. I wasn't ready to go to Montana and get more knowing looks from my brothers. Two of them had married for the trust money, but their marriages had lasted more than a year. They were real. I had yet to prove mine was.

Nobody missed our moment of hesitation. Savvy and I had no idea what we were going to do or where we were going to go. Lex's brows crept higher the longer it took us to answer.

I took the chance of speaking for us.

Vaguely, because that was what I did best. "I'm afraid we'd only hold you up. Savvy's coworker is still in town and we need to arrange our things."

She nodded like a puppet was yanking her strings. "Yes. We're not done in Vegas yet."

I'd had a few more drinks than I should've last night, but I recalled her saying that she'd been looking for jobs in the city.

Did she still want that? Because if I was going to put down roots, it wasn't going to be in Las Vegas. Montana was in my blood. It was where I always came back to. Even away from Montana, I always stayed away from cities, crowds, and the worst pollution.

"Don't take too long," Chief said. His eyes crinkled like he was smiling, but there was a measure of warning in his eyes. "I can't do without my best assistant."

Savvy's lips pursed. She'd thought he'd let up after she was married. She must've thought it was a slam dunk after she'd found out who I was. But it was dawning on both of us that he'd be more tenacious than ever, because Dad couldn't say no to a company his new daughter-in-law worked for.

I guess we were going to Washington, DC.

CHAPTER 5

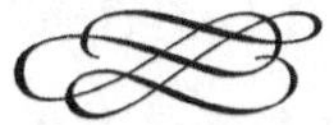

avvy

I NEEDED A DIVORCE.

We stood outside the restaurant, our dads and Lex gone. Xander faced me and I avoided looking at him. Chief had given Xander a hearty handshake before leaving. Lex had murmured, *Call me if you need anything.* Like I needed a rescue. Like I'd go to *him* for a rescue if I did.

No, I'd only married one of the few

people in the world that the Chief would approve of.

Way to go, Savvy.

Chief's collar around my neck would stay secure until he landed the King Oil account. And then he'd yank it even tighter. Last night, Xander's world travels had sounded exotic, worldly, and full of all the adventure that'd bring me closer to the planet I was trying to save. But under the harsh casino lights today, our future looked bleak and uncertain.

I didn't have a home. He didn't have a home either, and the way he'd evaded his father's questions, it didn't sound like he planned to make one anywhere close to Montana. That left my side of the country. With my parents. With Chief parading me and Xander around so he could show all his friends how his daughter had married into an oil empire.

We could make our own start somewhere. Which was what? Flying across the ocean and backpacking the world?

While I would love the opportunity, I wanted to make a difference in the world. To carve out my own little niche. I'd thought Vegas was the start of that. I thought I'd land King Oil and become a leading consultant in future energy technologies. Now I'd torched that. I was tired of needing my hand held while I navigated life. If I was going to recover my dignity and build a professional reputation, I had to be responsible. That might mean sucking it up and working for Chief and saving money. My own money. Money I could use to build my future. A future that I'd earned and hadn't been handed to me because of who I slept with. My family's wealth was held against me. I risked that working for Chief too, but at least I'd know I'd earned every cent. He was a demanding boss.

"Savvy. Talk to me."

I dragged my gaze up to Xander and his dark eyes, just one reason why looking at him was a bad idea. He was too good-looking for my sanity. And then there was last night.

My body certainly wasn't on board with researching how to annul a marriage. I couldn't even consider whether a divorce would be better or worse while he was in my line of sight. I just wanted to be with him again and pretend our life was wide open and easy to navigate.

I had to be smart about this, to think through the repercussions. "We can't stay married."

His concerned expression fell. "Because of who my dad is?"

As callous as it sounded, yes. "Xander, I got married thinking it'd be the big coup I needed to keep my parents from taking over my life. Chief's going to double down on making me his prize pony. Even if he does get the King Oil deal, he'll want to lock it down long-term, and having me work for him will do that."

"Then job hunt."

"Where? Here? All the money I have, I

got from Chief." My mother's family was loaded, but Chief made a healthy income of his own and he was the one that helped me out. It had been Mother's idea to call my Georgetown bluff and withhold any help for college. I'd be living in a dive with four roommates like Brady, one missed rent payment away from homeless, if it were up to my mother.

He lifted a shoulder and while I loved the casual look on him, his hoodie hid his muscles. Ones I'd licked last night. "Chief wants me to meet the family."

"And you think you want that?" My sisters were going to worm their way down my throat trying to get the answer to why I'd married him. Then they'd say *I told you so* and it wouldn't matter that they hadn't said it in the first place.

"What do you want, Savvy?" he asked quietly and I realized that he'd never agreed with me about the divorce. Was that good or bad?

If he announced that he'd do whatever it

took to dissolve our marriage, how would I feel?

I'd been broken up with before, but being casually divorced by my husband of less than twenty-four hours would seriously dent my ego. I couldn't even blame it on him being a gold digger.

"I don't know," I finally admitted. "I went to college and got a degree in something my parents thought was a waste of time. The first job I got out of college didn't pay enough for me to move out. Now I'm married and unemployed. I wanted to stand on my own, make a difference, Xander. Instead, I'm more dependent on my father than ever." My globe-wandering, struggling photographer of a husband was from a wealthier family than I was. I couldn't even rebel right.

He studied me for a moment. My body heated more with each heartbeat. Sex was the last thing on my mind, but my hormones weren't getting the message.

"I've been meaning to go to Kosovo," he

said. "There's an interpreter I met once in Macedonia when he was there for the military, Hector Morales. He lives in Kosovo now and said I could come stay with him and his wife anytime. We could both go, get to know each other before we decide what to do with our lives."

What had he said to Chief? *More remote regions, less popular if you will.* He wasn't kidding. "What would we do there?"

"I always start by finding work. Usually some simple labor to pay for food and a place to stay."

"You're not going because your pictures *are* the work?"

His jaw clenched and his gaze dropped. Last night, his experiences had been catnip to my sheltered self. A starving artist making his way in the world. But he wasn't starving—he was a King. So where was the artist part? "I wasn't lying when I told you that I wanted to be independent from my family and that I'd left home to travel. I support myself. Not my dad, and not the company."

Grudging respect replaced a portion of my mounting panic. Neither of us wanted to be reduced to our last names. We wanted our privileged upbringings to go toward being more than just a drain on society.

But to do that, we needed jobs, and between us, I was the only one who had one. I couldn't support the two of us on the salary Chief paid. Add in housing in DC and I'd be working for Abbot Security until I retired. I didn't care that Chief had a good pension plan. "If we go to DC, we'd be living with my parents. Where would you work?"

"I'd do the same thing I always do."

"What about your photography?"

"Savvy . . ."

I was willing to work for my future, not coast through my present like I was starting to suspect he did. "No, I'm sorry. I'll meet up with Brady and go back to DC. I'll give you my contact info so we can resolve everything. This marriage wasn't a good idea, and it's my fault. I brought it up and I'd had too much to drink and—"

"Is it the money?"

"What?"

"You want freedom to do what you want professionally without being dependent on anyone, right?"

"I want to be free to make my own decisions." My family's money came with strings attached. *I'll pay for college, but you have to get the degree I tell you to. You can live here, but you need to come to dinner with me and be nice to Lex. You can work for me, but you can't pursue your silly environmental ideas.*

"What about fifty million?"

I laughed. "I thought you didn't use your family's money?" He could stay in the Four Seasons, or the equivalent of it in any country he wanted, with that amount of money. Not couch surf with a friend in Kosovo.

"I'll tell you the story on the walk to your hotel." He stepped in close. My head tilted back. He was only four inches taller, but he towered over me. My lips parted like my body anticipated a kiss when we'd done nothing more than hold hands since leaving the hotel room. "But after you hear it, I want you to remember that getting married wasn't just about Grams or the money. It was about being with you longer."

He held his hand out and we both stared at it. *Getting married wasn't about Grams and the money.* Did he really have fifty million?

Why had he married me? We'd been carried away, bitching about meddling parents and grandparents, and then I'd brought up a Vegas wedding. He hadn't hesitated more than three seconds. And I hadn't asked myself why.

Grams or the money. I had to hear this story. I twined my fingers through his and nearly sighed. Touching his skin shouldn't have such a drugging affect.

He walked slow. "How are your feet?"

"Oh. Good." I'd been too distracted to think about them. Listening to Xander's voice on the way back would help keep my mind off these shoes and when I could clean and donate them.

He talked low, keeping our conversation private from the gamblers and tourists flowing around us. How many hungover couples were questioning their nuptials right now? "Not long after we were born, my mom's parents, Grams and DB, sold off some lease holdings. They gave Mama the money to put away for us. And she put it in a trust."

A *fifty-million-dollar* trust? That was stupid-rich money. That amount would make Chief salivate. Even my mother would lift a finely manicured brow.

"Only this trust has special stipulations." His hand tightened. "We have to get married by our twenty-ninth birthday and be married for a year by the time we're thirty."

"Why would she do that?" Though did I really have to ask? I could imagine my parents putting similar restrictions on my trust. They would attempt to control me in death as they had in life.

"I have no idea. The thing is, if we fail, the money goes to our neighbor, Danny Cartwright. He's a jackass of epic proportions. And he's got a daughter a few years younger than us, but I can only guess from the way Bristol acts that she despises us as much as he does."

"Why the hard feelings?"

"The Boyds and Cartwrights used to be close but had a falling out over money. Cartwright claims Grams and DB screwed his family out of mineral rights and drilled on land my grandparents had sold them. Then the Cartwrights turned around and screwed my dad's family, the Kings, out of some land, I guess because trying to buy land the legitimate way had bitten them in the ass with the Boyds. Then my mom married my dad and not Danny Cartwright, who for some reason had been sure Mama would forget everything and fall into his arms."

I struggled to keep up with the story. "Whoa. I think that rivals the gossip I hear at my mother's dinner parties."

"Yeah, it's a mess and one reason why I stay away. Danny Cartwright is a mean drunk and he's always plastered. Bristol is a thorn in our ass too, but I can't help but feel sorry for her. Growing up with Danny couldn't have been easy."

"So your birthday is tomorrow and you got married." He'd married me for money? Not even *my* money, which would somehow be easier to brush off. It would've meant there was something about me that was irresistible. But it was his own money that was tied up in a trust. My hand went lax.

He gave it a squeeze. "Remember what I said. That wasn't my reason. Until I met you, I was ready to let it go."

But now he didn't have to. I'd thrown myself at him and made it easy. I swallowed my hurt. I could deal with it later. I needed details. "And if we stay married for a year, you get fifty million?"

We stepped out of the casino. The sun shone bright, but we were shaded by the overhang. Vehicles cruised through the loop in front of the building, dropping off and picking up tourists. "No, Savvy. If you wait to divorce me until after my thirtieth birthday, then you get half. The trust is one hundred million. You'd get fifty."

Xander

SAVVY WAS quiet all the way to her hotel. I'd expected excitement. I suppose that was too optimistic after the way she'd shut down at lunch. But surely she'd tolerate me for a year?

I let her work through everything I'd told her. I'd meant what I'd said. I wanted to be with her for much more than a year, and when she'd come up with the idea to marry, I'd jumped at it.

Yes, I wanted the money. I didn't need it, just a small portion that I would keep. The total amount was staggering, but I could do a hell of a lot more good in the world with it than the Cartwrights. They'd buy up land and businesses in King's Creek, where my family had been for generations, and do their damnedest to push us out. Or worse, Danny would kill himself drinking it away, but only after he'd spent every penny, whether it was on boats, lakes for that boat, or a herd of horses and cattle he couldn't take care of. And the one thing he wouldn't spend that money on were competent employees to care for those animals.

I knew that better than anyone, except maybe Dad.

We wound through the hotel, the soft dings of the slots fading the closer we got to the elevator bank. We didn't speak as we rose to the thirtieth floor. The hallway was quiet and there were only a few doors on this floor.

Savvy let us into her suite. Music blasted from a Bluetooth speaker propped on an end table in the vestibule.

"Brady?" Savvy called.

"Savvy," a man drawled.

I wasn't a jealous guy. Never had been, but as Brady swaggered out with only a towel slung over his hips, grinning at Savvy like he knew her better than I did—because he did—my vision turned a little green.

He was about Savvy's height. His hair was fresh from the shower, but styled with more effort than I'd ever given mine a single day in my life. His was the wiry sort of muscular.

He stopped when he saw me. "Well, well, well. I can guess part of your long story."

"This is Xander." The bold, confrontational woman I'd met last night had vanished once we'd met with Chief, and she wasn't making an appearance with this Brady either, who was supposedly one of her best friends.

Brady stepped forward, his gaze guarded, but I couldn't tell if it was for Savvy's benefit or because he thought he should be in my place. And since he didn't know my place was as her husband, I was even more curious. He held his hand out and I shook it. "Brady Younger. How'd you two kids meet?"

"On the Strip, not far from here," Savvy answered easily. "He was taking pictures."

"Oh yeah?" Brady ran a hand through his dark wet locks. "Then you focused on Savvy?" He grinned at his pun.

This was weird as hell, but more comfortable than meeting her dad. Brady didn't dismiss me like Chief had. But he didn't size me up like Lex had either. He wasn't overly concerned that Savvy had brought a strange man back to their suite. My muscles eased. Towel or not, I didn't sense any animosity from Brady.

"That's about how it went, yeah." She'd been my focus since I'd met her.

"We, uh . . ." Her gaze flicked to me. "We got married last night."

That wiped all of Brady's humor away. "Be serious now. I'm not hungover, but I haven't gotten much sleep."

"I am serious. It seemed like a good idea at the time."

Ouch.

As the story spilled out, Brady's brows shot up and for the first time, I could see real concern. When it came time to tell him about the money, she glanced at me and I nodded. All my brothers knew about the trust, so it was only fair she had someone in her corner who knew.

Brady shook his head. "Savvy, if what he says is true, that amount could be revolutionary. But do you even know this trust is real?"

Savvy looked at me, vulnerability and uncertainty mixing in her expression. She hadn't thought about not believing me.

"I can have Grams fax you a copy of it."

"Maybe you should send it to my family's lawyer." She grabbed her phone, her fingers flying. "I'll send you his info." She paused and glanced at Brady. She chewed on her lower lip a moment before asking me, "What's your number?"

Brady barked out a laugh. "You exchanged vows but not numbers? Classic Savvy."

What was so classic about that?

As if he'd heard my thoughts, he added, "Our Sav can be impulsive. Hence how she's in debt with her parents for majoring in something that isn't business or, I dunno, how to be pretentious."

I got the part about owing the parents for college money, but Savvy hadn't mentioned that she was in debt to them for it. Her cheeks flushed when she met my gaze. "I insisted on majoring in environmental science, and I had to pay for it. Fiscal consequences and all that. But they paid my loans when I moved home, and I'm repaying them. Saves me from interest."

I'd thought the cost of living in the city was the reason she was still with her parents, but after meeting Chief, this explanation made more sense. He was willing to let her stretch her wings, but he'd make sure she lost a few feathers for it.

Brady's head bobbed. He'd heard it all before. "What'd your sisters say?"

"They don't know yet."

Brady's mouth dropped and he put his hand to his bare chest. "The proper Mrs. Abbot?"

"I'm sure Chief's told her by now."

Brady's gaze slid to me but he addressed Savvy. "You gonna tell them about the trust?"

Savvy shifted from one bare foot to another. "They don't need to know. I'll tell the lawyer I'm the one paying for him to look at it so he'd better not say anything. I'd rather work this out without the extra pressure."

"Yeah, I wouldn't tell them either. Otherwise, the Chief will keep you too busy to file for divorce." Brady looked between us. "Then once you get the windfall, you're home-free."

"You're right about that," Savvy muttered. "I got a notification from Chief that he put more money in my account. For Xander to fly home with us."

She worried her lower lip. Chief had invited me to DC whenever we were ready to leave Vegas. She hadn't. Leaving me would be easier if I wasn't around.

"I have no problem flying home with you," I said and her forehead crinkled. "It'll give you time for your lawyer to review the trust."

Please take me with you.

Brady's smile was wide. "Do it, Savvy. If what he says is true, you'd never have to worry about being cut off again. You won't find yourself in a flat with asshole roommates like me."

She folded her arms and studied me,

then Brady. Her gaze swept around the room. The sitting room. The TV that took up half the wall. The bedrooms on either side that she'd said came with private master baths. An extravagant room that Chief was paying for since her old boss couldn't.

"Brady, can you give us a minute?"

Brady held his hands up as he went to his room to dress and pack. "It's your decision. Just remember that you're still paying for the last one."

"College?" I asked.

"I hadn't eaten for three days when Brady asked me out. I only said yes 'cause I hoped he'd buy me dinner."

"You and Brady dated?"

"One date. He found out my parents cut me off for college and took me under his wing." She sighed and trudged to the sofa. I leaned against the small part of the wall the TV didn't take up. "We both wanted a friend more than an easy lay. My roommate had no sympathy and laughed at my privileged ass. Brady comes from a family like mine, but they kicked him out when he graduated high school. He worked a couple of years and then went to college. I couldn't even figure out how to cook ramen."

"You didn't get any help?"

She shook her head. "Not until I graduated. I guess I proved something to them by sticking it out, so they let me move back home and humored me while I worked for Saving Sunsets. I guess it was another lesson they thought I would learn. Like they knew I'd eventually go into the family business."

"But you said your mother doesn't work."

"She doesn't. I don't know what her deal is. She's stricter than Chief with money, yet it was her idea to pay off my student loans and have me pay them back directly—to save on interest. And while she let me live at home after I was done with college, she set a time limit. I had six months to find a job. She didn't think much of Saving

Sunsets, but she didn't insist I look for something else. Hopefully working for Chief is good enough to keep living with them."

Fear welled in Savvy's eyes. She didn't want to be that hungry girl who couldn't cook for herself. "Why'd you marry me, Savvy?"

She chewed on the inside of her lip and lifted her gaze. "In school, I would've quit and gone back home without Brady's help. I live with my parents and I lost my job. Chief stepped in. I can't say no without being kicked out again."

"And I seemed like a guy who could live on nothing with no one's help." Only I wasn't the pauper she wanted.

She squeezed her eyes shut. "I'm pathetic."

I hooked my hand in hers. My family didn't have to worry about money, but Dad and Mama had made sure we knew how to take care of ourselves. I could make a meal and do my own laundry, which were the first steps to living on your own. I doubted Savvy had learned basic life skills, but she was expected to navigate loans and rent without help. "You're human."

"What's worse is that I'm thinking of what you said. Staying married for money. That seems worse. That even after college I got married so I would be taken care of when I quit my job with Chief and that I'll stay married to get the payout my parents won't give me. Yet, if I get divorced, or annul the marriage, or whatever, I risk the wrath of Chief. I don't know what Mother would do. I can't see her explaining a Vegas wedding, but I certainly don't know how she'd handle the embarrassment of a Vegas wedding and subsequent breakup."

I swallowed my disappointment. I'd asked her why she'd married me and I'd gotten a brutally honest answer. I had an answer too, but she didn't ask. Those moments she was thrilled about who I was and what I did had burrowed under my skin. I wanted more of them and more of her.

"Either way it sounds like it's better to stay married," I said as casually but as seriously as I could without sounding desperate. As long as we were still together, I had a chance to win her over.

She tugged her hand free of my grasp and buried her face in her hands. "Then I'm selling myself out. Or selling myself out even more than I did last night."

Guilt gnawed at my insides. This would've been prevented if I'd been the reasonable one. If I'd thought through any part of a marriage beyond getting to be with this woman and fulfill the terms of my trust. "Whatever you choose, Savvy, it's no one's business but your own. You don't have to justify what you've done to anyone."

She was going to go through with ending things between us. To preserve the identity she was struggling to build for herself, she was going to ask that lawyer to draw up a divorce contract instead of reading the trust.

She dropped her hands from her face. "If we stay together, I need to go home. I'll work for Chief. I'll build my skills so when we divorce next year, no one can say that I freeloaded until I had your money."

I heard what she didn't say: just in case she was left without a dime to her name, she wanted to have a foundation. A fallback plan that wouldn't burn bridges with her parents or leave her without resources.

Hardly the most romantic reason to stay together. But it gave me a year to win over the woman I wanted to spend my life with. The romance could come later. I'd make sure of it.

CHAPTER 6

S avvy

I GOT out of the Uber and faced the historic Tudor mansion before me. Slate gray with miles of pristine white trim, the two-story house was covered in square windows, all gleaming due to the teams of people my mother hired to care for the place. Home, sweet home.

Our lot was just as ostentatious. We had two acres on the edge of Chevy Chase,

Maryland, and each bush and tree was manicured to within an inch of each leaf's life.

How pretentious did Xander think this was?

Or was this his normal? I mean, he came from a family as well off—or even more loaded—than mine. He ranched, but that didn't mean he'd grown up in a shack. I had no idea what ranch houses looked like. Or a ranch, for that matter.

"Nice place," was all he said. His backpack was slung over his shoulder and he rested our suitcases at his feet. While I had stared at the family home I'd seen nearly every day of my life, he'd gotten my stuff. I was used to our driver, Davis, getting it for me.

"It is." I pointed to the far right corner. "That's my room." After what we'd done together, my throat shouldn't be closing off from swelling panic. I'd have to share a room with him. My parents thought we were married. And we were. I'd decided on the trip home that I'd stay with him. Money aside, I had to save face, and being married at least a year would help. That didn't change that our marriage was nothing more than a business transaction.

"We're staying in your childhood bedroom?" His voice rang with doubt, and as unflappable as he'd been on the ride to the airport and while getting tickets to come meet my mother and sisters, his expression now said he'd rather run than sleep in some room better suited to a five-year-old girl.

"Relax, it's not pink. Anymore."

"It used to be?"

"With a canopy bed and ruffles. After you meet Mother, you'll see." My family had fallen into a well of stereotypes and never been rescued.

I hadn't had a chance to warn him about Mother's and my sisters' idiosyncrasies on the plane ride. After the rush of getting tickets and boarding, and after a short night and stressful day, I'd passed out on his shoulder each leg of the trip. I suspected he'd slept too, but we hadn't talked much. The car ride had been more silence as the magnitude of what we were about to do sank in.

We would pretend to be happily married.

I might as well mitigate what I could now. "My mother is a Stepford wife past her prime. Her fashion is on point and she participates in all the committees expected of someone of her station. She takes her role in society seriously. She'll smile and say all the right things until I don't know what she really thinks or what she thinks she should say."

Xander ducked his head, having no reason to question me after I'd told him about Chief. He'd seen for himself how right I was about that.

I sucked in a deep breath. "You already know about Chief. My father grew up being told he was the best and then proving it. He used Mother's money to get status he couldn't earn with his military clout. And since his career in the military was mostly dominated by males, I don't think he knew what to do with three daughters."

He thought my sisters and I needed guidance and direction instead of fatherly support. I wish I hadn't proved him right.

"He thinks marrying you each off is a good first step?"

"Basically." I twisted my fingers and glared at the beautiful house I should have been glad to see standing before me. I should have felt relief and happiness to be back home. I didn't. "That's what he did with Em. She's the oldest. He won't try it with Pearl. She wanted to join the military and he wanted her to go to an Ivy League school instead. So after she finished high school, she told them she was going to study abroad for a semester. Then she ran off and joined up, didn't tell anyone until she got to her first post."

"How'd Chief take it?"

"He set Em up with a guy that worked

for him, but he actually let me go to school somewhere else besides Georgetown." As if I'd ever be brave enough to outright leave like Pearl. "Pearl's back home now to get her degree." At Georgetown, but not with our parents' money. She'd earned what she needed through enlistment benefits and savings. Chief never demanded she work for him or get married. "Her room is next to ours."

Xander adjusted his backpack as his gaze swept the lawn. Old snow that held only a few rabbit prints spread over the expansive lawn. Growing up, that lawn was the most nature I'd seen outside of field trips.

"Em's husband is like Lex?"

"You probably won't see him much. He works all the time like Chief. Em doesn't, so you'll meet her. She's into volunteering and stuff." Em was our mother, minus thirty years.

The front door opened and Pearl came out. Her smile was sly, and mischief glittered in her eyes. Her blond hair was growing out from the bob she'd kept in the army. She flew down the front steps, no jacket and her feet stuffed into my boots that were kept in the front closet.

"Oh my God, Savvy. I thought Chief had gone out of his damn mind when he told me what you did!"

Mild curiosity seeped into Xander's expression. "This must be Pearl."

"If she'd been born a redhead, she would've been named Ruby." Mother said my eyes were so blue there had been no question they'd stay that way. Thus, I was Sapphire. "But she's a blond, so she got Pearl."

My sister barreled forward, her arms out. I thought she'd slow, but I should've known better. Pearl didn't do subtle.

"Oomph." My breath whooshed out as she swept me into a giant hug.

"I'm so glad you're home."

"I've only been gone a few days." But I sank into her hug. Pearl was the devil on my shoulder, daring me to be my impulsive self. But the older I got, the more I realized that it was only me dealing with the outcome, and Mother and Chief were left thinking I had to be cared for.

Pearl stepped back and waved her finger between us. "Since Mummy dearest found out what you did, she's been in a reception-planning frenzy and somehow hasn't figured out that I don't know the slightest difference between steel blue and cobalt."

Mother had been planning? Ugh. Xander might rethink how much he was willing to do for money.

"And you're my new brother-in-law. The knight in cheap armor that turned out to be platinum. Chief sounded downright giddy on the phone."

Xander held his hand out. "Xander King."

Pearl shook it, then crossed her arms, eyeing him. "I can't wait to hear the unabridged story, Savvy."

"That'll have to wait. Is Mother home?"

"The Dame is in the study, picking out announcements." No nicknames for Mother ever stuck. She was very much just Mother, but Pearl kept trying. "Marriage announcements."

Warmth leeched from my face and the cold seeped in for the first time since we'd landed. My family and Brady knew about my Vegas wedding. And Lex. And of course Xander's family had to all know by now. But all our extended relatives and everyone in our social circle?

That made it so . . . real.

Pearl bounced on the balls of her feet and I fortified myself against the next bit of news. Her voice was strangled, like she couldn't contain her glee. The military had done nothing to dampen her annoying sister qualities. "I heard her booking a photo shoot for the two of you."

"Oh God. She's going all out."

"She is. And I'm going to be so off the hook for at least a month. Chief might not be bugging me to get married, but she's been asking me if I met any nice officers while I was at Fort Jackson. Thank you!" She threw her arms around me once more, then withdrew so fast I stumbled backward.

Xander's hand was on my elbow in a heartbeat.

Pearl chucked him on the shoulder. "You've earned the best brother title already."

"Happy I could help," he said dryly. His hand dropped from my arm and I missed his heat.

"Come on." Pearl bounded away. "Let the fun begin."

I watched her go. I didn't move and neither did Xander. I had no idea how long he planned to stay, or what we were going to do together as a married couple while we were here. Xander was used to leaving when he wanted. How long would he stick this out with me before he said *enough is enough, have your lawyer call me next Valentine's Day?*

Had the lunch with Chief really been

yesterday? Yes. It was early in the day. I'd been married for nearly forty-eight hours. A detail niggled at the edge of my mind. Right!

"Happy birthday," I said. He hadn't reminded me.

"Thanks," he said, his eyes on the house.

"I didn't get you anything. I hope the millions you'll get next year will make up for it." What would a whole year bring? Would we still be together? Would we be married in name only until we cashed in? Too many questions when we'd known each other for less than two days.

But that didn't mean that the answers weren't important.

~

Xander

I WANTED TO LEAVE. Hitch a ride to the airport and fly out. I'd go anywhere there weren't reception halls, matching color schemes, or portrait sessions for invitations.

Less than two hours after we'd arrived at the Abbot estate, my arms were stretched to the sides and a dude I'd met only minutes ago had his hand in my crotch. Another guy was at my back with a measuring tape, getting the width of my shoulders. The suit Mrs. Abbot wanted me to wear for the photos was going to be the most impeccably tailored garment I'd ever worn. Which was a low bar to step over, but still.

I'd grown up with money. My family worked hard for what we had, but the stress of managing wealth was different than managing debt, or living without money altogether. A difference I knew and that my brothers didn't. But that didn't mean we'd grown up like Savvy. We bought our clothing from the farm and tractor place in town. If we needed something fancier, we went to the mall in Billings. My shoes and cowboy boots had always been off the rack, never special ordered, like the pair crotch-measuring guy had just put a rush on.

He'd even politely suggested a brand of underwear and undershirts that he could order. I'd agreed since I didn't have much more than what was in my backpack and I was certain this photo shoot wasn't the only one Mrs. Abbot had lined up.

Normally, I'd feel bad about the expense, but it wasn't like Savvy or I had asked for pictures, marriage announcements, a "small" gathering to celebrate our nuptials, or any of the rest of it. I'd rather leave the country until next February and find some good, hard work to sink into until then. Then I'd try my hand at selling a few snapshots.

But this wasn't about me, and despite what my dad thought, I wasn't selfish. All I had to do was stay married in order to get my share and pay Dad back for what I'd pilfered. In order to stay married to me, Savvy needed more. She needed me to put on this dog and pony show. She was doing what I couldn't—facing her family, determined to justify her choices in life. I wasn't going to leave her hanging during my first week of being a husband.

"All right." The man from the floor rose, one of his knees cracking, but that didn't slow him down. "I think I have all I need. Marcus would like to go over colors and styles with you."

"Is basic black an option?"

The guy, Harold maybe—this place didn't do name tags—smiled. "There is no such thing as basic black here." Humor laced his tone, as if he and I were in on the same secret. There was nothing simple in this store, otherwise their clientele would go elsewhere.

I followed him to a back room that had racks of jackets and a table full of swatches. The ornate chair behind a massive desk must be where I got to sit.

I looked around for Savvy, despite knowing she wouldn't be here yet. Mrs. Abbot had asked the driver to drop me off at the tailors while they went to a dress boutique. I guess the really high-end places specialized in only men or women.

It could be worse. Harold and Marcus hadn't asked me anything more probing than whether I liked the feel of a material.

Taking a seat behind the desk, I shook my head at Marcus's offer for a drink, especially once I spotted the same kind of brandy Dad would drink. He wouldn't approve of the Abbots paying for my tux, and the fitting, and everything else. I'd add them to the debt I had to pay.

An hour and forty minutes later, I was regretting turning down the drink. I couldn't take one more sable, slate, pitch, or onyx swatch coming at me. Then I made the mistake of asking about a navy blue suit.

A frenzy of messages went between Marcus and Mrs. Abbot until Marcus confirmed the exact shade of Savvy's dress.

"Sapphire," he announced.

"Wouldn't that be gauche?" I asked. "Dressing her the same as her name?"

Harold blinked and Marcus covered his mouth with his hand and looked at the ground.

"It's uh . . ." Harold licked his lips and scratched the back of his neck. "It's um . . . expected of the Abbots. No one questions Opal's choices."

"Is her dress going to be mother of pearl?"

Harold coughed a laugh and Marcus's eyes flared wide, but his cheek pinched like he was biting it.

"I don't mean to be insulting." I truly didn't, but I'd only been in this world for a few hours and I was dog tired from a night of traveling and sleeping on planes and in uncomfortable airport chairs. My day wasn't over after this either. When Mrs. Abbot had learned I didn't have more than a suitcase and a backpack, anticipation had gleamed in her eyes. She enjoyed planning and purchasing, and Savvy and I were the perfect excuse for more.

Opal Abbot wasn't what I'd expected. Savvy had said Stepford wife, but there was a lot going on behind my new mother-in-law's eyes. She didn't beam because I was Xander King, son of Gentry King and part of the King Oil empire. She also didn't look down her nose at a struggling photographer.

Savvy had introduced me, I'd been assessed, and that'd been it. I was Savvy's husband and for now, that would do. The rest was left up to me. Which was why I would suck up my fatigue and get whatever clothing Mrs. Abbot thought was befitting of the family image. For now, it was the only way I could repay her.

"I'm just trying to figure the Abbots out." It wasn't a lie. "This wasn't how I grew up."

Harold nodded like he'd assumed at least that. I doubted any of his other clients had worn a hemp hoodie in here.

"I grew up with manure on my boots.

Not polish." I don't know why I felt like I had to explain. They weren't judging me. But damn, this life wasn't anything like what I'd lived.

Marcus's eyes crinkled at the corners. "I used to show horses when I was a kid."

With his perfect posture and deliberate movements, I could picture him in long boots and a Beagler hat, taking his horse through the movements. But horse shows were nothing like the 4-H shows Mama had entered us in before she'd died. Scrawny kids with tucked-in white shirts, blue jeans, and dusty cowboy boots. Still, it made me feel better. Someone else knew the smell of horse sweat.

A flurry of giggles reached the selection room. I picked out Savvy's laugh, no doubt a result of something Pearl had said, and based off Mrs. Abbot's faint admonishment, I was right.

"Oh, husband of my sister," Pearl called.

"Pearl," Savvy hissed.

"Ah." Marcus clapped his hands

together. "I think we're done. It sounds as if the rest of your group has arrived."

"I'd better go before they tear your store apart."

Harold chuckled nervously. "The Abbots are always a delight."

Since he probably dealt with Chief, I understood the thread of anxiety in his voice.

I returned to the show floor, where the finest suits were displayed and rows of subdued colored shirts lined shelves.

My steps slowed. Pearl was behind a mannequin, attempting to do a *who wore it better* pose. Savvy was doing a version of the robot, mannequin style. Her back was to me, giving me a full view of her ass in the tight jeans she wore. They were stuffed into the fluffy boots Pearl had used earlier. Her coat was cinched at her waist, but the way she twisted and bent gave me a stilted, yet erotic show. Way more erotic than any robot dance I'd ever seen before.

Pearl giggled. "Better watch out, Sav. It

looks like your husband wants to consummate the marriage right now."

Savvy froze and peeked over her shoulder. Her cheeks burned red, but she turned back to Pearl and hissed, "Oh, it's been consummated. So. Hard."

Pearl sputtered and guffawed.

"Pearl. Sapphire." Mrs. Abbot's voice whip-cracked a warning through the store.

Pearl straightened, rolling her lips in, struggling to keep from laughing.

Savvy spun around and lifted her chin. "Why dah-ling. However did the fitting go?"

That earned Savvy a glare from her mom before she turned her back on us to finish conversing with Marcus. She probably had to clear my choices before they could be purchased.

When I reached Savvy, I leaned into her. "I'll be suited up as befits a prize stud in seventy-two hours." My arm slipped around her waist and I kissed her neck.

A hitch in Savvy's breath made me pull

away at the same time she did. Pearl's gaze bored into her sister, then me. For the first time in the hours since I'd met Pearl, she didn't say anything, just went to her mom's side.

"Sorry. It's just . . ." Savvy played with the ends of her long ponytail hanging over her shoulder. "Sorry."

Right. What had been magic on our wedding night was now pretend. She was willing to go only so far with the illusion. "No worries. Whatever you're comfortable with."

I meant what I'd said. If my wife was more comfortable while I slept on the floor, so be it. But that didn't stop my heart from sinking down to my toes. Didn't she want more than pretend? Didn't she want to explore the fire that had brought us together? Didn't she want . . . me?

It was early yet, only the beginning of our marriage. I had a lot of work to do. Double if I was the only one putting in the effort.

CHAPTER 7

avvy

THE ROOM WAS BLISSFULLY QUIET. Mother
had left me alone as she finished planning
various festivities for the upcoming weeks.
I had a reprieve from voicing my opinions
on venues, color themes, and VIP attendees
who meant nothing to me but everything to
my parents.

I was in the library Mother had created
on the first floor, a little-used room full of

boring military history tomes and a desk that hadn't seen an ass behind it for years. My sisters and I thought this room was the most unexciting space on earth, but right now, it was quiet and offered a wide view into the backyard.

Pearl stopped in the doorway. She eyed me, then the window. I ignored her devilish smirk as she danced in and peered out the window. I shifted in the wingback chair that looked like it had been pulled straight out of a Civil War–era plantation mansion. It probably had been, and no extra padding had been added either. But I'd been sitting here for an hour already.

"Stalker," she said triumphantly and flopped into the matching chair across from me. Both seats flanked the window. For a friendly visit. For natural light while reading. Or for spying on my husband, who'd been helping our lawn service clear snow from the outdoor seating area.

It was the end of February, but Mother

had insisted the backyard be as presentable as inside the house.

Xander laughed with the landscaper. I didn't even know his name, but by now, Xander probably knew the names of the guy's wife and children. Hell, he'd probably even been invited to their house for Easter.

I could go out there, but I never talked to the staff. I knew the names of the housekeeping staff. We exchanged pleasant greetings but nothing beyond "How are you doing today?"

We weren't a horrible household to work for, but natural turnover made it hard to get to know people. After a lifetime of seeing familiar faces turn to strange ones, I'd eventually stopped trying.

"I'm not stalking," I grumbled.

She curled her legs under her. "Didn't you get enough of him last night?"

I shot her a glare. Her room was next to mine, but I knew very well that she couldn't hear a damn thing. There was nothing to hear. Chief hadn't made me come into work yet, but I'd been exhausted all the same. I'd collapsed in bed, thanks to the travel and emotional roller coaster of the last few days. I'd burrowed under the covers and Xander had slept on top. I could only assume he'd gone to bed shortly after I'd fallen asleep, since he'd been in the bathroom when I'd conveniently passed out.

"What?" Her expression wasn't even trying to be innocent. "Seriously, though. I can't believe you aren't trying to milk him for all he's worth—and you know damn well I'm not talking about money."

My gaze shifted outside. Xander had produced a heavier coat from his luggage. The dark blue material did nothing to conceal his wide shoulders. And those jeans he was in hugged the muscles of his legs. The bunch and flex as he shoveled last night's snow was mesmerizing, casting some unique spell that kept me rooted by this damn window.

Mother had forced a couple new outfits

on him and not a one had included jeans. Yet that was what Xander wore.

"It wouldn't be right," I finally answered, my gaze lifting to his easy grin at something the other man said. Xander did the shoveling while the landscaper used a broom to sweep snow from between the crevices of the stone patio.

I waited for Mother to march into the library and ask why on earth my husband was clearing snow, but she hadn't made one comment about the way he dressed. She had to know he was outside. She knew everything that went on in and around the house.

Pearl's fists landed on her hips. "Why the hell not?"

Brady was deep in job hunting and couldn't afford to meet me for a coffee to talk. Pearl had been busy with school and this was the first time we'd been alone. Everything that had happened in the seventy-two hours before I'd returned home crowded on my tongue. "Close the door."

I explained it all—from getting canned to the trust. Pearl and I had always been closer than her and Em. My oldest sister and I had gotten along great when we were younger, but then during her high school years, she'd started emulating Mother while Pearl was still willing to do forbidden activities like play in the trees surrounding our property or take our dolls under the stairs so we wouldn't get a lecture about how it was time to move on from such juvenile activities.

I finished with "The lawyer confirmed everything Xander said about the trust. So that's what we're doing." And waited. Pearl was the strong one. What was she going to think?

"Sapphire Jewel Abbot, you're fucking crazy."

"I know. It's awful. I survived college. It wasn't like I was on the streets. Why am I so scared?" I'd been terrified I'd fail my classes because I was too hungry to study. I'd had enough in loans to pay for the dorms, but not a meal plan.

"No, you're an idiot if you think that's the only reason you didn't sever this marriage when you woke up the next morning."

"I had the lunch with Chief. And Lex."

She lifted a pale brow. *"Reeeally?* That's the only reason? It's not because he's hot? It's not because he's not a D-bag, he's considerate, and he's really into you?"

My heart leapt at her last words. "He's not that into me. He has a stake in this too."

"A stake that he was willing to walk away from until he met you. You don't think he could've been married by now if he wanted to be?"

Denial died on my tongue as I glanced outside. He was grinning at something the other guy had said. He stooped and pushed a swatch of wet snow with the shovel like it didn't weigh more than foam peanuts. His powerful muscles bunched and flexed, helping me recall our wedding night in vivid, steamy detail.

"There it is," Pearl gloated. "You want to eat him up."

"I already have." Yeah, it sounded like I was bragging.

"Then do it again."

Didn't she think I wanted to? "I'm not a fifty-million-dollar hooker."

"I doubt hookers would complain about making fifty-mil from a client."

I scowled at her. "If I was just me, and he was just him, we would've been nothing but a one-night stand." A memorable one. One that every guy afterward would have failed to live up to. "But I have Mother and Chief. He has his trust, and here we are. Married and acting like it was meant to be."

"Why can't it be more?"

"What do you mean?"

"Why can't you two fall in love? Do it backward. You're married, now start dating."

I wasn't like the women Xander had

dated. I didn't have to interrogate him about his history to know. He'd grown up in a rural, small town. He'd worked for a living. He didn't eat at three-Michelin-star restaurants like the Abbots did. Or use chauffeurs. I doubted he even used room service. He'd dated women who could take care of themselves.

"You said it yourself—you're scared." She shook her head and sat forward. "Come on, Savvy. Don't let anyone have a say in this marriage other than you and Xander. Get to know him."

"Maybe he's a cheater." I didn't think so. But my mind sifted for as many arguments as possible. I was prepared for a divorce in a year.

Was I prepared to stay married?

She wrinkled her nose. "He passed the sister test. How many guys have we dated that failed it?"

My attention sharpened. My sisters and I were close enough in age that it had caused more than a couple uncomfortable moments over the years. Like when one's boyfriend hit on another sister. One Abbot was as good as another to some guys.

"What do you mean?"

"Xander was coming out of the bathroom when I was going in." And with a house full of women, Pearl didn't wear much at night.

"Don't tell me."

"I had a shirt on."

"Did it even go past the top of your underwear?"

She shrugged and picked at a thumbnail. "Didn't faze him. Other than jumping and apologizing profusely like he was the one that had walked in on me, I don't think his eyes dipped below my collarbone. He beelined for your room."

Where I had been fast asleep. "Good to know." I wasn't jealous of my sisters, but it was nice to know Xander didn't have roaming eyes. At the airport, I hadn't caught him eyeballing any of the gorgeous women walking past us. One woman had slept in the terminal with us, a supermodel type with long glossy hair, glowing skin, and a willowy body. I swear she'd picked her seat so she could stare at Xander the whole time, but Xander had only read a mystery novel he'd picked up at the gift shop.

When he'd finished the book, he'd given it to a guy reading another book in the terminal we'd exited from. The smooth way he'd passed off the book told me that he did that all the time. He traveled so much, keeping extraneous items wasn't an option.

Pearl watched me, then opened her mouth. I wouldn't like what she said. She could read me better than Brady, and be blunter about it. "You're afraid he's with you for the trust."

"He says he's not, but it's a lot of money, even in our worlds."

"I'm telling you, Sav, you've sold yourself short your whole life. You're a strong, capable woman with the world at your fingertips. Making a few mistakes doesn't mean you're a hopeless loser who can't do anything for herself."

"Says the army private."

"I was a sergeant."

I rolled my eyes. "Even worse."

"Different paths in life doesn't mean one is better. If you got out of your comfort zone and stayed there, you'd find that out."

I got out of my comfort zone all the time. But dammit, she'd hit the target. I never stayed there. "I'm a privileged snot, is that what you're saying?"

After a beat of silence, she said, "I think you're afraid *Xander's* going to think you're a privileged snot."

I averted my gaze to the bookshelves. I couldn't look at my new husband, who was outside doing more manual labor around the house than I ever had. "I don't know him well enough to know what he'll think."

Pearl stretched her hands above her head. "Then go get to know him."

The movement caught the attention of the men working outside. I glanced over, right into Xander's direct stare. He lifted a gloved hand. They weren't the traditional puffy winter gloves meant to get him from a warm house to a heated car to a ski lift. These were grungy, beaten-up gloves that had been used for years.

I waved back.

Pearl rose and drifted toward the door. "You have a year. Just sayin'. You licked him, you can keep him."

Xander was back at work, this time clearing a path from the patio to the shed, where the landscaper stored much of the lawn equipment he didn't need in the winter. The landscaper said something and he turned around.

I jumped out of the chair before I could be busted staring again. He was my husband, but Pearl's stalker comment would hit too close to home if I sat here longer.

Get to know him.

What would it hurt?

For once, I was going to escape the

endless loop of questions in my head and do something. I went down the hall, my slippered feet whispering on the cherrywood floors. I stopped at the closet. It was full of fluffy ski gloves, snow pants, and parkas. Gear we packed and took to Aspen once a year, then had cleaned and packed away for another year.

Opening the door, I peered in like I was in the middle of a horror movie and the killer was going to jump out at me. I yanked on the chain hanging next to the bulb. When the light turned on, the closet went from dark and creepy to fluffy and colorful. I grabbed my fuchsia winter coat and shrugged into it. The boots I'd worn yesterday were in the closet by the front door. They should be good enough. They weren't made for actual snow, but they'd keep my feet warm.

I found gloves on the top shelf and made my way through the silent house to the front door and located my boots. Carrying them, I went back through the house toward the door to the patio. Mother stepped out of her office, her reading glasses perched on her nose and a paper in her hand.

"Oh, Sapphire." She took the glasses off and dropped them to her chest. I'd teased her that the 1950s was calling and wanted their reading glasses chain back, but it didn't bother her. For good reason: she rocked it and I'd told her that too. Mother was a lot of things, but unstylish was not one of them.

She tilted her head at my coat, her gaze dropping to my boots. "Is something wrong?"

"Xander's outside, so . . ." I didn't even know what I was doing, only that it seemed weird he was out there working and I was bored inside.

"Yes, I saw him helping Michael. He's . . ." Her smile wavered, then solidified. "Different than what I expected."

"You don't mind that he's helping Michael?" Not only did she know the landscaper's name, but she didn't mind if the neighbors saw her new son-in-law helping the help?

She blinked. "Why would I?"

I had no answer. I'd spent a lifetime not getting my mother, and times like these hammered it home. "Yes, he's certainly different."

Her eyes crinkled at the corners. "I imagine that's what got your attention."

Sometimes she surprised me with what she saw and understood. It was too easy to assume she was oblivious or uncaring, an unthinking follower of her status's demands. Then there were times like this. "His looks helped."

Her chuckle was like the tinkling of chandelier crystals. Mother had more sophistication in her left pinky than I did in my whole body. "The fireplace in the sitting room is electric if you two get too cold out there. Just go in and turn it on."

Her words summoned a long-forgotten memory. Me and my sisters would spill inside after building snowmen. We'd find Mother and Chief sitting by the fireplace, deep in conversation.

Those times were some of my favorite memories. The thought propelled me out the sliding door to the patio. Xander turned at the sound.

I hadn't been in the backyard during winter in years. Now that I was out here, faced with my new husband, I had no idea what to do.

Xander

My little snow bunny's gaze darted all over the yard like she was looking for shelter before a predator could snatch her up. She took a tentative step. And another, her boots crushing the remaining snow that Michael intended to sweep clean.

Overkill in my opinion, but he didn't

mind doing it and the Abbots didn't mind paying. It also gave me something to do, which in this house was a godsend. I'd never been so bored. When I went back home, Dawson always had chores for me. If I traveled, I had to worry about the necessities or I could fall back on taking pictures. The Abbots had staff do any and all manual labor. They had their groceries delivered, and they had a driver. The only reading options were the military history paperweights on the shelves in the library. I'm sure there was a TV somewhere, but I wasn't one to sit and binge shows. And there was no one to talk to.

Mrs. Abbot had retreated to her office to rule the Abbot world. Chief was gone and I got the impression he was gone a lot. Pearl was around between classes, but she wasn't who I wanted to talk to.

Since we'd had lunch with our fathers, Savvy had been a different person. Skittish. Uncertain. Subdued. The bold, determined woman who'd challenged me when I was taking pictures and marched to the altar with the confidence of a card shark approaching a high-stakes poker table hadn't made a reappearance.

I missed that Savvy.

I had to do something that'd break the ice between us, but small talk in the snow wasn't it. I stooped down and grabbed a handful of snow. Straightening, I packed it into a loose ball and eyed her.

Her expression turned wary. "You'd better not be thinking about—"

I lobbed the snowball, a gentle toss that wouldn't take her out.

A squeal escaped and she darted out of the way. It landed with a splat behind her. I grabbed another handful.

"What are you . . ." She narrowed her eyes at me and dove for her own handful.

In the second that she was turned and bent over, I aimed and threw my snowball at her ass.

Snow splattered her pants and she jumped, losing what she'd gathered for snow. "I can't believe you hit me with my back turned."

"You don't grow up with three brothers and pass up these opportunities."

"Sisters aren't easy either." She swooped down and loaded both hands.

My laughter was eaten by the wind as I loped through the snow to get out of range. A *thunk* hit next to me. A solid thump landed square in my back.

"Nice," I called and made another snowball.

She was advancing until I faced her and sprinted, my work boots cutting into the snow.

With a yell, she spun and ran across the lawn. The snow was slushy enough to slow her. She was wearing snow pants and I wasn't, but that didn't stop me. I dropped my snowball and tackled her, spinning her to keep from plastering her into the snow.

Her holler rang across the lawn as she landed on top of me. Her breath whooshed out, the condensation cloud dissipating with mine. I wanted to laugh, but I waited, my heart clogging my throat until she let out a full-bodied laugh.

She slapped me on both shoulders. Her thick gloves hampered the hit even more than my coat. "Xander! You're going to be soaked."

"It'll be fine. It's not like I'm two miles away from my cabin in a heavy forest full of bears and an impending snowstorm."

"That sounds scary."

"Newbie mistake in Alaska." I kept my arms around her. Her weight on top of me wasn't enough to warm me and the longer I stayed in the snow, the more soaked my jeans would get. But I'd lie in a glacier for hours just to keep her here. "No bears found me worth feasting on."

"The scariest thing I've ever had to face in the winter was a snowman Em put a Friday the Thirteenth mask on. She built it right outside my window one night after I went to bed. I couldn't sleep for a week."

"How old were you?"

"Ten." Her cheeks glowed red and her breath puffed out. Sexy and adorable at the same time.

"We can build a snowman right now. Make it a pudgy, cute one."

"You need to get into dry clothes."

"That'll wait."

She pushed off and my body mourned the loss. "If we hurry up and do it, will you get inside and change? I'll come up with something warm to drink. Is that good?" She held out a hand.

I was tempted to grab her hand and pull her down on top of me again, but I didn't want to backtrack on the small amount of progress I'd made. "Yes, ma'am."

I rolled up, taking her hand to help me up though I didn't need it.

"I'll start with the base." She crouched and wadded some snow together, then rolled and packed it.

I wasn't the kind of photographer whose camera was never far away. On the road, I had to earn a living. Sometimes, I kept it with me in order to make sure it was safe and secure. Other times, it was less hazardous to keep it in my luggage or find a lockbox. But I regretted not having it hanging around my neck right now.

Savvy's joy radiated off her as she crawled in the snow. To keep from staring and making her so uncomfortable she'd scrap the snowman idea, I dropped to my knees to start the snowman's midsection.

While we worked, we only chatted about our project. *How big should the base be? Should I start on the head now? I don't think we have any regular carrot sticks, just baby carrots.* But it was enough. The Savvy I'd met in Vegas emerged and took charge.

She rose and brushed off her knees and clapped her gloves together to shake snow loose. "Why don't you assemble it and I'll find eyes and a nose?"

"You got it."

She tromped away and I did as she asked. My legs were turning numb, but I kept on. Getting frostbite on half my body was worth waiting to see her reaction at the finished snowman.

"Here we are." She appeared behind me as I was packing snow between the connections to keep it stable. "Black olives are going to have to work for the eyes. I'm not hunting down charcoal. And we were out of carrots but had celery."

I stood back to watch her push in the eyes. She produced a purple fedora and a gauzy scarf she'd probably stolen from her mother's part of the coat closet.

She took a step back next to me and we eyed our work. She rolled her lips in and tilted her head.

It didn't matter how she looked at it, the effect wouldn't get better. "He looks like he's ready to catch a show on Broadway."

Her head dropped back and she laughed, a hearty sound that rang across the white lawn. "An Abbot snowman *would* be more likely to go to the theater than sledding like Frosty."

We grinned at each other, the dry air growing charged between us.

"Oh!" She clapped her hands. "The milk is probably warm for the hot chocolate. You need to get changed."

"Hot chocolate?" I'd drunk a lot of things over the years, but I hadn't had hot chocolate since I was a kid. Probably since before Mama died.

"Yes. I threw a pot of milk on the stove to warm up while we finished. You must be freezing."

I was, but I'd build an army of snowmen to have another afternoon like this again.

She took off inside, rattling off instructions for putting my clothes where they would be laundered. I took that to mean neither her, her sister, nor her Mom —and definitely not Chief—did their own laundry. I couldn't see her lugging a basket of wet jeans outside to hang on the line like I usually did.

In Savvy's bedroom, I took off my wet clothes and found the one pair of flannel pants I lugged around the world. This house didn't invite lounging in pajamas, but the skin on my legs stung as I warmed and flannel wouldn't add to the discomfort.

I was rolling on a sweatshirt when there was a soft knock on the door.

"Yeah?"

Savvy poked her head in. She'd thrown her hair up into a messy bun that bounced when she moved. She still wore the black leggings and pink long-sleeved shirt she'd had on this morning. "The hot chocolate is ready. I turned on the fireplace in the sitting room." She shifted and bit her lip, her hand still on the doorknob. "Want to watch a movie or something?"

I wanted to spend more time with her and that sounded perfect, but to keep from scaring her back into her shell, I kept it light. "Turned on the fireplace?"

She rolled her eyes but couldn't stifle a smile. "Yes, Montana boy. It's electric."

"All right, city girl. But I'm gonna have a hard time calling it a fireplace."

That earned me a head shake as she turned to go and I followed her downstairs to the den. We passed her Mom's office, but the door was closed.

The house was quiet. We weren't alone, yet I had her to myself. As she turned on the big TV over the fireplace, I settled on the plush couch that didn't fit in with the estate feel of the rest of the house .

I yanked the brown cashmere blanket off the back and spread it over me and my rapidly warming legs. Other things were going to demand my blood flow if she kept standing in front of me like that, her shapely legs glowing from the light of the fake fire.

She flipped through streaming services, holding the remote even though she was standing a foot away from the TV. "What do you want to watch?"

Careful of the steaming cup on the coffee table in front of me, I put my feet up. "Come sit and we'll decide together."

She looked over her shoulder at me,

then at the rest of the couch. I purposely hadn't left much room. She could sit on the love seat, but I patted the cushion next to me, hoping she'd choose to help me warm up.

The longer she took to decide, the more I gave up on making any more progress with my wife today. But finally she skirted the coffee table and perched next to me.

I held up a flap of the blanket. "Don't worry, I'm harmless. I'm still thawing out. You can even pick the show."

She studied me for a moment, her eyes going back and forth between mine. I thought she was going to insist on the blanket arrangement we had in bed, but she said, "What if I pick a chick flick?"

"What if I like chick flicks?"

She fought a grin. "What even is a chick flick?"

"*Die Hard?*"

She laughed, carefree, just like outside, and scooted close until she was under the blanket. I leaned forward and grabbed our drinks.

She accepted hers and flipped through the options, her shoulder bumping mine as she took a sip, her body heat seeping into me. I soaked her up, every bit she was willing to give.

"How's this?" she asked as if I didn't want to haul her on top of my lap and taste the hot chocolate on her tongue.

I didn't bother to read the title. "Perfect."

CHAPTER 8

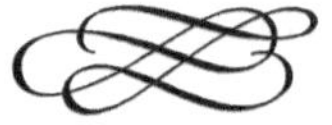

avvy

My sister pounded on the bathroom door. "Are you hiding in there?"

"Of course not, Pearl. Wait your turn!"

I'd only been done for the last twenty minutes, sitting on the toilet because I'd forgotten my clothes to change into. Twenty-plus years of getting myself dressed in my room was a hard habit to break, but I'd been doing well in the few days I'd been sharing a room with Xander. With my husband. The husband I couldn't bring myself to change in front of.

It was hard enough not to climb him like a sexy telephone pole after sitting next to him for two hours watching . . . I couldn't even remember what we'd watched. I hadn't paid attention to the show. All I remembered was picking something I knew didn't have sex scenes that'd make a pleasant afternoon uncomfortable.

That'd happened anyway. He had been solid next to me. A wall of cozy muscle and a blanket of heat that put my mother's cashmere throw to shame. There was no reason I couldn't have curled into him, slipped my hand under his shirt and felt his hot skin on mine. No damn reason.

But I hadn't.

Just like I slept between the sheets and he slept on top, not pushing me, not cajoling me, not pressuring me in any way to do what we'd done only minutes after saying I do.

Confusion swirled inside of me. Why couldn't I bring myself to be intimate with him again? Every time I looked at him, I noticed the way his broad shoulders filled a doorway, or how his hair flopped over his forehead and blunted the hard edge of his manliness, or the way he walked with a swagger that made desire coil in my belly until I wanted to match his swagger with a sultry saunter until we met in a flurry, seeking pleasure at each other's expense.

Yeah. Why couldn't I do that?

He could have any woman he wanted and he'd married me. I didn't want him to only be with me for the money. Yet I wasn't exactly enticing him with X-rated sex.

Whatever you're comfortable with.

He'd said that to me in the suit shop. What was he comfortable with? We shared a room, pretended our marriage was real, and then we built snowmen and watched movies together. We might be husband and wife, but we were, at best, friendly. A one-night stand, stuck together and trying to make the best of it.

There was another knock. Couldn't a girl get any privacy in her own home?

Maybe if I had my own home, I would. But I'd need a well-paying job first to afford anything decent in the city. I had an okay-paying job, but I hadn't worked any hours yet. Chief had been hinting hard that I should make an appearance at the office soon.

"Wait a damn minute, Pearl."

"It's me." Xander's deep rumble stirred up the butterflies in my belly.

I sank my head into my hands. The start of this day better not be a sign of how this party was going to go. "Sorry."

"Can I get you anything?"

I was about to announce that I'd forgotten my clothes, but the words wouldn't spill off my tongue. *I'm twenty-five, dammit, not five. I don't need a man to save me.*

Obviously, I did, or I wouldn't have this gold band on my finger.

I glanced at it for a moment before I squared my shoulders and rose. Ensuring the towel flap was tucked in above my breasts and wouldn't fall in the middle of the hallway, I opened the door.

Xander's gaze dipped to my cleavage, then drifted down. Yet he didn't go running like Pearl claimed he had when he'd encountered her in the hallway.

I smiled with a serenity I didn't feel. "Thanks for the offer, but I'm good. Just have to get dressed."

I wasn't the only one. His pristine white shirt hung loose over the half-buttoned slacks of his tux. A bow tie was draped over his neck. Did he need help tying it? I could probably YouTube how to do it.

He followed me back to the bedroom and as we got closer, the swirls in my stomach went wild. I wanted to shove a hand through my hair, but it'd been flat ironed and secured in an elegant bun. I dropped my arm.

"I can wait out here while you finish up," Xander said quietly.

The image of him lingering outside my door, looking bored and sexy, was enough to get me past the last hurdle of shyness. He'd already seen everything, and I didn't need my parents questioning this whirlwind relationship they had readily accepted.

"No. Come in. You can help with my zipper." How did I manage to sound so casual? I had to drop this towel to put that dress on. Though I'd rather drop this towel and take his shirt all the way off and run my hands over his rock-hard abs.

We slept next to each other, but I couldn't bring myself to find out if our chemistry had been that off the charts or if it'd been the hard cider. Having sex would complicate our simple arrangement. *Stay married. Get the trust.*

I crossed to the closet where my almost-a-wedding dress hung. Mother had exquisite taste. The color wasn't so white that I'd mock the virginal bride look while washing myself out, and the silver butterfly accents running crosswise from shoulder to waist picked up the colors around it. In my room, they had a hint of sapphire, and the thread connecting them took on a brown hue. The effect paid homage to my love of nature and was Mother's way of ensuring I didn't snub the dress.

The tulle on the skirt was loose enough that I'd be comfortable and could leave the Spanx in the drawer. It was sleeveless and the bodice had a wraparound appearance that stopped at the waistband. I could even wear a seminormal bra.

Mother knew what she was doing.

Sneaking a peek out of the corner of my eye at Xander, I relaxed. His back was turned as he tucked his shirt into his slacks. I used the moment to toss my towel in the laundry and slip on white lace underwear and a matching bra.

Taking the dress down, I slipped it over my head. I got lost in the poofy skirt and struggled with the zipper. Whispers of fabric could just as well be shouts while I searched for the elusive flap of the zipper.

"Here."

Xander's wall of heat hit me and I froze. His capable hands picked through the fabric until he found what I couldn't. He undid the zipper and bunched the dress up, then held it up to help me slip it over my head.

I suppressed a shiver as his fingertips grazed my shoulder. "Help women into fancy dresses often?"

The breath of his chuckle wafted over my nape as he worked to straighten the material in the back. "You're the first, but maybe I missed my calling. Hold still."

I did and he zipped up the back and hooked the zipper. I exhaled. The fit was perfect.

Neither of us moved for a heartbeat. He traced his fingers over the fabric, brushing my skin. I swayed back, seeking his heat, and my eyelids drifted shut. I missed his touch. Our night on the couch had included layers of blankets and clothing, not skin on skin.

He dipped his head down, his lips grazing the bare part of my shoulder. With only the faint touch of his lips, I was ready to strip down and demand he put his hands all over me until we were both shaking. It scared me more that not only was the sexual explosion between us real, but it was more powerful without the dulling effects of alcohol.

"Xander," I whispered, not knowing what to say.

He wrapped a hand around my waist and pulled me into him. "You look fucking gorgeous," he murmured against my neck.

I tipped my head to the side. "It's the dress." I barely had on more than a few swipes of mascara and lip gloss.

"It's not the dress, Savvy." His grip tightened and I was pressed into his body.

"When I turned around and saw you in nothing but a bra and underwear, I about came in my shorts like a damn teenager."

"They're barely more than plain white underclothes." I bit my bottom lip, loving every word, afraid to believe them. The chemistry was there. What did I do with it?

"I wasn't looking at those." His lips brushed a path of wildfire up my shoulder until he landed on the shell of my ear. "I want to taste you again."

My hands fisted in the gauzy skirt. Yes. Please. "The party . . ."

"Fuck the party, Savvy. What do you want?" He skimmed his hand up my bodice and splayed his fingers across my chest. My nipples hardened until they ached, until the bra I had thought comfortable only a few moments ago chafed unbearably.

"I want . . ." You.

He slipped his hand into my top until he cupped one breast. A groan resonated low in my throat as he nibbled on my ear.

I tried again, licking my dry lips. "I

want . . ." I wanted to ditch this party, just like he did. I wanted to forget that I was an aimless environmentalist going to a celebration bash that was nothing but waste. I wanted to forget that I'd panicked and married the first guy I'd met because I wasn't strong enough to stand up to Chief. I wanted to get to know the guy I slept next to every night.

I wanted . . . our marriage to be real.

The words clogged in my throat. We were together for the money.

"Sav!" Pearl called. "Wasn't I going to do your hair?"

"Shit." I'd forgotten to let her know I'd decided to go with a simple bun. "Sorry, Pearl, I already did it," I called.

Xander didn't let me go, but he removed his hand from my chest. "Say the word, and we'll leave when you want to tonight."

"You don't want to go?"

"I'm going because of you. But if you don't want to be there, we won't be there."

I spun in his hold. "I have to."

"Do you?"

I blinked but before I could ponder whether I really had a choice or not, Pearl knocked again. "Did you do a low ponytail again? You know you look like a renaissance boy going to his bookbinding apprenticeship when you do that."

A laugh sputtered out of me, more at Xander's perplexed expression. "She's not wrong." I reluctantly pulled out of his embrace. "The party will be fine. I'll be fine. I've been doing this stuff my whole life."

He dipped his head and I turned away before I could tell Pearl that I didn't care about my hair, or the party that was for my parents' benefit and not mine. I turned away before he could see that I wasn't brave enough to step out from under my family's umbrella when he'd been doing that for the last ten years.

Xander

.   .   .

MY TUXEDO WAS comfortable enough and I
didn't make the bow tie tight enough to
choke me, but I wanted to dismantle every
stitch and burn it. The few times I'd had to
don a tux before hadn't been as
uncomfortable as this one.

It wasn't the impeccable fit or the silk
lining that was like heaven on my skin—
Mrs. Abbot had spared no expense. It was
the fact that I was the only one in a suit like
this. Same for Savvy and her outfit. We
didn't exactly stand out, but everyone knew
we were the couple du jour.

Friends and associates of the Abbots
mingled in designer suits and cocktail
dresses that would fit the red carpet.
Women in slinky gowns that hugged bodies
of all ages stood in groups, holding
champagne flutes, laughing while the soft
glow of the chandeliers lit their highlights
and sparkled off the jewels adorning their
necks, ears, wrists.

Cream fabric covered the tables and chairs, and the drape over each chair was secured with a sapphire-colored rope. The ballroom screamed money and elegance. Both things I didn't have.

I'd grown up with money, but Dad had raised us like we had to work for every cent that was already in the bank. I'd hauled manure, worked cattle, and cleaned the damn toilets.

Had anyone in this crowd scrubbed shit-stained porcelain?

Three women zeroed in on Savvy and Pearl as soon as we entered. Savvy didn't have a chance to formally introduce me. The ladies evaluated me like a prize bull. I missed what they murmured to Savvy, but from their approving expressions, it was good. Then they carted Savvy off in a whirlwind of giggles and expensive perfume.

Mrs. Abbot took pity on me and guided me through the crowd. She introduced me to the owner of a new bank going up on the north end of the city, the headmaster of the private school the three Abbot girls had gone to, and Emerald's husband, Carter.

"Nice to meet you," I said and extended my hand. Carter was a lighter version of Lex. Same build, same crew cut, but unlike Lex, his expression wasn't frozen in arrogance.

Carter shook my hand and looked over my longish hair that Pearl had gelled until I looked like I walked off a *Mad Men* set, then studied my rigid stance. Whatever rubric he used to evaluate me, I either failed miserably or passed with a perfect score. "Nice to finally meet you. Chief's told me a lot."

"I can imagine." If Carter worked at Abbot Security, then yes, he knew all about me. But his tone said he didn't hold it against me. Neither did my last name impress him. Savvy had pegged Carter wrong. I could tell a minute after meeting him that he was nothing like Lex.

Carter turned his congenial smile

toward Mrs. Abbot. "I'll track Em down for you." He walked toward a group of women that must contain his wife, leaving me alone at Mrs. Abbot's side.

"Oh, there's Walter." Mrs. Abbot curled her hand around my elbow. I let her guide me toward a crowd that was laughing boisterously.

Lex stood next to Chief. He was the first to spot us. I didn't like the Cheshire cat grin that spread across his face as soon as he saw me. Tension crept up my spine, making me stand straighter.

What the hell did that bastard have in mind?

Chief's grin, at least, was genuine when he saw us. He ignored his wife and held his arm out for me, beckoning me into the fold.

"There's my new son-in-law," Chief boomed, his strong arm clutching my shoulder. "Xander King of King Oil."

Nothing about me was "of King Oil" except my Dad and the small amount I still had left in the bank. This time next year, I'd have a shit-ton of money thanks to King Oil, but I'd feel less guilt about each dollar of those millions than the meager amount I was sitting on.

Introductions took place, a round-robin of names and titles thrown at me. One was a barrel-chested man about Chief's age. General Something Or Other. Darren Cornantzer was about my age and in military intelligence, and the third gentleman also had a military background and was affiliated with West Point. I was the only member of the group who hadn't attended the military academy.

The general was the one who asked the question I dreaded whenever I had to socialize with Dad's associates. "So, Xander. Tell me, what do you do?"

"I'm a photojournalist." Like always, I kept the answer simple and hoped there were no further questions.

"What do you cover?" Darren asked.

I went through the usual song and dance. International locations that have no other notoriety than their residents and the struggles they face. No, I hadn't been featured in any reputable publication. No, I didn't work for anyone.

"What branch of the military where you in?" This was the West Point guy. Based on the rigid stances and close-cropped hair of the men in the room, I was one of the few, if not the only, nonmilitary men here. I was sure many of the women were military too.

"I didn't serve," I said. I had no excuse. Recruiters had approached me in high school but I'd grown up getting told what to do. I'd wanted freedom after graduation. "I needed more flexibility with my travel."

That earned me a laugh.

Lex swirled the wide-bottomed glass in his hand that held a giant square ice cube. An old-fashioned. "What'd you go to college for again?"

The tone of his voice sent prickles of awareness down my spine. It wouldn't be hard for someone like Lex to dig into my school records and find a whole lot of nothing.

"I started in business media."

The men lifted their chins, waiting for more that I wouldn't give them.

"What degree did you end up with?" Lex took a sip of his whiskey, his glittering blue eyes pinned on me, his expression smug.

I wasn't about to confess to this group of men something my own father didn't know. "Nothing that sounds impressive." I opened my mouth to excuse myself. Unlike my wife, I didn't have to put up with men like Chief or their attitudes. I could go where I wanted when I wanted.

But Lex beat me to the punch. "You did graduate, didn't you?" He laughed, and glanced around the group. "No need to be modest. The man that married Sapphire Abbot must have some impressive initials behind his name. How would you travel the world otherwise?"

I stuffed my hands into my pants pocket and bowed my head. At my side, Chief's eyes narrowed on Lex. Chief might not like the tidbit Lex was gleefully revealing, but he had an image to uphold, and more importantly, a client to attract—my father.

True to form, Chief joked, "His last name is credential enough."

As the group laughed, I gave Lex a perfunctory smile. "Good thing I never claimed to be anything more than humble. If you'll excuse me."

I nodded to Chief. Like it or not, he was my father-in-law and he'd done nothing but respect me. My last name might be the only reason why, but it was enough for tonight. Whatever I was doing to get my trust was between me and Savvy.

I wove through the crowd, nodding greetings at random guests as I sought a snack table, or guest book, or *something* to keep me occupied for a few minutes so I didn't have to talk to anyone.

"What'd he do?"

I turned as Savvy caught up with me in the far corner of the room. A table held elegantly wrapped gifts, gift bags that somehow matched the aesthetic of the room, and a basket of cards.

It hit me. This was my wedding reception. Complete strangers thought we were married for real and wanted to send us forward on the best footing possible. If I hadn't been humble before, I was now.

What had Lex done? Nothing more than knowing more about me than my wife did.

I swept my gaze over Savvy. She carried herself like a queen. Around Chief and her mother, she was meek and uncertain. But when he wasn't nearby she stood straighter with her shoulders back and her chin lifted.

"Did Chief say something?" she asked.

"It wasn't your father. He was cordial."

"Right. Of course. With you he would be." She peered at me. "Then what's wrong? You looked like you'd mow down anyone that got in your path."

I took a deep breath, my gaze straying to the group of accomplished men I'd just stood with. My secret wouldn't be a shameful one if I didn't come from the family I did. If I hadn't lied to my dad and then avoided the truth around others like Savvy's entire social circle.

"I dropped out of college."

She frowned, her plump lower lip sucking between her teeth. "Okay?"

"I'm guessing Lex wants to use the information to humiliate me in front of Chief's crowd."

Crossing her arms, she kicked a hip out. "Good luck with that. Chief won't stand for it."

No, he wasn't that kind of man. And since he was trying to land King Oil's account, Lex could lose his damn job over a little pride.

Yeah, I'd be pissed too if I thought I was about to be handed someone like Savvy on a silver platter of prestige and opportunity, only to lose her at the last moment. But she was a person who could decide for herself whom she wanted to marry. It wasn't my fault Lex hadn't even tried to win her over.

"It's not just that." Partygoers glanced at us, but as if sensing the deep conversation we were about to have, they kept their distance, offering us a little privacy. "Lex must've also seen how little money I have. Money that's left over from my college days. Money that Dad gave each of us to go to school."

"It won't matter to Chief. You're a King."

I hadn't told anyone what I'd done, and if I said that much, I had to tell her the rest. "My dad doesn't know."

Her mouth formed an 'o'.

"I know," I continued. "Shitty thing not to tell your dad. But, Aiden has a financial degree and helps run King Oil. Beckett went to Princeton, started his own business, and is worth millions in his own right. Dawson was given the ranch, but even he finished college and uses what he learned to make the ranch more successful than it ever was."

Then there was me. I couldn't wait another three years to get out of Montana, so I'd cashed out and traveled. Using the excuse I'd pay Dad back when I hit it big was growing weaker each year. So, I just never went home.

I'd taken all my college money and the cash meant for living expenses for four years and blown it. Not frivolously, but I'd gone through nearly all of it. I had no job and no home to show for it. I had a wife who thought I'd married her in order to get more family money that I'd done nothing to earn.

"My family's extremely accomplished." And rich. Each one of them. My brothers would never need the trust or to live off Dad. "I just didn't tell them."

Her smile was small. "And then kept not telling them."

"Gets worse each year that goes by." A huge weight rolled off my chest by admitting that. It was a pittance compared to what was still sitting on it after years of lying, but telling someone what I was most ashamed of brought relief I hadn't expected. "He thinks I graduated and everything."

Her eyes widened. And there it was. Not finishing college when I was given money and opportunity was one thing. Pretending that I had attended for four years and graduated was another, more pathetic, more pathological thing.

She cocked her head, no doubt trying to understand a preposterous scenario. "He thinks . . . Didn't he visit? Didn't he ask about the ceremony?"

"I brushed all his questions off. We weren't close and Dad, during those years, wasn't an invested dad." The pre-Kendall years had been ugly. Dad had been a playboy, traveling the world for King Oil and living the high life. My brothers and I had been grown and on our own, officially severing him from any responsibility, and he'd used his newfound freedom to never be in Montana. He'd done the same thing when Mama had died. Cut loose. Stopped caring about what anyone thought, including his own kids.

Reconciling the current Gentry King with the dad of my teen years and early adulthood wasn't easy. His marriage with Kendall was only a few months longer than Beckett and Eva's. But by all accounts Dad was a changed man.

Didn't mean he'd like finding out that he'd been lied to and essentially stolen from for almost a decade by one of his sons. His least favorite son especially.

Her gaze strayed to the left and I followed. Her mother was heading for us, her determined stare telling me everything I needed to know. We'd been on our own too long. Time to mingle and show everyone what a happy, well-adjusted couple we were and put to rest any accurate rumors that we'd just met a week ago and gotten married within hours of our first words to each other.

"I'd like to say you should talk to him and it'll all be okay, but I don't know your dad, and I can see why this money is personally important to you."

"It's not just the money." Mrs. Abbot was nearly on us. "It's my mom's last gift to us. Something she created with us in mind. I don't want to be the one to lose it when she created the trust to make sure we were okay. I can't steal from my dad and then lose the trust money on top of it."

Too much sentiment was wrapped up in that money. I hadn't planned on fighting to keep it, but now that it was attainable, I couldn't just let it go.

More importantly, after confiding in Savvy and having her listen to me, I couldn't let her go either.

CHAPTER 9

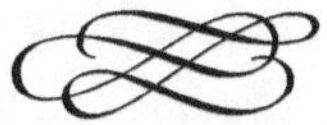

Savvy

I HOVERED between asleep and awake, those peaceful few moments when nothing mattered but how comfortable, cozy, and warm I was. So warm. I snuggled further under the blankets. A hard body was at my back and a strong arm was banded across my waist.

I opened my eyes and stared at the wall across from the bed. A wall that had once sported a One Direction poster and my ticket stubs to one of their concerts in London. Now, it had a modern abstract painting with only a spark of color among the earth tones, done by a local artist and purchased for top-dollar. Remembering the day Mother insisted I redo my bedroom as befit a young woman helped take my mind off where I was right now.

And that was pinned against Xander's hard stomach with an even harder appendage prodding my bottom. I didn't want to move.

I should, but after he'd confided in me last night, I couldn't disrupt this moment of closeness between us. I might not be able to jump him quite yet without a healthy dose of hard liquor, but I could snuggle. I could wish that we'd married for real, and were staying together because we were deeply in love.

I was in lust. But that didn't change why we were there, together.

He nuzzled my hair, destroying my

hopes that he was fast asleep and didn't know I was actively engaged in snuggling. "What are you thinking about?"

I chewed the inside of my lip. To tell the truth or not? The fact that he lied so well to his family bothered me, but didn't at the same time. His remorse and shame were clear, but he hadn't confided in me until he'd been busted by Lex, as if he hadn't wanted me to know how personal his trust fund was to him.

I was staying married for the money so that when I let down my family, I had a safety net. He was staying married so he wouldn't let down his family.

I wasn't sure how I felt about that. I thought we'd been growing closer, but all last night had done was remind me of our true motivations. That safety net wouldn't protect my heart if I fell in love with this man. So I lied. "I wish I didn't have to go to work tomorrow."

"You don't have to."

"Unless your dad has said yes, then I do.

My dad would kick me out otherwise." It was a long year until next February.

"What about moving out first? We can go somewhere besides Montana or DC."

I looked over my shoulder. "What? It's the middle of winter, a bad time to roam the world with no home or money."

"It's not winter everywhere."

"I can't afford an international flight. Can you?"

"All we have to do is afford the flight there. We'll earn enough for a trip home later."

I chewed my lip. He made it sound so easy but my entire being rebelled at the thought. I might be well traveled, but I was well traveled on well-funded trips. "Room and board?"

"I earn that too." His cadence kicked up like he was getting excited. "You really learn about the world, and the people, and what they need. I think you'd really like it. Depending where we go, you'll be closer to the earth than ever before."

"Like camping?"

"Maybe. Depends."

I sat up, letting the blankets drop from my torso to pool at my waist. I'd been wearing a T-shirt to bed since Xander had come home with me. "Depends? I can't just go and not know." I couldn't quit on Chief and leave and then expect my parents to save me when I called begging them to help me get home.

"You wanted to work with my dad about environmental issues regarding oil. So we can go to places where oil has decimated the land. Alaska? Hell, there's been pipeline leaks in North Dakota. And—"

"—and it's not winter everywhere, but I'm pretty sure those places are currently buried in snow." I didn't need to get stranded in a blizzard.

"Texas has oil fields," he continued as if learning about where oil was drilled hadn't been part of my college education. "Or even better—offshore drilling. We could investigate how the seismic techniques used to look for oil underwater can damage marine life. And then travel up north when it's summer to look at fracking. You've heard the controversy around that, right? There's always part-time work to be found in the oil areas. "

I tuned him out. What he said made sense, but I couldn't escape the subtle undertone of *You don't know what you're talking about, Sapphire* that I'd heard my whole life. "No offense, but I'm already well researched on those topics."

"Research is different than living it." The simple way he said it cut into me until the ache I'd felt earlier turned to hurt. The whole reason I'd chosen him in the first place was because he took me seriously. After seeing what a spoiled rich girl I was, had he changed his tune?

"I'm sure Chief will agree that's a lesson I have to learn too." I stood and gathered my clothes to keep from looking at how devastatingly sexy he was in my bed. He was right. He could pack up and go and that's why I'd married him, but when push came to shove, I couldn't do it.

He ran a hand through his messy bedhead. He'd washed all the gel out and was back to his sexy, haphazard self. "Look, I'm trying to help—"

"I know. But I can't go rushing off. We have almost twelve months still. I can't burn all my bridges before the end is in sight."

"Your parents should support you if you want to move out and find a different job."

I leveled him with a stare. "Is that why you came home with me and didn't fly to Montana with your dad?"

His jaw flexed. "Touché."

"I'm sorry." As long as I was stuck, he was stuck with me. It couldn't be easy to accept after the freedom he'd had for years. It wasn't easy for me to accept that he'd married me for his own monetary reasons and not because I'd swept him away.

"Don't be. You're right."

Didn't mean it hurt any less. It was like I

had channeled Chief. We needed a better topic to land on, to bring back the lightness of playing in the snow. I spotted his camera bag. "I think you picked a fine career."

He sat up and draped his arms over his knees. Unlike me, he wasn't wearing a shirt, so every mouthwatering ab was on display. "You want to look at my pictures again?"

"You haven't pulled out your camera since you've been here." He'd taken no pictures of my home, my family, or . . . me. Us. Unease combed through me. Why would he? We weren't a real couple trying to capture memories.

"The older ones are in the cloud."

"Get your laptop. Let's see them." It had worked last time to bring us together, get us talking. Last time, he'd offered, but today he wasn't going for his camera or his laptop. "Unless you don't want to show me."

Hurt snaked through me. That's what was wrong between us. We'd been so passionate that first night—before we'd taken our clothing off. We'd talked about our plans, our dreams. But reality was different. Reality was hard. Besides the night I'd met him, he hadn't taken a picture in my presence. Likewise, I hadn't done more toward my chosen career than toss a can in a recycling bin.

"I don't mind showing you," he said. Then he rolled out of bed and padded to his camera, like I'd imagined his reluctance. With his back to me, I ate up the sight of his carved back tapering into his boxer briefs.

This was where the marriage would be hard. *He* was what had attracted me in the first place. Him, doing his thing. If we had married based purely on our blazing chemistry, then it would have been easier to survive this year as a couple.

It was about being with you longer.

Was that part true?

He lifted his laptop out of his bag and I spun before I could get caught staring. "I'll be right back."

I scurried to the bathroom. I doubted

my mind would get any clearer in there, but I needed to clean up anyway.

When I returned, he was dressed in his jeans and his untucked blue plaid flannel, looking so out of place in my *young lady elegant* room, but the truth was, I felt out of place here too.

Xander scratched the back of his neck, his laptop open as he held it in one hand. "I've gotta use the bathroom. Do you want to go to the library or something when I get back?"

I wanted to stay holed up in my room with him and keep the rest of the world away while we figured some shit out. "We can do it here."

After he left, I threw on a Georgetown sweater Pearl had gotten me for laughs and a pair of maroon leggings. I was pulling on fluffy socks made from recycled jeans when Xander entered. He pushed the door shut and joined me on the bed, sitting on the other side. I leaned over as he clicked through his pictures.

Flashes of people flew by. He didn't say much about each one, just gave me a rundown of the location and when he'd taken it. In several photos, one woman in particular kept reappearing.

"Girlfriend?"

He stopped, his jaw ticking as he studied the picture. My throat grew thick. For fuck's sake, did he still have a girlfriend? One in each country? These were questions I should've asked before we married.

God, I was naïve. I didn't know this guy.

Finally, he sighed. "She and I dated, but it wasn't serious and it ended before I left."

"There's a lot of photos of her."

"She liked to pose and her parents loved the pictures." He leaned across the bed closer to me and flipped through the rest. The woman was stunning. Burnt-umber skin, long dark hair, glittering dark eyes, and a round face that managed a level of innocence and sexuality that shouldn't mix.

"She's beautiful," I murmured, more

disheartened with each snapshot. "Why the Philippines?"

"I stayed for several months doing a story on the parallels of rural farming there and here in the States." He glanced at me and, seeing my blankness, explained, "Many farmers in both places have heavy debt and struggle to feed their families while growing food for the nation."

"Did you write the article?"

"Not yet."

"Is it the writing stopping you?" I stretched across the bed, which brought me closer to his fresh linen smell. Other than minty toothpaste and my shampoo, he didn't use products. A simple man but a complex individual. I had to get to know the individual.

"Yeah. I like action. Sitting at a computer and punching out the details is something I'd do on a long flight, not when I could work or take pictures." He flipped through frame after frame. There was a man bent over a crop I didn't recognize, dressed in basketball shorts and a T-shirt. Another with a red and white tractor of some sort. Was it similar to anything Xander had used as a rancher? Photos flew by of people swarming a field, then more of fields submerged in water. Rice. That was the only crop I could identify.

One thing was clear in each picture. He had talent. Maybe it was raw. What did I know about photography? But he had passion and that gave him an edge many photographers didn't have. He could focus on what was most important in the photo without making it the focus. In each of the farming pictures, it was obvious how hard they worked, that the odds were stacked against them, and that they loved the land.

He kept going back until he hit green plains disrupted by buttes and a river.

"Where's that?"

"Home."

I peered closer. Cattle dotted the pastures and the green was offset by the twinkling blue of the river. Fluffy white clouds dotted the sky. The image was a burst of color that was pleasing and relaxing. A meditation on the screen. The clarity was stunning, as if I could walk from my room right into the scene and stay there. "It's gorgeous."

"This was when I was home a little less than a year ago to work cattle. My favorite time is the spring."

"Do you go back often?"

"Sometimes Dawson calls and asks for help working cattle in the fall. If I can afford to fly home, I'll do it." He smirks at me. "Then I can use his Wi-Fi to upload all my pictures and clear up some space."

"Do you blog or anything?"

"No."

"A website?"

"Nope."

Then what did he do? Query here and there and give up when he was rejected? I wanted to ask, but photos of handsome men stalled my questions. Each one had a chiseled face, dark eyes, and dark hair.

He stopped at one brooding man a little older than me. He was sitting at a table with a pretty woman by his side, but he was ignoring her and on his phone. "That's Aiden, the uptight workaholic, and his wife, Kate."

The picture and his description answered any questions I had. Kate's expression and demeanor screamed that she was a kind soul, but also lonely. Aiden looked exactly like an uptight workaholic—rigid posture, pristine clothing, and a permanent scowl. He could walk into Abbot Security and even my father would think he worked there.

The next handsome man had softer features but only because he was looking at a petite woman with a pixie haircut.

"Beckett and Eva, the newlyweds."

My heart twisted. They looked so in love. How I'd wanted to look when I'd married. But we didn't have any photos of our impetuous, happy day.

The third man had a devil-may-care

grin and a relaxed stance that matched Xander's.

"My baby brother, Dawson."

He was the last thing from a baby. Four good-looking men from a dad they all resembled, but out of all of them, Xander was the hottest. In my humble opinion.

As he showed off image after image of his ranch—his most obvious inspiration—I asked about the farming details, startled by how interested I was. The only data I had on farming and ranching and their effects on climate change were from books and papers. I'd learned about all the big, bad ways they hurt the environment and I'd studied a little about the attempts being made to offset and reduce the effects. Hearing it firsthand, how the Kings decided what to do on the ranch and thought about how it'd help or hurt them and the cattle and the land, was fascinating. From testing the soil to determine what minerals they needed to supplement the cattle with to what they grew for hay. Protein mattered for cattle too. Who knew? It was like learning about a foreign world for years and then someone opening the door and inviting me inside.

The analogy described my career in a nutshell. I learned about everything, but from the outside looking in. I was in this glass bubble, privileged and protected. My parents weren't the type to take me and my sisters camping in a nature preserve. Mother wanted spas and fine dining. Chief was the uptight workaholic of our family. He went where she wanted and brought his work with him.

I'd only learned about the world, I hadn't experienced it. Xander had.

"Researching it is different than living it," I said.

Xander paused, his finger hovering over the arrow key, ready to bring up another picture that would prove how inexperienced I was at life. "We can change that."

"The last impulsive thing I did ended up with us both here."

His brow furrowed. "And that's bad?"

I sighed and rolled to my back. "No, but I feel responsible. I want to do it right, Xander. I know that if we stay married for eleven months, some huge treasure chest will unlock and rain money down on us. But I want a plan. I want a plan A, B, and C, all the way to Z if necessary."

"I'm not big on planning."

I turned my head, gazing up at his hard profile. "How's that going for you?" The muscle in his jaw jumped. "All I'm saying is that I should work for Chief, for a little while, save money. Then . . . we'll see. Maybe you can work on that article."

His gaze slid to his screen and the stunning sunset. Purples and reds layered across the sky, making the green of the buttes stand out like a lawn of emeralds. That land called to me. It was his home. Was it the same for him?

No, otherwise he'd be there.

Was there anywhere he could stay and be happy?

~

Xander

"IT'S NO PROBLEM," I assured Mrs. Abbot, hating that I had to explain myself, where I was going, and how I was going to get there. I was twenty-nine damn years old. "The bus is fine."

Mrs. Abbot feathered her fingers along her collar. From her expression, one would think the bus stop was rife with muggers and murderers. "You can use our driver. I'm working in the office all day."

Three weeks had gone by and I still had no idea what Mrs. Abbot did for work. Savvy said she volunteered and ran the house. I only had childhood memories of my mother running our house. She'd also run the cattle, which included the tractors, the trucks, and anything else with an engine that could turn over. Mama had done chores with us, spent some time in the office to pay bills and balance the accounts, then come back out for more chores.

I had no idea what it took to volunteer or run a house that only held a wealthy couple and two of their three grown kids, but it must take all damn day.

I tried my best placating smile and edged toward the door. So close to freedom. "I like experiencing the city and I can't do that with a driver."

"Sapphire," Mrs. Abbot called, her hand still on her chest. If I gave the woman a heart attack, I'd feel bad, but seriously. It was the *bus*. I could come and go wherever I wanted according to the bus schedule and not have a driver huffing and looking at his watch while I roamed and took some pictures. "Wait here."

When she was out of sight, I dropped my head back, fed the hell up with Savvy's controlling parents.

Last week, I'd used a cafe to work on that farming article I'd told Savvy about and Davis the Driver had lapped the coffee shop every fifteen minutes on the dot. I'd gotten all of one page written because by minute twelve, I was staring out the window to see if he was going to do it again. Then I'd spend another three minutes after he passed stewing about the gilded prison I'd landed myself in with my wedding vows.

I had a cell mate, but she was doing nothing to escape her bindings.

She spent her days working from home, or meeting Chief at his office, which I'd never been to. At first we'd gone for walks, even held hands a few times like shy thirteen-year-olds. She'd been back at work over a week, but she'd ignore me and bury herself in her computer. She'd even taken up working in the dry, boring library that repressed my inspiration just walking by it.

I was bored and going out of my damn mind. Opal didn't seem to mind having me around, and Chief broke into a grin whenever he saw me—the few hours he was home a week. I couldn't take eleven more months of this. How did Savvy live it every day?

She thought this was the best course for now, but how would she know if she didn't try another route?

The front door opened behind me and a swirl of expensive perfume traveled on the cold air. I guessed who it was before I turned.

Em. Where Savvy was a tropical bird swinging in her cage only to be adored by approved onlookers, Em was a bird of prey, swooping down on the weak. After enduring people like Lex, I should be ready, but Em hadn't been able to corner me alone yet.

She unwound her scarf and gazed down at me, despite being a solid six inches shorter. "So. At last I get a chance to talk to the college dropout that's using my sister to get a free ride."

She spoke quietly enough that no one else could hear unless they stood in the same room with us. Maybe she wasn't so unlike Savvy after all. She, too, was afraid to rock the boat too hard.

"I see you've been talking to Lex."

I must've passed some test. Her gaze softened, but only from cast iron to stainless steel. "My husband and Lex gossip like old ladies in the bingo hall." She shrugged out of her knee-length black coat and looked around like someone was supposed to come and take it from her. When no one did, I took the coat and hung it on a hook. I'd disappointed my dad in a lot of ways, but lacking manners wasn't one of them.

"It's been a month and you're still here," Em said. "Your family must not share their money either. You're not holding out hope that ours will, are you?"

What would Em think if she knew it was the reverse and I planned to share?

More respect, or less? "I'm not here for the money."

Wasn't I? I couldn't stop the question drifting through my mind. In the last couple weeks, the only time I saw my wife was in bed, where she slept on her side and I slept on mine. She'd heaped all this pressure on herself to make her own money before we were married for a year. She didn't go out with friends, she didn't have time to talk to Brady anymore, and she didn't socialize with her sisters. She'd doubled down on work since we'd looked at pictures on her bed. She was working for the present and I wanted to leave and start *living* our present.

Em crossed her arms, inspecting me from head to toe. "You're sticking around for my sister?"

I wanted that to be the case. "We're married."

Em cocked a cool brow. "Marrying and living with the 'rents. How's that going for you?"

I'd never had to answer to anyone like I had in the last month.

Before I could answer, Mrs. Abbot appeared from the library, Savvy trailing after her. Em smiled primly. "If you'll excuse me."

"Emerald!" Mrs. Abbot's delighted greeting wiped the scowl from my face. She was letting me live with her, allowing Savvy and I to stay here and eat her food. I wasn't going to be a pouty child at twenty-nine. Mrs. Abbot directed her grin at me. "I've already phoned Davis."

I held back my sigh. I had plans today to do the work I'd told Savvy and her family that I'd been doing since I left college. I was doing research on rural family farms, corporate farming, and what kind of publications would be interested in an article comparing them to any other country's. Then I had to write the damn article. Edit my photos. And just . . . work.

I'd grudgingly admit that having a driver would help me do that. But it was stifling. This town was stifling. This house was stifling. The people in it too . . . my wife included. Mrs. Abbot had recruited her to do just that. Would she go for it?

I looked from Mrs. Abbot to my wife. Her shoulders were tight, and stress pinched her eyes. Chief was a harsh taskmaster and even though Savvy worked mostly from home, she put in long hours.

I was whining about roaming the city during the day and working at my own pace. Still, I had to try to regain my freedom. "I appreciate the offer, but I'm taking the bus."

Savvy chewed on her lip. "I'm sure he'll be fine, Mom. He's taken buses all over the world."

"But this is a big city."

I focused on Savvy again. She met my gaze and an apologetic smile flickered. Mrs. Abbot thought this was a simple request, asking her to talk me into taking the driver, but it only added more pressure on Savvy.

She needed a break. "Would you like to come with?"

Savvy blinked at me. "Aren't you working?"

"Yes," Mrs. Abbot chimed in. "Davis can take both of you."

Dammit. If she was trying to block me from public transportation, she'd probably stroke out if Savvy took it. I'd have to roll with it. "Pack your laptop. We can go together."

"Chief doesn't want me using public Wi-Fi."

Em sidled past us. She shot a disappointed look at Savvy and a knowing one at me.

Savvy noticed and straightened. "But I'll figure something out."

Mrs. Abbot's smile was serene. She'd gotten her way. "I won't need Davis's services today so take as much time as you need."

As much as I appreciated her looking out

for me, and the pang of longing a concerned mother figure inspired inside me, I didn't need her permission. If Dad could see this, he wouldn't believe I was the same kid he'd told a hundred times to quit standing on his horse's back while out riding. The same kid who'd ridden off whenever he wanted and been gone for hours.

I had to use a driver now.

"I'll grab my coat," said Savvy.

She wouldn't need much this time of year. Winter was giving way to spring and we were in a city covered in buildings. I had a shirt under my flannel and my jacket wadded up in my backpack. My camera was slung around my shoulder.

Savvy got her jacket out of the closet. I held a hand out to help her shrug into it, but she didn't see as she twirled it around to put her arms in. I hooked my fingers in the laptop bag's strap across my chest but that didn't make me look less awkward. I didn't dare glance at Savvy's sister in case she was silently laughing at us.

Savvy zipped her coat. "I'll grab my computer and be right back."

"How lovely," Mrs. Abbot said as Savvy scurried away. "Where are you going?"

"A coffee shop, probably."

Mrs. Abbot lifted a manicured brow, waiting for specifics. I had none. I changed it up each day. I had a feeling Mrs. Abbot wouldn't understand.

Savvy came down the hall.

"Well, you two have fun." Mrs. Abbot led Em the way Savvy had come.

An engine idled outside. Davis. Our ride.

Savvy stopped in front of me. "Are you sure you don't mind? I have a lot of work to do, and I don't want to interfere with yours."

I thought about how the last several minutes had gone. And how uncomfortable our afternoon would be if we kept up like this. Two adults, leaving on a chaperoned trip.

"What do you say we ditch Davis, find a

nice place to get some work done, and then fuck our work and have some fun?"

Her eyes flared. She mouthed *fuck our work* and peered down the hall where her mom and sister had disappeared. Her wide eyes turned to me, but instead of being scandalized, they were filled with mounting excitement. "Why do I feel like I'm skipping school?"

A slow grin spread across my face. "Ready to sneak out together?"

CHAPTER 10

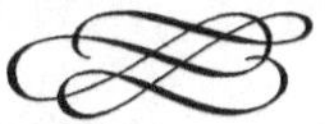

avvy

I TRIED to decipher the rail map, but it was a mass of rainbow lines. We'd been in and around the city, then we'd taken to riding the metro all over.

Xander leaned in, his hot breath tickling my ear. "You're so lost."

I giggled and traced my finger along the map kiosk at the station. "Correction. *We're* so lost."

"Why don't we find a place to eat while we figure out how to make it back home?"

I shot him an accusatory glare. "You could get back, couldn't you?"

His grin was unrepentant and chased away the chill, infusing my body with warmth, reminding me how my favorite part of the day was waking up with him in bed next to me. How I wished I could roll over and wiggle into his embrace.

But as each day passed, the space between us grew further and further until an emotional chasm separated us, one so expansive I didn't know how to cross it. So I kept working. It was what I knew. Work for my parents, prove myself, then try to be brave again and try not to fail. Again.

This day was what I needed. What both of us needed. We'd worked at a coffee shop after Xander had somehow talked Davis into leaving us alone the rest of the day. After a few hours, he'd asked if I'd ever taken the bus.

And there we were.

"I could, but this is more fun."

"Watching me get lost?"

His grin widened and I turned back to the map, a smile dancing over my lips. This *was* fun.

My stomach rumbled. We hadn't grabbed more than a drink and a snack between rides. I pressed my hand to my belly to keep it quiet.

"You're hungry. Come on."

"Shouldn't we get back?" I wasn't sure where back was, and I was in charge of figuring that out. I didn't even know where I was now.

Wow, I'd lived a sheltered life.

"We don't have a curfew," he said.

I sighed and rested my hip against the kiosk. "It's bad, isn't it, the way Mother insists on Davis driving you everywhere."

The humor faded from his face. "It isn't good." He crowded closer to me until I tilted my head back. Was he going to kiss me?

Lowering his head until our lips

touched, he kept the kiss light until I was ready to go out of my mind. *More, dammit. Give me more.* I'd been craving this, only to starve without it each day.

He continued teasing me. Then he pulled back, his gaze sweeping over my face.

My lips formed a troubled line. He didn't want to kiss me as badly as I wanted him to.

"You look disappointed," he said.

"I am," I admitted.

He leaned in again and pressed his lips along my jawline once, twice, until he reached my ear. His hot breath tickled my ear and sent shivers exploding over my body, but it didn't help the confusion clogging my brain. "That's only a taste of what going to bed next to you and not touching you is like. I've been hard as a fucking rock every day since we first met. I want you, Savvy. That hasn't changed. Ever."

My breath hitched. That's what it was

like with him when we were on our own. Fun. Light. He was an assault to my senses. A delectable dessert I hadn't been able to indulge in.

"I feel the same," I confessed.

"What are you going to do about it?"

I licked my lips and his eyes tracked my tongue. I clenched his flannel, unable to believe what I was going to say. "Is there a hotel nearby?"

He cocked his head like he hadn't heard me correctly. "A . . . yeah. I'm sure, but—"

"No 'buts.' You gave me a taste of life today and I don't want it to stop. We both want the same thing, so let's do this." Do it now, before all the reasons why we shouldn't jump into bed again could stop me. Before I wondered if he just wanted to get laid while suffering through Mother's smothering.

He brushed his rough thumb along my lower lip. "First, we get you food."

Xander

IT WAS ALL I could do not to carry my wife caveman style down the street. There was a little hotel along this stretch, an old refurbished one that promised more ambiance than comfort. As long as it had a bed, I was fine. We didn't even need a bed, just a door that closed and people on the other side of it that we weren't related to and wouldn't have to see again.

Savvy took a bite of her salad. I'd wolfed down most of my meal already, but her salad took time. Patience was hard to come by. Spending the day with her was exactly what I'd needed. I was ready to take it to the next level. I was ready to take this whole marriage to the next level, but I had needed some sort of sign from Savvy beyond the glow of her face behind the laptop.

"You're still going to need to find our way back." One of my favorite pastimes was watching her forehead furrow as she followed bus lines along a map.

"I would've starved down there."

"You were getting the hang of it. When should we do it again?"

Her fork paused before another stab into her organic greens. "Maybe the weekend?" She speared her lettuce and a cucumber. "No, wait. Chief wants me to go into the office and take notes while he conferences overseas."

"You're going to sit beside the camera and take notes?"

"That's what I do. Personal assistant to Walter Abbot, security consultant." She brightened. "But tomorrow's payday."

I hated being reminded what was paying for the hotel—my wife working her ass off. "I set up my account on Upwork."

"Any hits?"

"Not yet, but I also started setting up accounts on the stock photo sites." I had to bring in money somehow. Then I could convince Savvy to go away with me. Except roaming all over the world for the last ten years had left me more out of touch with the technological possibilities out there. It was time I entered the gig economy.

The grudging acceptance that settled in with each profile I set up must be what being a real adult felt like. It's what I had to do.

"When should we go?"

"I'll finish as soon as I can." She shoved a forkful in her mouth.

"No. When should we leave DC?"

Her chewing slowed until she swallowed. "I thought we were going to stay for the year."

That was her plan, but it wasn't mine. "Winter's ending. You've worked for a month."

"Is your article done?"

Frustration mounted. Writing wasn't my strong suit. I was working on being more than an amateur photographer and I hadn't put that same work into being a journalist. I'd left school before getting to those classes. "No. Article's not done. I can work on that anywhere."

I didn't tell her that the Philippines trip had been three years ago. I'd had the idea when taking the pictures but hadn't put a word down. I hadn't remembered my idea until I'd showed those pictures to Savvy.

Mustering the interest to do all the research had taken more energy than I'd anticipated.

She took another bite, her expression troubled. She stuck her fork through more arugula and impaled a cherry tomato.

"Wouldn't you rather travel sooner than later?" Didn't she want to travel with me?

She pushed her plate away. "Yes, but all I have to do is be predictable and responsible until next February. It won't be long in the grand scheme of things."

Every day equaled a hundred in the Abbot house. "We can live a little until then."

"Isn't that what we're doing?"

"One day a month isn't enough, Savvy.

You didn't commit any crimes. You aren't in a work-release program for the rest of the year."

Her pretty lips turned down. "A date night then. Weekly?" When I didn't answer right away, she worried her lower lip. "It's the structure, isn't it? You don't like it."

"No, it's fine." It chafed. The routine I lived by wasn't one of my own making. I'd held jobs where I had to abide by a time clock. Hell, ranching's punch clock was the sun and the weather and there were no days off. This weird purgatory in DC was nothing like anything I'd done.

"It's not fine. Even at my most impulsive, I am still pretty restrained."

"Impulsive?" Except for Vegas, I hadn't seen that side of her. "You've mentioned it, but I married responsible Savvy."

"Well, there was the time I wanted to go to a high school Halloween party as Ariel. But my boyfriend at the time had an ex who was going as a Disney princess too. I had to be better, so I dyed my hair bright red instead of wearing a wig."

All I could imagine was Savvy wearing seashells over her breasts—damn, I wanted to see that someday. "Red hair, huh?"

"Not red hair. Cartoon red. Mother paid a fortune to get it stripped out and not leave me bald."

"Okay, but that's normal teenage impulsiveness."

"I told you about college."

"The degree ultimatum." The decision that had left her in debt to her parents.

She tipped her head and the lights of the cafe gleamed over blond highlights that had to be from the sun. She didn't treat her hair. Too hard on the environment. Getting dragged to the salon for chemical treatments had probably killed young, budding environmentalist Savvy. "So, in college, I almost got arrested."

I sat back and crossed my arms. "I haven't heard about this."

Pink dusted her cheeks. "I was out with

some friends I'd met through Brady. They dragged me to a football game our senior year and it's so not my thing." She bit her lower lip. "You played, didn't you?"

"My brothers and I made up half the team." It wasn't much of an exaggeration.

"Well, I wasn't a sports kid. No big shocker there. So, the girls latch on to these guys and they're drinking." She huffed out a breath and lifted her gaze to the ceiling. "Drinking six-packs, right?"

"Okay?"

"With the rings?"

I couldn't stop my grin. "With the rings we're all taught will strangle the sea turtles and penguins?"

She squeezed her eyes closed. "Let's just say, I tried to provide some education."

"They called the cops on you for informing them of the dangers of six-pack rings?"

"They were making fun of me and started tossing their cans and bottles at me instead of the trash. So I threw them back."

Another hard breath blew out. "I may have ruined a vehicle paint job or two."

"Holy shit, Savvy."

"It was bad. Chief had to come down and deal with things, which included claiming self-defense and threatening to sue all of those involved. That's when he told me to move home after I graduated and look for a job in DC. I was in no position to argue. I was glad I couldn't see Mother's face when he told her."

"I can't believe Opal Abbot is such a hard-ass."

"About coddling me, yes."

"Then why Davis?"

She lifted a shoulder. "I think she's trying to spoil you, or she thinks that's what you're accustomed to and she wants you to stay."

"I'm more accustomed to tractors than drivers."

"She only knows her little part of the world."

"Regardless, what happened in college

was passion, not impulsiveness." What she described was the Savvy I'd met in Vegas.

She lifted a shoulder and her eyes dimmed. "Either way, it ends with my parents saving my ass. They tried to warn me away from Saving Sunsets." She winced. "I hate how right they were."

"We all make mistakes."

"I'm ready for a success."

"We're working on it." I meant it. Even if I didn't have the trust, I'd want to build on what Savvy and I had. Our attraction was a lightning bolt with enough electricity to power a lifetime. "I want to take you to that hotel, Savvy."

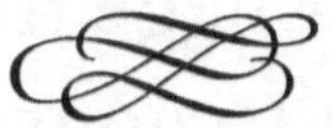

avvy

WE NEARLY RAN out of the cafe. My legs quivered, my belly fluttered. It'd been weeks since Xander and I had been intimate.

Xander clutched my hand and we hurried toward the hotel. He wove between people, towing me with him, and not letting me go.

A giggle escaped and he grinned down

at me, his eyes twinkling. I was ready for a win, and at the moment, he was my prize. With him, I reverted to the old Savvy. The one who took chances. The girl who shrugged off the college threat and moved to North Carolina to go to school. The girl who stood up to strangers for what she believed in.

We reached the door and he stretched a hand out to open it. My phone buzzed. I stopped, yanking on his hand. He whipped his head around. "You okay?"

"My phone," I said lamely. No one called me other than robots and my parents. I dug it out. "Chief."

Xander shoved his hands in his pockets and waited. The decision to answer was mine. Since I was technically on the clock, I flashed Xander an apologetic smile and answered.

"Sapphire, where the hell are the summaries for next week?"

"I have them written up. I'll send them when I get home."

"Home? Where are you?"

My teeth ground into my lip. "I went to lunch with Xander."

"It's three in the afternoon, Sapphire." The disappointment I was used to dripped from his voice.

"I've been working, but I know how you feel about public Wi-Fi—"

"Then get home and finish your job."

"Won't tomorrow work—"

"Do your job, Sapphire. I hired you for a simple position."

I met Xander's steady gaze. His mouth was set in a line. He could hear Chief's boom through the phone. "Sorry, Chief."

"You know what we've told you about apologies."

"They're useless words if you don't follow up."

"Get it done." He hung up.

I tucked the phone into my coat and raised my nervous gaze to Xander. "I need to get home."

"A hotspot won't do?"

"He barely tolerates me working from home." *A simple position.* The last month working for Chief had been hell. He was a demanding boss. I didn't understand how some of the assistants he hired could tolerate working for him. Was he only a tyrant to me? Was it another life lesson for me? "I'm sorry."

Tears burned the backs of my eyes and I blinked rapidly. I would not cry in front of my new husband because my dad was a hard-ass. Xander stepped close and wrapped me in his strong arms. His warmth closed around me and we could have been the only two people on the sidewalk.

"It's not your fault," he murmured.

"I really wanted . . ."

"I know. Me too." He gave me a squeeze. "But you know, we do sleep together every night."

"It's so weird." My words were muffled in his flannel.

"It is."

I tipped my head back. "I suppose it's time to get past that."

His lips lifted. "How quiet can you be?"

Xander

I DIDN'T HAVE a chance to find out how quiet Savvy was. Her dad had come home late, found her in the library wrapping up work while I was in the shower, and then kept her pinned in his office discussing impromptu travel plans.

She'd been in Boston the rest of the week, helping Chief evaluate the organizational security of a new client. But as she'd informed me while packing, *He usually travels a lot this time of year . . . through the summer and fall.*

Perfect.

I'd prepared for her return tonight. A new restaurant had opened in the city that touted locally sourced ingredients, used metal straws, and donated any oil used to some biodiesel place in town. Savvy was supposed to arrive this afternoon and I'd made reservations for this evening.

It was the first date I'd actually planned.

Waking up next to Savvy and not touching her had been a special form of torture, but waking up alone and surrounded by nothing but the natural lavender and vanilla fragrance she preferred sucked worse.

To kill time while waiting, I retreated to the sitting room to watch a show. I chose a documentary with stunning visuals and minimal narration. Writer's block had hit me hard. Photojournalists didn't have to write much, but every word I penned sounded inane and empty. I needed guidance and inspiration and Netflix would have to do.

Voices trailed down the hall. I looked at the time. Too early to be Savvy.

Pearl poked her head in and spoke to

someone outside the door. "It's Xander." She danced in. "What's going on? You've made yourself scarce this week."

I had. Usually when I hung out at someone's place, even lived there, I contributed somehow. Since I was still doing a whole lot of nothing, I'd made sure to be gone as soon as I woke up, not coming back until evening. I'd managed to sneak out before Mrs. Abbot could insist I use Davis. Apparently ditching him earlier this week had sent a message—or Mrs. Abbot thought I'd learned my lesson when public transportation had added extra commute time and Savvy had incurred more of Chief's wrath for taking the day off.

"I don't want to be underfoot."

Pearl scooted over and Em pushed in next to her. Em was the opposite of Pearl. Dark haired and serious. "He's waiting for his wife."

"She's supposed to be home soon," I agreed.

Em folded her arms. "I hate to break the bad news, but they're going straight to the office when they land. Chief doesn't mess around with afternoons off."

"But she said . . ." I reread the messages. She'd said they were flying in, not coming home. "Shit."

Sympathy oozed out of Pearl. "Yeah. We used to make that mistake a lot. Learned not to wait for Chief for the dance recital."

Em nodded. "Carter didn't go on this trip, but when he flies back, his nights are often later. Chief wants to be caught up from being out of the office before he goes back the next day."

"I wanted to take her out tonight." I could still do it, if I could change the reservation. It was just dinner and catching up.

"She'll be exhausted." Pearl stepped in. "Really, if you wanted to spoil her, you'd run her a bath and get her fluffiest pajamas ready."

"Especially if they're turning and

burning to Houston the day after tomorrow," Em added.

"Houston?" My plans were obliterated. Like a selfish jackass, I'd wanted to pick up with Savvy where we'd left off before she'd gotten the call from Chief. The need pounding through my body wasn't as simple as getting laid. My wife was coming home. I hadn't seen her for four days. We were supposed to have the whole weekend together, but now she was leaving Sunday.

"Welcome to Abbot Security," Pearl said lightly. "This is how Chief socializes and the rest of the office is dragged along. It's why he can't keep an assistant."

Em exchanged a look with Pearl. "I think it's why he pushed Savvy to work with him. She won't quit like the others."

"So you're saying not to make too many reservations this summer?"

Em snorted. "I get annoyed at Carter's travel schedule, but Savvy's is going to be heinous since she's Chief's assistant. His executive assistant doesn't even travel as often as him."

They both give me *oh so sorry* smiles and left me to ponder my suddenly open night. The hours ticked by and I didn't pay attention to what was on TV. I ran options through my head, but I would make no decisions until I talked to my wife.

The front door opened and Chief was rattling off details. "Make sure you confirm our ride from the airport to the hotel. We'll also need a driver to get us from head offices to the warehouses."

"Yes, Chief. I've got it all down to verify in the a.m."

His heavy steps pounded up the stairs. I darted out as Savvy slogged up the stairs after him, dragging her suitcase behind her. I trotted to catch up and lifted the luggage from her grip.

I didn't like how wan her smile was. "Hey. Sorry I'm late. Did you get my message?"

"Yes." I lifted my chin for her to

continue to her room. Hers, not ours.

I struggled to keep my eyes off her ass the entire way. Getting sexually worked up before a *what the hell are we doing about us* talk wasn't the way to go. Her snug brown cashmere sweater and long red skirt made it hard.

She turned into her room and I followed her in and shut the door. "I should've expected this," she said on top of a yawn.

"You're leaving Sunday again?"

She nodded and sank onto the bed. "And Minneapolis the week after that. So many travel plans." She groaned and flopped back.

"Any way you can get out of them?"

"What do you mean?" She propped herself on her elbows, and I forced my eyes off the way the position made her breasts jut out.

"It sounds like you're going to be traveling constantly for months. Is there any way you can maybe . . . not?"

The weariness vanished from her eyes and she sat up. "It's part of my job, Xander." Ice crystals punctuated her words.

"You don't have to work for Chief."

She pushed a stray hair out of her face. It looked like she'd put it in the bun she favored so much for most of the day, then released it as soon as they'd left the office. "We talked about this."

"You told me what you thought you should do. We didn't really discuss our options other than you didn't want to travel with me."

"These are work trips. Funded by Abbot Security."

I leveled a stare at her.

She looked down at her hands. "It's a short amount of time. It'll be next February before you know it."

Each day this week had stretched into eternity. For each hour that went by, I'd sworn it was eight. As soon as Pearl and Em had informed me of what Savvy's work schedule would really be like, I'd realized I couldn't take months of it.

"So you're not going to try to change it?"

She frowned. "Why do you want me to?"

"This isn't my home, Savvy."

"You don't have a home." She clenched her hands together. "You don't have a job. I'm trying to build a good foundation in case what we want doesn't work out."

A foundation that was her plan B. *Her* safety net, if we didn't work out. "Aren't you committed to making this work?"

"Of course I am, Xander. That's why I'm doing this."

I nodded but I wasn't agreeing with her. This was what, round three of this same talk? "Your parents are your security blanket."

"Excuse me?" She rose until we were facing off.

"You're afraid of failing, so you're clinging to them because you think that once you get the money, you're guaranteed not to fail."

"No." Her arms were folded so tight across her chest that her fingers were turning white. She leaned forward to emphasize a point I wasn't going to like. "I'm sticking around, like an adult, to clean up a mess I made. I'm not running from it like a scared teenager."

I recoiled. She thought I wanted to run? I wanted to *live*. This wasn't living, it was hiding. I admired her dedication to her job and to her parents, but the cost was us. If she was taking care of herself in case we failed, then I'd do that too. "I'll be leaving too."

"What? When?"

"Tonight." I shocked myself with the decision. Her eyes went wide but I'd said it; I had to commit. "We won't be seeing each other anyway. This won't be any different."

"Wh-where are you going?"

"I have that friend. I messaged him and he needs help with his business. I can work for him for a while."

"But your career—"

"Isn't going anywhere in DC. I can find another story with Hector." And maybe take some pictures again. I didn't bring my camera with me when I left each day to work.

"You can't just leave." Her lower lip quivered and her eyes were glassy.

"You did." I nearly relented, but I thought of Sunday and repeating this last week for several more months. No, thank you.

"It's only a few days at a time. A week at the most."

"We're fooling ourselves, Savvy. If we can't make this marriage work without money, we don't stand a chance being millionaires together. It's better to part now than wait and hope for another ten and a half months."

She opened her mouth to argue, but shut it again. I didn't know what else to do, what more I could say. That mic drop moment said it plainly.

I moved around the room. Packing my

things took ten minutes, tops. I didn't include any of the clothing Mrs. Abbot had purchased. Savvy stayed in the same spot and watched me.

When I was done, I stood at the door with my beat-up suitcase and my backpack slung across my shoulder. "I'll send the address, in case you need it for any papers. Whatever your decision, I understand. Let your mom know I'll pay her back for all the clothing."

She nodded and a tear rolled down one cheek. My hand itched to wipe it away, but touching her was the last thing I should do. I wouldn't leave if that happened. I wouldn't stop touching her and our wedding night had shown that it wasn't enough.

So, I turned and walked out. The house was dark and empty. Savvy didn't come racing after me. Darkness blanketed the night and the neighborhood was as quiet as the house I'd never see again.

CHAPTER 12

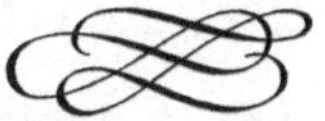

avvy

SIX WEEKS LATER . . .

MY iPAD LAY on my lap. The screen had long gone black, concealing the travel itinerary I was supposed to be double-checking. How long had I been in the library, looking out the window and wishing Xander was out there with

Michael? But where there had once been snow and the snowman we made together, there was green grass. Michael worked alone, sweeping grit out of the patio blocks and trimming the edges of the lawn with military precision that I think my mother loved more than the Chief.

I sighed and tapped the home button. My screen woke up, but I was no longer interested in which hotel was closer to the venue for the security conference Chief had to attend next week. I closed the file. Next week would be our seventh work trip and I was exhausted. Chief should have two assistants, one just for travel.

He got a helluva deal with me.

Done for the day, I left the library and headed for the sitting room and the oblivion TV might bring me. But when I was just outside the door, heavy footsteps sounded down the hallway behind me. My shoulders crept up to my ears as I ducked inside and hoped Chief would keep walking. At least the disapproving looks for chasing Xander away had tapered off. He didn't quite buy my excuse that Xander had a deadline that he needed to travel and do research for. It sounded good, even if it wasn't true. Mother bought the lie, but my sisters didn't. Yet they stayed out of it.

My solitaire diamond sparkled on my hand, a signal that I was still married. Xander had said he'd understand, whatever I decided. I wasn't sure what my choices were beyond stay married or don't. Thinking about each decision was depressing on the best of days.

How much did the money matter to me? Enough to let my husband live in another country while I stayed here? Enough to quit and run after him?

The idea sent my pulse racing. We'd tried to connect while we lived under the same roof and we'd failed. I couldn't quit my job and race after him. I couldn't leave one mess behind to chase another.

"Sapphire," Chief's voice broke in. "I need you to get started on the paperwork for the King-Abbot Security contract negotiations."

God, how I hated putting together Chief's ever-changing paperwork: I was killing more trees than I was saving. "Gentry King said yes?" Did Xander know? Had they talked during the last six weeks?

Chief broke into a rare smile, one that crinkled the corners of his eyes. "He just sent word. We need to work out the terms before we can officially get started." Before he left the sitting room, he turned to me and said, "Good work."

Good work. My first instinct at hearing those words was to jump up and down and pat myself on the back. Chief was actually proud of me! But it wasn't from anything I'd done other than get a little too tipsy and marry someone with the right last name. I wanted to be congratulated for doing more than spreading my legs.

To be fair, I'd been married for two and a half months and hadn't spread my legs since.

Good work for marrying Xander and helping Chief land a contract? Did Chief see the irony? The guy who'd told me to think through my actions my entire life had given me a rare atta boy for the most impulsive thing I'd ever done.

Regret welled up like it always did. For the first couple of weeks after Xander had left, I'd been incensed. He'd abandoned me because he wasn't getting laid.

Regrets. Looking back, I might've done things differently. Packed a bag and gone with him. But I couldn't fly halfway around the world and find him in some country I'd never been to before where I couldn't speak the language. My two years of French in high school wouldn't get me far.

He'd sent me the address of where he was staying in Kosovo. He'd gone to work for that interpreter friend of his, but if I couldn't face him in my own house, I couldn't face him thousands of miles away.

I was sitting on the couch, staring into

the fireplace, when Mother walked in and stopped.

"Oh, I'm sorry." She glanced around, probably searching for what I was concentrating on when she'd busted me and the wall having a face-off. "I thought I left my reading glasses in here."

She barely came in here to relax and hardly ever watched TV, but Chief had been home last night, a rare Saturday night with his wife.

"I haven't seen them."

Mother hesitated, her shrewd gaze raking over me. Then she closed the door and took a seat on the overstuffed chair by the couch I'd spent way too much time on the last six weeks.

"How are you doing?" Her voice was full of motherly concern.

"Fine."

She tilted her head, calling me on the lie as easily as she'd done when I was five and had gotten caught coloring on my bedroom walls. "Sapphire. You haven't been fine for a month and a half, and I don't think you've even talked to Pearl about it."

I'd talked to Brady. *Suck it up with Chief until you can afford a plane ticket to Kosovo. Nail down that money, Sav.*

So, no. His advice wasn't stellar.

My throat thickened. I never talked to Mother about my love life. Never. I'd seen who they'd rather have their girls date and marry and it wasn't who I was interested in. It was easier not to discuss it and save my energy for the wedding battle that I had ended up preempting anyway.

So what made me want to talk to her today? I was already married? I had a husband who'd left me and Mother had managed to stay married to a hard man like Chief so maybe she knew something I didn't? Maybe it was that I needed a mother more than a sister or friend right now.

"Xander figured he might as well go since I refused to quit working for Chief. He thinks I'm too scared to move out."

"Are you?" So much for the *That's absurd!* motherly support.

"No. Maybe," I whispered.

"You've had plenty of time to think. Have you changed your mind about staying here, or staying married to him?"

Tears burned. I wanted to be mature around my parents, but in the end, I was in the sitting room, crying about a boy.

She exhaled and wrapped her hands around her knees, sitting forward. "It wasn't the fairy tale you expected?"

"I didn't expect a fairy tale." Had I? Handsome man sweeping me off my feet. Promises of kings, castles, and rescuing. "But I expected . . ." I closed my eyes as I said what Pearl had guessed before. "I wasn't sure I could be enough for him and it was easier not to try than to find out the hard way that I'd failed."

"Whatever makes you think you'd fail?"

"You and Chief." I covered my lips with my fingertips. I hadn't meant to say that.

Mother's face didn't dare wrinkle with her surprise. "What about us?"

"You're beautiful. You're intelligent. But all you've done is house stuff and Chief calls the shots." I opted for chewing the inside of my lip instead of gnawing it between my teeth.

Mother's sharp inhale was followed by a long, weary exhale. "I was happy you didn't want to go to Georgetown."

The sudden subject change left me shaking my head. "What?"

"I was. I would've paid for it, but I wanted you to have the chance to get some real world experience."

I sat forward. My melancholy morphed into simmering anger. "Like being too broke to buy food?"

"Sapphire, don't be silly. We'd never let you starve. Your father and I kept an eye on you."

"You made me move back home."

She lifted a meticulously manicured brow. "How did we make you?" My mouth worked but nothing came out. "Chief wanted you home. He's such a worrier."

"Mother. He's . . . he's . . ." Demanding. Domineering. Overbearing.

"Provided for you? Given you everything you needed? He at least agreed that you needed to learn how the world works for yourself. I wanted you to learn to care for yourself instead of depending on someone, especially a husband."

The irony that I was depending on my husband to hand me money so I could do just that constricted every vessel in my chest. I sucked in a hard breath. "You've been so hard on me because of how Chief treats you?"

"No, dear. I was being hard on you so you could learn everything I wasn't allowed to." My eyes widened and she nodded. "I care for the house and take charge of the staff because it's what I know how to do, and I enjoy it. I can donate to any charity I want without asking for permission. I can volunteer for the local food pantry for eight months if I'm so moved. Unfortunately, I was worthless to them and they said that my financial support was more than enough."

A chuckle escaped my lips and grew to a laugh. I couldn't picture Mother stocking shelves in her Louboutins and pencil skirt. "Mother. What about Em? Chief shoved Carter on her."

"Dear." Mother rolled her eyes, a wry smile twisting her matte red-stained lips. "Emerald begged your father to introduce her to Carter. The poor boy didn't stand a chance."

My eyes narrowed. "But she doesn't work and she acts . . ." *Like you*. But I was learning my mother was more than how I'd pigeonholed her.

"She can't decide what she wants to do with her life. Carter is understanding. Happy wife, happy life. She's been talking about going back to school."

"She went to Georgetown."

"She also did more outside of the house

than you. You can't tell Emerald what to do, you know that."

"Pearl? Never mind. None of us worry about her."

"She was always headstrong. But you, Sapphire. You were too scared to contradict us and when you did act out, you withdrew into your shell so deep and for so long . . . I worried."

She'd worried some man would sucker me into marrying him so he could get to my family's money. Her gentle shoves out of the nest had turned into an expensive heel to the ass. "Why did you keep insisting Xander use Davis to get around?"

Her hands fluttered on her lap and for the first time in my life, I witnessed my mother blush. "Well, I wanted to make sure he wasn't using you . . ."

"You were testing him?"

"Yes. The way he looked at you—I didn't think it was necessary. But I bought him all those clothes and he didn't argue."

"He was being polite." My voice was a screech. Mother was diabolical.

She lifted a shoulder. "It made me nervous. Then he didn't wear them, and he started leaving before I could offer Davis's services." Concern crinkled her eyes. "Then he left for good and I'm afraid you're too far into your shell to do anything."

She hadn't wanted me to get married for money, but I had and it wasn't mine. Mother didn't know about the trust, yet she was talking about Xander like she knew he was important to me.

"I don't know if he wants to be with me."

"I thought he left because he couldn't be with you." My mouth turned down and she shrugged. "Thin walls."

"I work for Chief. I can't just leave."

"Sapphire, if you want something enough, you go for it. That's how your father and I know when you're on the right track. You lack focus until you decide not to. Why didn't you go with him?"

"I was trying to be responsible." I was getting so sick of those words.

There went that shaped brow. "By forcing him to live here and be miserable?"

"I woke up married in Vegas because it was either get married to someone I picked or get stuck with Lex."

"Yes, that. Em and Carter worked out so well, Walter thought you and Lex could too, but I do admit, he seems rather arrogant. I might've had to step in if you'd shown real interest."

I feared what her interference would've looked like.

"You made it to twenty-five without breaking down and getting married. Do you really think you did it as an act of rebellion?" Her voice softened. "I saw you two in the snow." She patted my knee. "You fight for what you really want."

Had I used my parents as an excuse, my path of least resistance? It had taken a quarter of a century, and just one five-minute conversation, to learn that my parents were a weird mix of smothering and shoving me out of the nest. That didn't change the reason why Xander had married me. Mother didn't know the story, but I needed her advice. "What if he married me for his own reasons and isn't interested in a relationship?"

"The young man I met was very much interested in you. Whatever you two told yourselves about why you married, I think you've overlooked the obvious."

"What if I fail?" Would there be a shell deep enough I could climb into?

She patted my knee. "What if you don't?" She rose and turned to go, unconcerned about her reading glasses. A ruse to check on me? Mother was crafty. How did I not see it? "But Savvy, whatever you decide, wherever you go, make sure you're living life on your terms and not someone else's. You've done that long enough."

Xander

SUN BOUNCED off the trees around me, making it seem like I was working in a forest of emeralds. The base of the Sharr mountain range was gorgeous this time of year. I hadn't arrived in time to help my buddy with his ski business, but he'd put me to work as a hired hand, slash hiking, and camping guide.

I was more hired help than buddy. I'd been piss-poor company since I'd arrived. I'd given Hector an abridged version of what had happened. Considering Savvy and I had been together only a month before I'd left, it wasn't really all that abridged. Which made me pissier.

I stomped the shovel into the garden bed. It might be a little too early to work the beds, but the harder the labor, the more peace I felt. I'd hauled logs all weekend so Hector and his wife, Eris, could put in firepits.

I admired him, making so much progress in the handful of years since we'd last talked during one of my rare trips home. He'd gushed then about how he'd left the military and moved to the country he'd met his wife in while serving. Working as a contracted interpreter, he'd banked money until he could afford his own slice of paradise.

A grunt escaped as I stabbed the spade into another mound of hard dirt. The ground was only mostly thawed, but I didn't care. I could work it again in a couple of weeks. I would still be here.

Thunk. Flip. Thunk. Flip.

I stopped only to shrug out of my flannel. It had gotten ripped on an old fence post I'd fixed by the river last week. A strip hung loose at the bottom, but if I ripped it off, I'd look like I was wearing some new torso-baring fashion in plaid flannel. I didn't want to waste money on a new one. I wasn't a millionaire yet. And since I hadn't heard from Savvy since leaving, I didn't know if I ever would be.

She'd be bold to give up that much money, but I could respect her decision. She wanted to live life on her parents' terms and there was a certain admirable loyalty in that. But as long as I wasn't served divorce papers—there was hope that something could be worked out.

How the hell was that going to happen?

I was across the world. It wasn't like I was in some mainstream vacation spot either. Not many people, much less Americans, said, Hey, let's vacay in Kosovo. I heard there's a cute new trail place that some asshole ran to in order to hide from his new wife.

Thunk. Flip.

I wiped my brow.

"I brought you water," came a voice behind me.

The one thing I hadn't factored in when I'd run to Hector was that his wife might have siblings, and that one of them, a sister, might be living with them. I hadn't considered that she might be single. Or that she might be undeterred by my marriage status.

She wanted the happiness that her sister had and here I was, new to town, and apparently a clear target to set her sights on. Hector or Eris must've told her that my marriage was on legs as shaky as a newborn calf's.

I cursed myself for not grabbing my water bottle. After the aggression I was exerting on this soil, I'd worked up a sweat.

"Thanks." I shoved the spade in the ground deep enough that it could stand on its own and accepted the bottle.

Rina kicked a hip out. Her black pants could just as well have been painted on and she'd tied her fuchsia shirt at her waist with a hint of skin peeking out. It didn't look like a work outfit, though for all her unabashed flirting, the girl could work. I hoped it meant she wasn't staying. Some days, I wanted nothing more than the oblivion manual labor would bring by the end of the day, but Rina talked my ear off.

At first, I'd hoped it was so she could practice her English, but then she got bolder, and as the weather got warmer, her clothing got more revealing. I often took meals to my room, risking coming off as rude, so it wouldn't seem like double-dating when only the four of us were around the dinner table.

I gulped down what turned out to be lemonade. Rina leaned against one of the wood posts that Hector had put in last year to keep the critters out of his garden. Someday they'd like to serve meals to hikers that featured homegrown fare, but for now, the garden fed him and Eris and their baby due at the end of the summer.

"Hector is making coffee. You come?" Her accent was thick, but she was learning my language much faster than I was learning hers.

"Hector's espresso is like drinking tar."

"I add milk." Her lips turned up and she

lifted her thick black hair off her shoulder. Her expression was rueful and for once not flirtatious. It was a common point of bickering among Eris and her younger sibling. Eris drank Hector's tar without a drop of milk or a granule of sugar. Occasionally, she made Turkish coffee, but Hector loved his espresso.

"I'll keep working. Thanks, though."

She said thank you back to me in Albanian and I repeated it, my American accent as thick around the words as Hector's espresso.

She chuckled. "Good try," she said in English. While I didn't want to date her, she wasn't a terrible companion.

She pushed away from the post and went to my camera bag. I'd set it by another post farther away to keep the dirt off. I stiffened, but there was nothing she could do to tank my camera. It wasn't like I was using it to pursue a story no one was interested in anyway.

"How do you— Oh."

The click of it turning on and the shutter snap made me glance back, my brows drawn down. She took another photo. I didn't care about pictures of myself, but they were useless.

"Model, yeah?" She laughed and took another shot.

"All right. I don't need to sacrifice storage on myself."

She pouted but located what must be the button to review the pictures. A smile spread across her face and she turned the camera around to show me. From my spot twenty feet away, I could see my scowl. If that's what I looked like just puttering around, no wonder Hector kept me away from paying guests.

As I worked up the soil, she looked at pictures.

"Where's wife?"

I jerked the handle and dumped a pile of dirt on my boots. Other than a few pictures of Ljuboten, the mountain peak that towered over us—because how could I not

—I hadn't taken many pictures. I hadn't come here for photography and that thought turned the lemonade in my stomach. I should be doing something career related. Savvy had at least been working on a future, even if it hadn't been the one she wanted. Or one with me.

Rina appeared at my side, standing closer than was necessary, her ankle boots sinking into the dirt.

"I don't have a picture of her." Humiliation left a sour note on my tongue. I'd never taken a picture of my wife. I had nothing to remember her by but the ring I kept in my luggage. I could see her in my mind, brilliant as the diamond that might still be on her finger. Would her image be so clear in six months?

"No picture?"

I bristled at her disbelieving tone. "No."

"Why is she not here again?" Rina's tone was deceptively innocent.

"Work" was all I said.

Thunk, flip. I shoveled my way down

the row. Hector wanted to get the onions in this weekend. Snow might line the Ljuboten peak, but with the seasonal temperatures and the river close by, this was good land.

I could already tell the grass was going to be thick and lush here. The grass at home was sparse, and only the heartiest varieties could survive there. This was why I liked traveling the world, experiencing how each environment was different. If I traveled deeper into the mountains, or farther out into the rural areas, the land would be different. It was fascinating, and like Savvy, I wanted to do my best to preserve it.

But that's not why you're here.

I ground my teeth together.

Why today? I thought that, with time, being here would become easier. That I'd quit wanting to count my cash and catch a ride to Pristina so I could buy a plane ticket outta here.

Thunk. Flip.

I was close to the end of the row, but not ready to turn around and see Rina. I wanted to be alone. I wanted to work the lemonade off, until I was sweating so bad I had to take my ratty flannel off. Then I'd collapse into bed tonight and quit thinking about what I should do. Quit thinking about her.

"Xander." Rina's voice broke in at the same time Hector called my name.

Had he been trying to get my attention?

I straightened and ran my gloved hand over my brow. I needed a shower. I tried not to wash clothes too often, but what I was wearing would stink by tomorrow. I was sweaty, pissy, and dirty, and I probably smelled like I'd been working all week without a shower.

I hadn't. Had I?

"Xander!" Hector called again. "There's someone here to see you."

That got me to spin around, spade forgotten as it hit the dirt. A spike of anticipation went through my gut, but I squashed it down. No way would it be who I wanted it to be. That was a fantasy that would never be fulfilled.

Had I upset someone in town? Often Hector sent me on small errands and either he or Rina went with me because of the language barrier. Sometimes, Hector stood back and let me muddle through the purchase while holding back laughter at my shitty attempts to speak anything but English.

I squinted into the sun, searching the area behind him. He stood on a stone patio he'd put in a couple years ago, having come out the back door of the tiny house he'd purchased only for the land it came with. No one else stood beside him.

"Who?"

Hector's mouth turned up in a shit-eating grin and the air froze in my lungs. "She says she's your wife."

CHAPTER 13

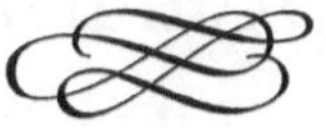

Savvy

ERIS LED me through her small, tidy home. I left my suitcase by the door and clung to my backpack as I trailed her. New smells assailed my nose. Coffee—strong stuff. Baked bread that reminded my stomach I hadn't eaten in hours. A mustiness that came with the age of the structure. We passed a set of wooden stairs that were currently stripped of all stain. A sander sat abandoned next to the railing.

From the outside, I'd thought the place would echo like an empty shell and have more drafts than DC during a blizzard, but I was wrong.

The main living area had a stunning wood beam ceiling that arched to a wall that made up the second floor. Furniture was minimal, but there didn't need to be a lot. The outside of the house needed some TLC that it appeared to be getting in stages. The inside was simple, yet elegant. The wood plank floors had recently been redone and served as the focal piece for the house.

"This place is nice."

"Thank you."

I hated how relieved I was that Eris spoke English so well. My years of French had come in handier than I'd thought on my trip here, but since I'd landed in Pristina, I'd been an earnest mess, hoping that if I looked pathetic, whoever I was dealing with wouldn't mind finding someone who spoke English or French.

As it was, I'd thrust the address at anyone who looked like they could get me where I needed to go. A bus ride to a smaller city and a cab ride later, I was here. I think it was a cab. By then, I'd been so tired and jet-lagged, I hadn't cared if I was in danger as long as I could shut my eyes in the next few minutes.

But I was here. I'd made it.

All by my damn self. A tremble went through my body. Had it really been the first time I'd traveled alone?

It had. And not to some tourist destination that catered to the traveler at every stop. I was in the middle of a new country, around the world from home, and as Eris stepped out the back door onto a stone patio, I was surrounded by the sounds of frogs and the fresh smells of spring.

How was it so green around here already?

Trees crowded the house, but it looked like someone had beaten them back. The cabins the driver—who thankfully spoke French—had told me about were hidden among the trees.

My gaze had no time for the small white structures. I desperately sought out one person and one person only.

There he was.

Xander's stunned expression told me what I'd known when I set out for my travels. He hadn't been expecting me—ever.

I gave him a tentative wave and he only cocked his head, his mouth dropping open and his eyes narrowing like he was focusing a lens on me, making sure I was real.

"Hey," I said as if the wave hadn't been enough.

"Savvy?" He snapped straight and shook his head. "What are you . . ."

What was I doing here? Wasn't that the question of the day? I wanted him. I wanted to talk about us.

I drank him in. Sweat wicked down the

black shirt he had under his flannel. It was one of my favorites, but it wasn't going to survive that rip. His sleeves were rolled up to show his muscular forearms.

He had no idea how much I liked that part of his body. Strong forearms, with a hint of veins that grew more defined when his muscles bulged. They did that when he worked with his camera.

Two strides and he was out of the garden, nearly bowling over the girl next to him.

My mind rippled with *Who is she?* but the closer he got, the less I cared.

"Savvy." His gaze swept behind me. "Did you . . . Did you come alone?"

"Someone should've told me in high school that German would come in handier." My chuckle was nervous. We still had an audience and I wasn't sure how he felt about my arrival.

He lowered his voice. "Why are you here?"

His tone wasn't combative. He sounded

downright mystified. Was it that unbelievable I'd packed up and left home to travel here by myself?

Hadn't I just been thinking the same thing?

"You," I said quietly.

He stopped in front of me and the corner of his mouth hitched up. He brushed a hand against my hair. I inhaled all that was him. He smelled like fresh soil, clean mountain air, and man. The best cologne money couldn't buy.

"Chief gave you time off?"

"I quit."

Surprise flashed in his rum irises. He danced his fingers under my chin. "I can't believe you're here," he murmured and stepped in.

I lifted my face. He was closing the distance when a female voice broke in. "Too bad she can't stay with you."

He scowled and straightened.

Eris shot the girl a hard look and said something in their language before switching to English. "Of course she can, Rina. She's Xander's wife and she's had a long trip."

Rina crossed her arms and spoke clearly, likely for my benefit. "You told me that I had to earn my keep, and I have been. Xander and I work this land as hard as you and Hector. The garden. The trees. The fence."

Acceptance crossed Xander's face. Rina wasn't exaggerating. They were earning their keep and not by doing menial chores. Those trees hadn't been cleared by heavy equipment. That had to be backbreaking work.

He glanced over at Hector, who'd only broken into a wide grin when I'd told him who I was looking for. "We can find a place in town."

Hector was about to brush him off but I caught the look on Rina's face. Smug.

"I can work," I said before I could scare myself out of it. I barely ever vacuumed. What did I know about fences other than some were metal, some were wooden, and some were plastic?

Rina raked a dubious look down my black leggings and cashmere sweater. They'd been comfortable to travel in, but would last no more than two minutes doing whatever Xander had been working on when I arrived.

"Savvy, you don't have to—" Xander started.

I lifted my chin, feeling every inch the petulant child I must resemble. "I can work. I catch on quick."

That lopsided smile sent my belly flopping. "I'm staying wherever you're staying."

I returned his smile. We drifted closer, only to be broken apart by a loud clap.

Rina snorted. "I'm sure Eris and I can come up with plenty to do. It'll be nice to have another strong back around."

Eris rubbed her back and I noticed a rounded belly under her baggy shirt. "Perfect timing. I wasn't looking forward to planting. Savvy can certainly help me there."

Rina huffed and stormed past us. I was grateful I didn't understand what she growled to Eris as she passed.

"Don't mind her," Hector said. "She's probably more disappointed to lose the challenge than to lose the guy. Xander kept her from being bored."

I locked eyes with Xander.

"We just worked together," he said softly.

"Is it all right that I came?" I hadn't allowed myself to have doubts the entire thirty-six hours that I'd been traveling. Xander didn't seem upset, but my presence had disrupted his routine, disturbed the peace he'd wanted to find here.

He didn't answer, but glanced at Hector. "Mind if I take a break and get her settled? I'm sure she's had a long trip."

Hector's knowing grin sent a flush up my neck and into my cheeks. He had more faith than I did that my husband wasn't bothered by my arrival. "Eris and I wanted to run to town for some more seeds for the container garden. We'll take Rina along."

"Appreciate it, man."

Hector and Eris disappeared inside, leaving me alone with Xander. I opened my mouth to ask once again if it was all right that I'd come, but Rina's shouts from inside caught me off guard.

"She doesn't want to go," he said.

"Sounds like it." I swallowed hard. "You and her . . ."

"Nothing happened. I didn't want it to, and like Hector said, she was bored more than anything. It's just us out here."

I nodded. We stood across from each other as Rina and Eris argued all the way to the car. Doors slammed and an engine fired up. Then the little red hatchback that had been sitting out front drove off toward the main road.

"Finally," Xander growled and closed in.

He captured my mouth and I dropped my backpack on the ground.

He tasted sweet, a startling contrast to the sweaty man I wrapped my arms around. I'd tried to fix my hair in every window I peered into, but at the moment, I didn't care how bedraggled I looked. Xander was kissing me. His tongue swept into my mouth and he devoured me.

I let him.

He picked me up and I twined my legs around him. He managed to walk over the stone without tripping and push me against the wall.

"Fuck, I missed you," he murmured against my lips.

"So, you don't mind?"

"What? No. Absolutely not." He nibbled down my neck. I needed a shower as much as he did, but the only difference was that he was sexy as hell after all the work he'd been doing. I was tired and rumpled from planes, buses, and cabs. "If it's a problem staying with Hector and Eris, we can rent a room in town."

"You're staying with me and I'm not letting you go again."

He'd told me it wasn't about the money and I'd kept wanting to believe it. The way he touched me now washed away my doubts. Any worries faded against the feel of his hot lips on my skin. My head tipped back against the side of the house. All those mornings I'd wasted when I could've been having this.

"Xander." I squirmed against him. His erection pressed into my center but our clothing muted the sensation.

He pulled back and my legs dropped to the ground. "I need to clean up." He looked down at himself. "I've been in the dirt all morning."

I feathered my fingers down his collar. "I'll clean up with you."

Heat seared his gaze, then he winced. "I don't have any condoms."

"None?"

His smile warmed my already blazing

insides. "I'm a married man and my wife wasn't around. I didn't need any."

"Well . . . I still have the IUD so . . ."

His expression grew solemn. "Only if you're sure."

I sighed. "Just as sure that I'd regret missing this opportunity as much as I have the last two and a half months."

He touched his forehead to mine. "You're going to be the end of me."

He picked me up again and swept us both inside. I'd deal with my backpack and suitcase later. I had lost time to make up for.

Xander

WATER POUNDED DOWN ON US. I'd admired the remodeling work Hector had done on this bathroom before, but my gratitude now was on a whole different level.

I kneeled on the wet ceramic tiles, barely having the sense to shut the water off so I didn't overflow his septic system, and cherished my wife. One leg was wrapped around my shoulders, I had two fingers inside of her, and she moaned my name over and over as I tasted her inside and out.

Hands twisted my wet hair. I'd washed both of us down in record time and I was finally where I wanted to be. Not just with Savvy, but between her legs.

I brushed my tongue against her clit in the slow, sensual way she'd loved on our first and only night together before this, but I didn't get long to play. She arched her back, her hands releasing me to press into the tiles of the wall.

"Xander. Oh my God!"

Heat flooded my face, and I lightened the pressure but didn't let up. Her hips bucked against my mouth as I drained every ounce of pleasure from the first orgasm between us.

When she sagged against the wall, I helped her put her foot on the floor and rose.

Wet hair hung behind her and moisture dotted her eyelashes. My own little water fairy was in the shower with me. I cupped her face in my hands and she met my gaze with her satisfied one.

"That's nothing like what I can give myself for orgasms."

I dropped a kiss on her lips. "It's a shame you had to do that for yourself." As if I hadn't been doing the same, in this very shower, in a rush so no one would know what I was up to.

Desire dimmed under her regret. "It's my fault."

"Shh." I kissed her again. "I said whatever you were comfortable with and I meant it."

"I want to get to know you. And myself. And . . ."

My erection pounded, my dick so hard my eyes could cross, but this discussion was open and honest. We were bared to each other in all ways. "And what?" I brushed my thumb across her lower lip. "You can tell me."

She flicked her tongue out, catching my skin. I was so close to her, just a little adjustment and I could thrust inside, but she wasn't ready. "I want this to be more."

There was that vulnerability again. She wanted us to be about more than sex and money. What she didn't get—and what I had to show her—was that we'd already been more on our blazing wedding night. We were more than that damn trust.

To put her at ease and give us both what we desperately wanted, I ran my hands down her sides and lifted her legs. She instantly wrapped them around my hips and I loved the trust it showed.

"It is more, and I'll prove it."

"Yes." The word came out breathy, needy. She ground her hips into me.

I stooped and placed myself at the entrance to heaven and thrust inside. Savvy cried out and hugged me closer, her teeth digging into my shoulder.

"Shit, did that hurt?" I shook from the effort of not moving, but dammit, I'd hurt her enough. I'd left her. I only wanted to pleasure her now.

"No," she moaned. "Keep going."

I pumped in and out. All my plans to bring us both to the brink and keep us there until we were about to collapse vanished. I only knew her wet body gripping mine, keeping me for herself.

Fucking without a condom blew my damn mind, but I had a feeling it was because of the woman in my arms. There were no barriers. Her body around mine, me stroking us each to climax. She clung to me so tightly, the movement was enough to tease her clit and send her soaring into another orgasm. I managed to last until she stiffened, a long groan leaving her as her muscles spasmed around me.

My hips jerked, hardly able to move thanks to the grip she had on me with her legs, but it was enough for my crest to slam into me. The biggest orgasm I'd known threatened to take my feet out from under me.

"Fuck, Savvy." I couldn't get out more eloquent words. My mind was gone, too busy enjoying the rapturous wave I rode as I released inside of her. My first time coming in a woman and it was exquisite. *She* was exquisite.

Somehow, I stayed standing. Her head was buried in the crook of my neck and mine hung next to it. I had one hand on the damp wall and the other helping hold one of her legs.

"That was amazing," she murmured. "I can't believe I can orgasm that close together with you."

Her warm body and honest words made my cock twitch. "Same."

She lifted her head. "But you only went once."

I jerked my hips, intense pleasure sending a rush of blood back to my dick.

Her eyes rounded. "Oh. So soon?"

"Let's find out." I pulled out and she dropped her legs. I spun her around and kissed across her shoulders.

"Aren't they going to be back any minute?"

"They probably just got to town." I nibbled her ears and caressed her damp body. We'd need another rinse off when we were done and if we were going to use the water, I'd make it worth our while.

Shivers broke out along her creamy skin. I felt them more than I saw them. My hands had free range. I wasn't fully erect yet, but everything was happening quickly, including Savvy squirming under my touch.

"You want it again, don't you." I nipped her skin.

"God, yes."

I slid my hand across her belly and down. She was still wet. She jerked at the touch to her swollen bundle of nerves. All I did was rest a fingertip on top and let her do the rest as I kissed and licked her skin. She turned her head to meet mine for a kiss.

It was an awkward angle, but I made it work. She swiveled her hips as our tongues met and danced. I used my other hand to stroke up her torso, cupping a breast, and rolling her hard nipple between my fingers, then back down.

This time took longer. She'd already climaxed twice, but neither of us wanted it to end.

When she was warmed up again, her skin flushed, and her body demanding more, I nudged her legs apart and placed myself. Her entrance was a furnace, scalding me with nothing but pleasure.

I pushed inside and took it slow. Long, solid strokes. We enjoyed each other. Her hands were splayed on the wall, her hips pushing back into me while I circled her clit as gently as possible.

"I missed you," I said into her wet hair. I'd said it already, but she had to know.

She'd left her home and I doubted she had any more cash than I did, all because of me. Because I couldn't stay in DC with her and get over myself.

Sure, I'd had my reasons. But here, in a different country, those reasons rang hollow. She'd followed me when I couldn't be bothered to stay.

"I dreamed of you," she said.

I captured her mouth again. "You won't have to anymore. I'll be right beside you." I pulled almost all the way out and thrust back in, loving the way her breasts bounced against my hand. "It's a twin bed so . . ."

A giggle escaped before she let out a little gasp as my thrusts gained momentum. "Are we both going to be under the covers?"

"I don't know." I pounded into her, the tempo picking up at the sound of her voice. She'd been in my dreams too, but her voice made it real. It wasn't dulled by memory or slumber. "You never did show me how quiet you could be."

"I'll make it work."

"You don't have to be quiet now." I couldn't last longer and neither could she.

She came with force, her cries bouncing off the tiles. She flooded my hand and my dick with her sweetness. I dropped my head and finished myself off in her slick body. Fucking amazing.

Never again. I was never masturbating in the shower again when I had a responsive wife who'd gone through so much to be with me.

I reached over and flipped the water on, angling myself to take the initial cold spray. The shock was exactly what I needed to get us both rinsed and dried off without taking her again. By the time I was dressed in my other pair of clean jeans and red flannel, I was fighting off another erection. Savvy's bags were downstairs so I wrapped her in a towel and led her across the hall to my twin bed.

"Eris is pregnant, right?" she asked as she perched on the edge and took in the small rectangular room with its bare walls and single chest of drawers. My empty suitcase was by the chest, next to the closet door, and my laptop was under the bed.

I nodded as I finished buttoning my shirt. "They're going to keep the baby in their room after it's born. They keep assuring me it'll be fine, but I think I need to find another place to stay. I can keep working here for a while, help Hector out, but . . ."

I faced her, hoping she didn't expect me to finish. There was nothing to add. I had no clue what the hell I was going to do, but Hector and Eris needed their house for their growing family.

With the sun streaming through the small window, Savvy's exhausted face was clear. I hadn't noticed the circles under her eyes before. She was ready to drop.

"Here." I dug a clean T-shirt out of a drawer. "I'll go grab your bags and see what they have for food."

"Thanks." She sounded as tired as she looked.

I left before her naked body gave my dick any more ideas. She needed rest more than she needed sex. I grabbed her bags but didn't stop for food. I could find something while she was getting dressed.

As I jogged back upstairs, I hoped things didn't get awkward between us. Or that our lust-induced haze didn't make barely having a roof over our head seem less dire than it was.

I pushed open the door. Savvy was curled on her side, fast asleep, wearing my shirt with the towel over her long legs.

She was on top of the covers. I set down the bags and took an extra blanket from the closet and covered her. Then I sat on the bed and let my mind wander. It wasn't often that I got the place to myself.

Savvy breathed softly beside me. We were together now. Newlyweds with our whole future ahead of us, however long or uncertain it was. And we had no idea what we were doing.

CHAPTER 14

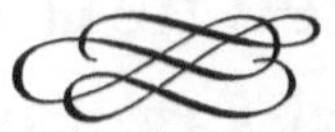

$\mathcal{S}$avvy

MY MUSCLES STRAINED. I pulled, tugged, shifted my weight, but I couldn't reach my goal. If only . . . All I needed was another inch, maybe two, but I couldn't fucking do it.

"Need help?" Rina's catty voice broke into my concentration.

It was just the push I needed to get the

heavy limb I was dragging over the mound of earth that'd been tilting my way.

"Nope. I got it." I had no clue how much farther I could pull this log.

Xander appeared next to me, frowning. "Let me grab a hacksaw and get those branches off for you. It'll be easier to drag."

"What about your work?" Rina's pout made me fantasize about scraping it off with those branches Xander was going to cut.

"It'll get done," he said tightly. Annoyance crossed his features as he shot a glare at Rina.

Rina could've mentioned that these branches and fallen trees would be easier to clear away if I cleaned up the limbs first. I should've thought of it myself, but my scraped and bleeding hands were telling me that no parts of me were used to this.

"I can do it." I dropped the ragged end of the branch. It was longer than I was tall and the base wasn't bigger 'round than my thigh, but it was heavy—for me. Xander could've cleared it within minutes.

"You . . ." Rina moved her arm back and forth. "Saw?"

"I can saw." How hard could it be?

Xander's expression went neutral before he turned to grab the saw. Rina stalked off.

It'd been a week since I'd arrived. I'd been put to work the next morning. Eris had had me help with dishes. At least I knew how to do that. Mostly. She had some tips and was a patient teacher.

There was only so much to do in the house. Kosovo had four seasons and there was a lot of work to be done to get the cabins up and the trails manicured for campers. They needed me outside more than sweeping the already clean floors.

"Here, let me show you." He squatted and he couldn't look sexier if he tried. Muscles flexed under denim and his shirt stretched over his shoulder. Today was cool, but with the work we did, there was no need for sweaters.

"I can do it."

He looked up and squinted at the sun dappling through the healthy trees. "I know you can, but I'm not Rina. I'm not going to throw you into the fire and walk away."

She'd do that too. Rina didn't flirt with Xander anymore. She'd given up on him. Her focus was me. Hector's initial insight had been correct. Rina wanted a challenge, and scaring me off of manual labor and out of Kosovo was her next one.

It wouldn't work.

It might work.

My arms shook each night when I carried my plate to the kitchen and helped Xander do dishes and clean up the meal. Then I gave myself a cat bath to keep from using their well water for a fifth person in the house they hadn't planned on. I was usually asleep before Xander entered the room. No chance to test how quiet I could be when we were having sex.

I brushed stray hair off my face. I'd thought about cutting it twenty times in the last week, but Rina kept her hair long and managed not to look like she was dying every day. So no haircut. I kept it piled on top of my head and hoped that I didn't miss brushing out the bits of debris that got caught in it before I went into the house.

Rina liked to point them out.

Xander positioned the saw. "These limbs are pretty small, so it shouldn't take too long. I know it seems self-explanatory to just saw back and forth, but you have to get a sense for pressure versus speed. The blade is thin and can bind if you wiggle as you're sawing." He moved the blade, adjusting the angle a few times before the limb hit the ground.

"Looks easy enough."

He rose and handed the saw to me, handle first. "It is. Don't worry."

I was more worried about looking inept in front of Rina.

The girl got under my skin. I couldn't pinpoint why. It wasn't because she'd tried for Xander. I mean, look at him. Wide shoulders. Powerful legs. Hair long enough to give him the bad-boy appeal, but anyone who talked to him would see what a good guy he was. Besides, *I* knew what he looked like naked. In the shower. In bed. On top of me. Behind me. She didn't.

Yeah, so jealousy wasn't it. But Rina's treatment bothered me.

I squatted like Xander and started to saw. It was simple, but there was a technique, and it took me a few moments to get the hang of it without binding the blade.

"Dammit." I readjusted and kept sawing. My triceps burned. I dropped to my knees. This was taking forever. Xander and all his muscles could cut a limb in a few swipes. It took me twenty to make a decent groove.

Sweat dripped down my forehead. Ick.

I stripped another branch. Each time I broke through the limb and it dropped to the ground I wanted to pump my fist in the air. But since neither Rina nor Xander celebrated after finishing part of a task, or even the task itself, I refrained.

I made a neat pile of branches that I'd have to haul to the wood pile later and went back to dragging the heavy limb. It was no longer as heavy and had fewer knobs to snag things on. At the log pile, Xander was chopping the limbs Rina and I cleared into similar bits that'd fit into a fireplace.

"Each cabin is going to have a firepit?" I knew the answer but I wanted to linger by Xander—and take a breather before I carried all the branches I'd cut and then gather even more.

"Yep, but Eris and Hector might go through a lot of this during the winter."

It was the end of May and they were stocking up for winter? Mother just paid the electric bill and there was my fire.

"What about the wood chips?" I asked.

"Those will get used for landscaping."

Hector didn't have a wood chipper, but he was supposed to pick one up in town. We'd have it for a day, maybe two, and that was why we were working overtime to clear the trees that Hector wanted to use for expanding his hiking and camping business.

Since a peacekeeping mission after the war in Kosovo had been the reason Hector was in the country when he'd met his wife, he knew how it had damaged the tourism economy. He'd fallen in love with the country as much as the woman, and his goal was to do his part to help it heal.

I was helping too. Pride welled in my belly, much stronger than the day Chief had told me good job for landing an oil tycoon's kid.

Yeah. This pride was better. Stronger. Like me. In that moment, the wobbly muscles I'd been building the last two weeks seemed like they could carry the wood chipper on the narrow road from town instead of waiting for a truck to haul it in.

There was an extra spring in my step as I went back to the branch pile. I arranged them in my arms and turned. Rina was eyeing a stack that I'd have to make another trip for. I'd been so preoccupied I hadn't heard her tromping through the grass.

"Took you long enough," she said.

My glowing bubble burst and I huffed out a hard laugh. "Why do you hate me so much?"

Her mouth pursed like she was inspecting a new bug we hadn't come across before, and we came across a lot of bugs and spiders. I'd had to readjust my fight or flight response to better ignore the less glamorous parts of nature.

"I don't hate you." Her English had really improved in the last few weeks, and it'd already been good when I arrived. My presence had made her more determined to get every nuance of the accent right. That I intimidated her that much made me feel better. "I get sick of you."

My brows drew together.

"Girls . . . *like* you," she amended, nailing the phrase she must've wanted.

Okay, that was less personal. I adjusted my load to keep a branch from poking me in the shoulder. "Like me how?"

"Everyone . . ." She waved her hand around. "Does things for you. You don't work hard. Don't know how."

"I work hard, just not like this." My words rang false. I hadn't worried about food or money until college. I hadn't grown up with many chores. My parents were alive and wouldn't let me suffer. Chief had been ready with a job when I'd lost mine.

"I bet in America, you are surrounded by people who do it all for you."

My mouth dropped open. How could she be so . . . *accurate*? So incredibly on the nose that it hurt to hear? Rina was obviously used to working hard, doing this for herself, and she was helping her sister live her dream. Was it because she didn't want to do it for herself? Or because she didn't have other options? Rina could be here, because like me, she had no other options, no job advantages, no money to make her dreams happen, and no one to pave the way to make it easier.

We were so much alike, only she'd had to work her ass off to reach the place I'd just decided to fly to on a whim. Without Xander here, I'd have landed on my ass. Unlike him, I didn't have friends and contacts all over the world. I didn't know how to work with my hands and my body for a living and I didn't have the skills to do it.

"God, you're right," I said and laughter bubbled out.

She eyed me warily.

"You're so right and that's why you bugged the hell out of me." She lifted a brow, but I continued. "You didn't do a damn thing to help me and I'm not used to that. I'm a pampered princess."

My parents had safety nets up all over the place. If they didn't, my sisters wouldn't let me go homeless. Then there were my friends. Others who'd been raised like me. And Brady, enabler extraordinaire. His motto was *take the easy way out* and he'd encouraged me to rely on my parents.

"You are a *pampered* princess?" she said, her accent thickening around "pampered."

"It means spoiled."

Understanding lit her eyes. "Yes, rotten." Her eyes twinkled and I knew she wasn't messing up *that* meaning.

"Sometimes rotten, mostly helpless."

Her mouth quirked in a smile and I couldn't hold back my grin.

"Everything all right over there?" Xander called. He'd finished the branch I'd brought him and was watching us, the ax impaling the stump. From his vantage point, we probably looked like we were facing off.

"We're bonding," I called.

"Okay?"

"Bonding?" Rina asked, a faint smile still on her lips. "Like, friends?"

"As long as you don't spoil me. I need a little more reality in my life."

She fought a smile and her gaze swept

over the small area I'd been clearing all morning. It was half the size of hers. "You have a lot of branches to haul and you've been talking too long. That kind of real?"

My arms were starting to burn for it. "You have to admit, you didn't think I would hang on this long."

She shook her head. "I thought you were going to cry after the first row of seeds."

The planting fiasco. Putting seeds in dirt should've been easier, but there were directions to read and details to pay attention to. This was how Eris and Hector made a living and they'd had to keep correcting me. I'd lost a crapload of radish seeds in one corner when I'd spilled the bag. I'd never get my pants clean after kneeling in the dirt to save as many seeds as I could.

But I'd done it. I'd also helped haul lumber off the truck that delivered the supplies for the next cabin Hector was building.

I was still grinning when I dropped my armload by the wood chipper pile.

"What did I just witness? Both you and Rina are smiling. At the same time."

"I think I need her." I swiped my gloves together, my grin triumphant. Energy infused my muscles and I no longer felt like dropping in a pile of blood, sweat, and tears.

I hadn't had much time since arriving in this country to get to know my husband, but I was getting to know myself, and maybe that was the real first step to making this crazy, impulsive relationship work.

Xander

Savvy was blooming like the wildflowers along the house that Eris had planted. She and Rina were fast friends after another week of playful bickering, and I could see why. Rina didn't coddle Savvy. She expected my wife to take care of herself and get shit done, and Savvy did.

We'd cleared another area in the trees and I'd started helping Hector build a small cabin. There was even a set of hikers in the first cabin Hector had erected two years ago. Eris was busy cooking and cleaning for them with Rina's and Savvy's help.

I propped a boot on the edge of a couple of two-by-fours, placed a nail at the joint, and swung my hammer. The pounding was a familiar sound. This would be a lot faster with a nail gun, but the budget didn't allow for it. Hopefully, once Hector got this cabin built he could rent it out enough to pay for itself and buy some extra tools to build more.

I was almost done with this wall. It was early morning but since the summer had started unusually hot, we worked early mornings and tried to hang out in the house in the afternoons. There wasn't AC, but the lower level was pleasant with the paddle ceiling fans running.

Hector emerged from the house and started through the field, along the little path that Rina and Savvy had made while clearing the land. It'd be covered in pea rock to keep from dragging mud into either dwelling, but we'd worry about that when we had a building that resembled something someone could sleep in.

I kind of wanted to see Savvy pushing a wheelbarrow. She'd learn to do it. Nothing stopped that woman. Admiration swelled in my chest.

We'd snuck some kisses here and there, and I'd had to reassure her that getting to sleep next to her each night on our small twin mattress was enough. I wasn't lying. I might be hard as granite when I went to sleep holding her and again when I woke her up with soft kisses down her neck, but we were together and that was all that mattered. She'd groan and complain about sore muscles. I'd massage the worst spots, fight a painful erection, and then let her get ready for another day of hard work.

Hector approached. I straightened and took a few steps to the left to hit a patch of shade. The strength of the sun diminished to tolerable.

"Great news. We rented out the second cabin for all next week."

"Awesome, man. How many?" My brain circled over the to-dos to get the place ready. Since they hadn't been rented, we'd worked on other tasks that were harder to do when snow was on the ground.

"Four. Two couples. They said they were okay sleeping on cots when I told them how small the cabin was."

"They just want a roof over their heads." Made sense. The customers Hector's business attracted were harder core than the average hiker. These people probably just wanted a dry place to store their gear while they explored and if they got the bonus of a roof over their head during rainy days, even better.

"Savvy offered to clean it up, but when she walked through, she said there might be a small leak in the roof."

"Want me to take a look?" I was in the middle of building a frame, but I offered anyway.

"Sure. Yeah." He puffed out his chest and clapped his hands. "I need to work off some of this energy. The summer bookings are filling up fast."

"For the outdoor sites too?"

"Yeah." He grinned. His dream was coming to fruition.

Damn. What would that feel like? He'd had a goal and he'd worked steadily toward it. I'd left my camera in the bedroom since that day Rina had looked through it. I'd seen plenty of photo-worthy sights. Sunsets. Rain clouds gathering over the peak of Ljuboten. Savvy and Rina squatting in the garden, pulling weeds and thinning out sprouts. My fingers itched to point and click, but my camera was in my room.

"Hey . . ." Hector scratched the back of

his neck. "Could you maybe take some shots of the cabin and, you know, anything that'd attract people to this area? I could use some more photos for the website. Eris thinks brochures are still the way to go."

"Yeah." Like those sunsets and rain clouds I had just been thinking of. Hell, any shots with Savvy and Rina would attract more than a few male campers. I should've thought of it earlier. "I'd love to. I didn't want to assume . . ." That was a lie. A total bullshit lie. Instead of using a pseudonym, I should just call myself the Shy Photographer. My tagline would be *I'm too much of a pussy to actually take photographs, but I couldn't sell them anyway.*

"I get it. Totally. I'll pay."

"Are you kidding? Consider it part of settling my tab."

"No tab. I couldn't have done all this without you. I wasn't sure about Rina, but she's been a rock star. And you and Savvy have been such a help. I don't know how long you're staying, but we'll take you for as long as we can."

He might think differently after he had a baby. With a booked-up summer, word would spread and he'd start taking reservations for cross-country skiers and winter adventurists who'd want to explore the mountains. Then he could hire his own help, help who had a home to go to after a day of work.

I left him to finish the frame. He vibrated with excitement, and swinging the hammer would help burn it off.

I walked down the path toward the main house, which served as headquarters, then angled off to the cabin that needed to be cleaned for next week. I didn't bring tools. I'd find out what it needed first.

That was me. Aspiring photographer, handyman around the world.

I stepped inside, letting the door creak shut behind me. Faint mustiness greeted my nose. I let my eyes adjust. The cabins had rudimentary electricity that could be spotty. With the sun shining today, I wouldn't need more than a flashlight.

I walked through the space, inspecting both the floor and the roof. Delicate footsteps displaced the dust on the floor. Must've been from Savvy's walk-through. The cabin wouldn't need more than a good dusting and mopping. The mousetraps in the corners were clear, so that was a good sign. I went back to the light switch and flipped it on to make sure everything worked. Same with the faucets, all the while looking for the leak that Savvy thought she'd seen.

Hector hadn't been lying to the campers. The cabins were sparse. They were a shelter and little more. Any cooking needed to be done via campfire and the pressure of the well didn't lend to more than spit baths and light dish rinsing.

I hadn't grabbed my camera, but I took out my phone. A few demo pics would tell me if there was any point in taking photos of the insides of the cabin. Rustic attracted just as many customers as plush.

A message I hadn't noticed before made me pause. *Working cattle next week. You in?*

It was the same message I got every year around this time.

Footsteps resounded on the floors and echoed off the walls. "Hey. Looking for the leak?"

Savvy's hair was up in its standard messy bun. The sunburn she'd suffered after her first week out in the sun had faded to an even tan, but her cheeks were red from the rising temperature and uphill climb to the cabin. She was in leggings today. She'd taken to wearing her one pair of jeans when we worked outdoors, but since she was cleaning today, the leggings made sense. She'd adapted quicker than I thought she would. She was thriving.

"I haven't spotted it yet."

She led me to the second room that wasn't quite a bathroom but was too small to be a bedroom so it was just an extra room that Hector had installed the sink and showerhead in. Pointing to a corner just under the roof, she said, "There. Is that a water stain?"

I walked around the room. Where the leak was didn't make sense until I thought about what was outside the cabin. "The old bathroom."

She wrinkled her nose. "What old bathroom?"

I chuckled and led her outside. The grass surrounding the base of the building muffled our footsteps. On the wall that had the water spot on the inside was an old wooden partition that Hector and I hadn't removed yet.

I pointed to the triangular hole in wood planks that made up what would've otherwise looked like a deck. "Bathroom."

She scrutinized it. "I don't get how— Oh!" Inching toward it, she bent to look down the hole. "Is it . . ."

"This place had been abandoned for years before Hector bought it. This was an original cabin so it had an old-school toilet." I gestured to the hole. "He filled in the reservoirs with dirt but didn't tear down the partitions. I should do that though, before we have campers thinking it's still good. I think it's where that partition is nailed into the wall that's caused the leak. I can seal it up."

"He must've put a lot of money into this place to get plumbing and electricity."

"He's taken it in stages, but yeah, he worked hard and saved up. I'm glad I could be a part of it."

Her expression went soft. "It's really taking off, and perfect timing with the baby."

Hector was older than me, and he'd had his shit together for much longer. I'd lucked into a marriage and was waiting out nine-plus more months until I could collect a shitload of money—that I had no idea what to do with. I was broke and aimless. I didn't want to be rich and aimless.

My phone was still in my hand. I didn't

have to see the message, I knew who it was based on the time of year.

"Not important?"

Was it obvious I was ignoring the message? I tucked the phone back into my pocket. "Dawson. They're working cattle next week." She waited for me to elaborate. Her look forced me to do more than ignore the message. "We're too busy here. I want to help Hector through the summer and get him set up for the winter."

Her head bobbed. "Makes sense." She bit the inside of her lip. Another move that forced me to think about what I'd just said.

Shit. "But I suppose I should talk to my wife about it first."

She blinked. Perhaps she hadn't been thinking about it like I had—or maybe not consciously. "The flight would be expensive. And long."

"Unless we take the company's private jet."

Shock rippled across her face. "They

would do that? To work cattle? Wait, what does working cattle mean?"

The sun had shifted and was blazing on us now. I held my hand out to her. She took it and I led her behind the cabin, where branches shaded lush grass. I sat and pulled her onto my lap. She settled against me with a sigh.

"Working cattle in the spring means vaccinations, tags, and Dawson usually does AI with part of his herd."

"AI?"

"Artificial insemination."

"Oh." Her smile was sheepish. "I have so many questions about that."

"I have most of the answers."

She giggled. "Not the conversation I thought I'd have today. So, you're not going?"

"*We're* not going, if it's okay with you."

She was quiet and I'd been around her enough that I could see her mind working.

"What are you thinking about?"

She didn't respond at first. A long

breath eked out of her before she spoke. "Are you going to talk to your family before you get the money? Do you plan to see them before then?"

I never *planned* to see them. Plans were for people who knew where their future was going. I'd planned to go to college. I'd planned to be a photographer. I'd planned to have accomplished more in life by the time I was thirty. Plans were for those who could get stuff done.

Seeing my family just happened. Some circumstance eventually brought me back to Montana. But that wasn't exactly her question. She was asking if I was avoiding them until I was a millionaire. Then what? I swagger back home, count out bills, and pay Dad back for all his money?

"You think I should?"

She rested her head on my shoulder, her face tipped up to the sky. The temperature in the shade was pleasantly warm. "I don't know your family, but I can say that I never thought talking to my mother about my issues with them would turn out the way it did."

"The only talking I've ever done with Dad led to him reiterating how disappointed in me he is."

She licked her lips. "You talked to your mother a lot, didn't you?"

My stomach sank. The one topic I tried to never think about. My mother and how she was no longer here. "Yes." We were quiet for a moment before I kept talking, something I'd never done. Previous women had never pushed me on the subject. Not that Savvy was pushing, not really. Maybe she would eventually, but I wanted to tell her about Mama. I wanted to tell a girl who'd become really fucking important to me about the woman who had been the most important in my life.

"She taught me to take pictures. Whenever I got into trouble, or in a fight with my brothers, which was all the damn time, I'd go to my room, or to a quiet space in the barn, or to ride my horse, and she'd find me. She always had her camera and instead of telling me how wrong I was, asking me what I thought, she'd take some pictures and then hand the camera over and give me tips."

"No wonder you're a natural. How old were you?"

I would've shrugged, but with her resting against me, I didn't. "I first remember her sitting with me when I was four. We took pictures of Buster, one of the blue heelers we had growing up. I was eleven when Mama died." When she had been murdered.

"I hope you're not mad, but I read the story."

"King's Creek doesn't have much to report on, and the paper covered Mama's death for a full year." Mama's death was so gruesome even a bigger town would have salivated at the story. The ranch hand our bastard neighbor had hired had thought something in our house could fund his next meth score. Instead, he'd found Mama.

"They constantly interviewed us and did stories about how we were coping and moving on. I hated that Dad could still read the newspaper. I hated a lot of things that Dad did after Mama died."

Savvy turned her head into my neck and twined her fingers through mine. She didn't speak and that was what helped me keep talking.

"He played the field. Less than a year after she was gone, he was sleeping with everyone and everything, like he was making up for lost time."

"That had to hurt."

"Yeah. It pissed us all off. Dad never really talked about it, but . . ." Savvy gave my fingers a squeeze. "Then I see him with Kendall and I wonder if he was just really fucking lonely and afraid to love again. Except I can't forget what those years were like, seeing him with other women in the bedroom he shared with Mama."

"Regardless of how hard it was for him, it was still hard for you," she murmured.

"Yeah. She understood me. Dad doesn't. To him, I just run from my problems. Mama got it." I wasn't into yelling, or proving myself, or arguing until I lost my voice. I had to go do something. Take that energy roiling inside of me and expend it on the world. At home, I used to ride my horse. Then it was photography. In college, I bought my own camera and struck out in the world, Dad's cash in my pocket.

"I want to understand you too, Xander."

A small smile hitched up the corner of my mouth. "Since you crossed the world to sit here under a canopy of leaves by an old cabin and talk to me, I think you do."

She wiggled in my lap to get more comfortable, and despite the gravity of our conversation, my manhood woke up and reminded me that my wife and I weren't able to have nearly as much sex as we both wanted.

I splayed my hand along her side.

"Xander?" Her voice was breathy, hopeful, or was that part just me?

"We should be alone for a while."

She sat up, her ass grinding into my growing erection and doing nothing to calm it down. Looking around, she squinted into the trees and went still. Then she ripped her top off and turned toward me. "I've never had outdoor sex."

My mind went blank as I was faced with perfect, creamy tits. "We'll have to remedy that—right now."

CHAPTER 15

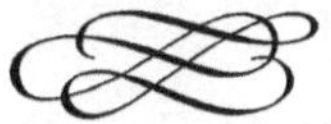

I shook my phone, as if that'd make the information upload faster. "Come on."

"What's going on?" Xander dropped down beside me where I was sitting on the stone patio behind the main house.

"I'm not sure. There's a message from Pearl that's not downloading."

I sighed and put the phone on the

ground in front of us. Sitting outside and waiting wasn't a hardship. I spent more time outside than inside these days. It was early September and I'd just finished a two-mile hike around the base of the mountains with the latest group of tourists.

My heart still raced when I passed the signs Hector had made that instructed hikers to stay on the trail as not all the land had yet been cleared of land mines. Real mines. Ones that exploded. I knew this country had been through a war—I even saw the soldiers from Camp Bondsteel when we went to different villages. But *land mines*. Hector talked about how an organization was slowly clearing the country, but demining only took place in the warmer months. He'd rather be safe than have someone hurt or worse.

I never left the trail, but I also couldn't believe that this was my life now. From being chauffeured by a private driver to walking beside explosive devices. Though I wasn't one of the brave, knowledgeable souls doing the clearing, it gave me a sense of bravery. Like, I could do this. I could go back home and tackle whatever I wanted.

The only problem was that since I'd lifted off from the US, I wasn't sure what I wanted to do with my life. The world was a big place, and I was just one person who didn't know a whole lot about it.

Whatever I did in life, I wanted to be effective. Look at Chief. I had a lot of issues with his work hours, but he was committed. He'd made his company one of the top organizational security firms out there. He was a consulting *boss*.

Mother was a boss too. I hadn't seen it before I'd quit working for Chief and left home, but she was in charge of her life all the same. Neither of them was necessarily saving the world, but I could take a page from their playbook and commit.

I just didn't know what I wanted to commit to. Not anymore. I'd thought I had all the answers. Recycle. Clean up manufacturing. Rely less on oil and nurture other forms of energy.

Hector and Eris weren't destitute, but they worked for everything they had. They reused what they could and it wasn't because of some trendy campaign, but because they had to. Those branches I'd hauled to the wood-chipping pile a few months ago? They were used in the flower beds and for mulching to help some saplings get through the upcoming winter. All the wood chopping Xander did was both a necessity and income for the business. Campers purchased bundles for campfires, ones that weren't a fun firepit like I'd grown up roasting marshmallows over. They cooked their meals over those campfires. Hector and Eris had even started a fire on the chillier nights that were common in the mountain region.

I'd bought a new outfit, but only to replace a pair of jeans that were torn in places that would make them indecent to wear—though not according to Xander—

and a lightweight shirt because hiking for miles needed moisture-wicking fabric. I'd had limited funds and limited shopping options, but Eris had turned it into a fun afternoon in Pristina. Rina had come with us and we'd run errands for the business and hit up thrift stores.

My perspective wasn't changing, but instead of the bird's-eye view I'd had before, I was in the thick of the environment. My hands were dirty and I loved it. The new Savvy still wanted to carve a niche, but after years of knowing exactly what I wanted to do with my life, I no longer knew exactly what that niche was.

Did I want to go back to an organization like Saving Sunsets and be another cog in a wheel? Or did I want to find a place where my voice was louder, where I had more input in the final decision? The latter option appealed to me more and more.

"There it is," Xander said.

It was a picture of Pearl, hair pulled back in a twist, uniform on. Her message read *Finished up during summer semester. Off to become an officer.*

Pangs of jealousy and fear didn't stab my chest like the last time she'd packed her bags and left without informing anyone of her plans first. I'd proved I could do the same thing. I could do it when I didn't know my plan first.

"What's up, bitches?"

I glanced up at my best friend. He'd flown across the world to check on me, arrived on the doorstep muttering about how Sapphire Abbot did not willingly leave Chevy Chase, Maryland, to spill radish seeds and cry. He had stayed for two months and showed no signs of leaving. When I'd asked him after he'd been here a week, all he'd said was "Job market's shit anyway."

"Brady, don't you have hikers to alienate?" He'd come here under the guise of being a camper, using next month's rent money to fund his trip. Xander and Hector had placed bets on how long he'd last. Rina had set the earliest date, calling him "city boy" instead of his name.

Brady hated it, and hated that he couldn't charm the pants off Rina, but he'd wormed his way into Hector's good graces and now he worked as a guide with me and Xander. I helped Eris the more pregnant she got. She taught me things in the kitchen that I would've learned had I not grown up an Abbot.

This was the best summer of my life.

Brady straddled one of the cheap plastic chairs Hector kept on the patio. "I saw them all safe to their cabins. Another tour done and another invite to come visit later tonight."

I wrinkled my nose. All of us got hit on more than I'd thought possible. For safety reasons, Xander and I kept our wedding rings in the bedroom and we swapped stories of bad pickup lines at least twice a week. The price of having young, virile folks coming through.

"Did she take the rejection well?" Surprisingly, I hadn't witnessed him messing around.

"Always leave them thinking they have a chance."

The door banged open and Rina exited. "They don't know you then?" she asked innocently.

I grinned at their banter and exchanged a look with Xander. We had our own bet and it was that my two best friends had a thing for each other and they were fighting it hard. I didn't know why, but if that made it all the more successful in the end, then I would support their bickering. As for me, I had my guy and the muffled sex was worth it.

Xander hooked an arm around my shoulders. With his body heat plastered against me, I wouldn't need the fire that Hector planned to start. It was our Friday tradition, and with Eris due soon, it wouldn't last much longer.

I stiffened and Xander gave my shoulders a reassuring squeeze. Neither of us had brought up what we would do once winter came. Hector would help with the baby, but he still needed to work. Rina would be here, of course. They had cross-country trails mapped out, along with winter hiking routes and ice-fishing plans. Anything that could be done in the winter to attract outdoor enthusiasts. If they were successful, and I was sure they would be, they'd need that much more help.

Xander and I could stay and work, but as much as I enjoyed it, I was growing antsy. If we stayed, we'd have to get a place of our own and neither of us wanted to put stakes down that deep. I had a calling. I didn't know which direction it would push me, but I wasn't going to figure it out here.

To distract myself from all the questions, I told Brady about Pearl.

"She always had a fancy set of brass ones. So, what about you?" Brady took a drink of lemonade. He'd never been a boozer, but this was the cleanest I'd ever seen him live. I guess the same went for me. My clothing fit differently. I had muscles in new places that Xander liked to explore. As for Xander, he lived the same way he always did and somehow got sexier every day.

"What about us?"

"When are you heading back?"

Xander's fingers squeezed my shoulder. He liked the question about as much as I did. "We don't know yet. We'd like to meet little Morales before we leave."

"Won't be long," Rina agreed. "I hate to see you go." She tilted her head toward Brady. "Him, not so much."

I laughed at Brady's scowl and hoped it'd be enough of an interruption to keep from having to answer. I wasn't sure how Xander felt. He'd mentioned the baby as a sort of deadline, but neither of us had followed up on it.

The issue that went unspoken was that there were months to go before we got any trust money. Working for Hector paid room and board and we didn't ask for more than that, it wouldn't be right. Hector had insisted, but they didn't know about the trust. I wouldn't feel right taking five dollars when I was supposed to be a millionaire right after Valentine's Day. So we'd put our earnings away for his family, and we'd give it to him before we left.

Rina rolled her eyes. "He's asking because he wants the room before it gets too cold."

Brady's grin stretched. "Rina just wants me closer to her." He dodged a pebble she tossed at him and laughed. "But Savvy here hasn't met the in-laws."

"I met his dad." I glanced at Xander. Did he agree that it was time for me to meet his brothers and their wives? The thought of meeting them made our situation real. We hadn't survived life in DC. In the mountains, in the middle of nowhere, it was easy to pretend this was some fairy tale we'd fallen into, one that only required sweat equity for a happy ending.

In the real world, I needed to get along with his family. I wanted to. My family liked Xander. They liked how he pushed me out of my safe zone. My goal for the year hadn't changed, but instead of working for Chief and saving money to build a foundation for whatever happened, I was working on myself—and this relationship.

Xander met my gaze, then scanned our surroundings like he was viewing the rest of the world. "We don't have to go to Montana. We could go anywhere."

Anywhere? The thrilling thought did nothing to clear up my confusion. We'd been together for months. He hadn't seen his family for longer than I had, and while he was used to long periods between visits, it wasn't every year he was married.

Xander and Brady started naming places. Romania. Rina told them about the salt mines turned tourist attraction and maybe we could find work around there. There was Macedonia and the birthplace of Mother Teresa, but Xander didn't want to go to a big city like Skopje.

Rina shrugged. "After doing the hiking tours, you'll have no trouble finding work. Some hostels are always looking for help, and I heard of a couple developing an ecovillage that might be hiring, but you'd want to do it before it snows."

"What do you think about an ecocenter?"

My smile was perfunctory. The three of them fired ideas back and forth, but I wanted to ask, What was wrong with Montana? What was wrong with introducing me to his family? Meeting his dad and Kendall had basically been an accident.

Was his hesitation about me or the money?

It could be me. He hadn't been taking pictures. He hadn't used the laptop he'd worked on at home. And he didn't talk anymore of photojournalism or his photography. There were those simple photos he'd taken for Hector, then he'd tucked his camera away and helped build another cabin.

I'd once thought I only attracted two types of men—those like Chief and those with Peter Pan syndrome who wanted to freeload through life. Xander didn't fit either description. Instead, he was a bit of both. He worked his ass off, but he avoided important parts of his life. His life was constructed around being able to leave at a moment's notice. When we'd first met, that ability had attracted me. But I'd been with him long enough to know that he'd built his life that way so he could avoid hard discussions.

I'd grown up wealthy, and I'd been able to see that money didn't solve everything. So what would Xander do when he got all that money? What would he do when he and I needed to have a long, hard discussion about us?

Anxiety churned in my stomach. The memory of watching him pack his bags when we'd had our first and last argument was still perfectly clear, even months later.

~

Xander

I LIFTED my shirt over my head. The chill of the room wafted over my skin, but I wasn't worried. As soon as I crawled into bed with Savvy, I'd heat up past the point of discomfort. I dreamed of the day we'd have a bigger bed and some privacy. I'd taken that first night together for granted. Our own room with a queen-size bed. That sounded like heaven.

At the same time, I'd miss this. Snuggling close, careful not to shove each other off the side. Cozy. Intimate, now that Savvy could stay awake for a little longer after she laid her head down.

She was fucking amazing and she got more unbelievable each day. She handled dude-bro enthusiasts with ease, channeling her mother like a boss. And every time we had female campers, they drifted toward her like moths to a campfire. Making friends with Rina had boosted her confidence.

Just when I thought she couldn't glow more, she'd see or experience something new and her expression would brighten like the summer sun.

Savvy wiggled in bed to make room for me. Now that she'd been here awhile, she was more impervious to the temperature drop when the sun went down, and neither of us wanted Hector and Eris to waste money on heat for us.

I crawled in and wrapped myself around her. She was used to my dick pressing into her by now, but each time it made her giggle. Tonight, I did it intentionally. She'd gone quiet outside when Brady and Rina had helped brainstorm about where we could go next.

"Aren't you ever tired?" she whispered.

"If I am, this thing wakes me up as soon as you're close."

"Can you imagine what it's going to be like when we don't have to sneak a quickie in the shower?"

"I'm gonna make you scream so loud."

She chuckled, then bit her lip to keep the sound down. As much as I liked Rina, she didn't need to know our sex schedule. Though Savvy probably gossiped with her about it anyway.

"Do you think Brady and Rina are going to get together?" she asked. Her head rested on my arm. I covered her shoulder with the blanket, leaving mine out. I was already warm enough and with her ass pressed against my half-erect dick, I needed the chill.

"I think she needs to make him work for it if she wants anything other than a hookup."

"I don't know if she does, but I agree."

I nuzzled behind her ear. "Is it bad that I hope he stays because I feel like shit leaving Hector and Eris once they have a baby? They'll want the privacy, but they'll also need more help than ever."

"But we are leaving?"

I winced at the timidity in her voice. A big decision loomed over us. "Only if you want to. I figured you wouldn't want to hang out either when the baby comes."

"Agreed. I feel like we'd be in the way." She went quiet, her warm breath caressing my arm.

"We have almost six months to go before we have some spending money." I could do my normal routine, roam and do odd jobs until I had a few bills for room and board, but I hated to risk Savvy being on the streets or stranded in the middle of a strange city with me.

"How do you feel about going home?"

"I don't have a home." At my sharp tone, she turned to look at me, her eyes brimming with concern. "I mean, Montana's home, but the place is Dawson's." Aiden worked for Dad, Beckett and Dad had mended their figurative fences, and Dad helped Dawson with the ranch every year. I was the oddball.

"You don't want to go because we won't have a place to stay?"

"No, Dawson has plenty of room and I have an open invite."

"Then why don't you want to go?" When I didn't answer she wormed her way around until she was facing me. "Talk to me, Xander."

She made it sound like talking would be easy. When I was a kid, Mama would talk to me, but she used her camera to do it. I sucked up my feelings through high school, riding my horse when I needed to work through my thoughts. No one came after me and when I returned home, no one asked questions. I'd been on my own since I moved out, but the only difference was that now Dad asked questions. But he wanted answers; he didn't want to understand.

Savvy wanted to understand, and she probably would. Didn't make it easier to talk. "The only good thing I've done for my family is to get married before I turned twenty-nine. Keeping the trust out of the Cartwrights' hands will be my only contribution."

Those pink lips I'd rather nibble turned down. "When you go home, you help your brother."

"Savvy, Dawson has employees and he's taken what Mama and Dad built with the ranch and expanded it. Beckett's a CEO—at a company he built—and lives in a mansion. Aiden is the CFO of King Oil and works sixteen-hour days. And except for Dawson, who's got a year left before his deadline hits, they've saved their trusts and they're still married."

"And we're still within the year where it looks like we're only together to get rich."

I feathered my fingers along her cheek.

"You know that's not why I'm with you. But they don't."

She furrowed her brows. "Then why not go show them?"

"It's not you, Savvy. It's not us. I don't give a shit about what they think about us." A pang of longing tugged at my chest. I missed home. I missed wanting to be home, and I hadn't had that for a while. I missed by brothers. I missed . . . having a parent I was close to.

As if she could read my mind, she said quietly, "You should talk to him and tell him everything. Not for him, but for you."

I stroked a lock of golden hair off her face. "For me, huh?"

"I can tell it bothers you. I don't know what'll happen after, but it's gotta beat avoiding your home and your family."

"I could tell him everything, and then what?" I go out and feed some cattle while I have no career and my Dad and brothers think I married for millions of dollars? I didn't care what they thought of me and

Savvy. I knew what we had was real. But . . . Aw, fuck. I did care what they thought. If I had something else in my repertoire to keep me from looking like a loser, it wouldn't be an issue. "I know you've noticed I haven't worked on my photography."

She stroked my chest, her fingers warm and soft. "If you could take pictures of one place in the world, where would it be and why?"

The answer was immediate. Montana, and because my mother had loved it. She'd lived and breathed home and family. She'd been the glue that had held us together as a unit. Now, we just traveled individually to and from the house, from King's Creek, rarely gathering as a large group. Four times. That'd been it since we'd all graduated high school. Dad's heart attack and all the weddings—Aiden's, Dad's, then Beckett's.

No one'd had a chance to gather at my wedding. *Typical Xander.*

Instead, I said, "I don't know." Her brow furrowed, so before she could call me out for my lie, I blurted, "New Zealand."

"New Zealand? Have you been there?"

I shook my head. "No. It seemed too commercial for my tastes at the time, but I can't deny the picturesque beauty of the place." All true. Stunning scenery that had been the backdrop of many movies. It was an easy answer, the low-hanging fruit of the landscape photography world, like Alaska, but more exotic to a Montana boy.

"But does it inspire stories?"

"I haven't been there."

There was that furrow again. "What are you going to do with the money?"

"I plan to stay married to you if that's what you're asking."

"Xander, your mother trusted you and your brothers with an enormous sum. What are Aiden and Beckett doing?"

"I have no idea what Aiden plans to do with his. He lives in a nice house, but he and Kate don't travel much other than going to King's Creek. He won't waste it, I know that. And Beckett and Eva have set up a lot of programs and charities to pay it forward."

"Then maybe if you had a plan, you'd feel better about going home."

"I don't plan," I answered automatically. I wasn't going to spend a hundred million I didn't have. I intended to keep my wife, but I wasn't the only one with a say in this marriage.

"That's been kind of the problem though, hasn't it?" Her tone was soft but no less chastising.

I bristled. The urge to roll out of bed and go for a walk hit me. I couldn't think with a pair of sapphire eyes stripping me bare. But I'd wake up the others. Buckling down and finishing a conversation with my wife shouldn't make me want to crawl out of my skin. "Fine, let's go home."

"Xander—"

I cupped her face and it was enough to shush her. "No, I mean it." I didn't. "I want you to meet everyone." That part was true at least. My brothers would love her, and I could withstand their side-eyes. "I can help Dawson work cattle."

Her gaze was guarded. "Are you sure?"

I answered honestly. "I'm sure Dad and Kendall would like to see you again too." I wouldn't mind proving to him that I had something real with Savvy. This girl was important to me.

She studied my face for several moments before she offered a hesitant smile. "I'm also a little homesick."

I hadn't thought to ask how she was doing being away from the States for so long. She might miss her family, but she might also miss being surrounded by everything familiar. She'd been unshakable —eating food she'd never had before, grappling with a new language, doing work she'd never done in nature that was unlike anything she'd grown up in. The least I could do for her was get us back to Montana.

I wrapped my arm around her and tugged her closer, grateful the conversation was over. I could deal with Montana later. Capturing her lips with mine, I deepened our kiss before pulling back to murmur, "Think we can keep the springs from squeaking?"

CHAPTER 16

avvy

THE AIRPLANE TOUCHED DOWN. I had my face plastered to the window for the last hour. Giddy that I was back in the States, but already missing Kosovo and my friends, I soaked up the sights.

"I expected more mountains," I said sheepishly. I knew nothing about Montana other than it had Yellowstone Park, mountains, and cowboys. The terrain out the window could very well have plenty of cowboys, but it was flatter. I'd spotted the river valley from Xander's pictures as the King Oil jet descended.

A private jet. What a freaking waste of jet fuel, but we were broke for a little over five more months. Saving the world was easier with a steady cash flow.

"They're there," Xander replied, his usual rugged, sexy self in the same blue jeans he always wore and his hemp pullover. The cowboy boots were more worn than before from his time in the country, but he'd mentioned getting another pair while he was back. "Just not so much in eastern Montana, where there's more buttes, and we're in a river valley. It gets really green in the summer, but brown this time of year."

I nodded. Yeah, green was giving way to brown outside the window. I'd expected to be surrounded by buildings and unable to see the land, but the airport at King's Creek was a little more than a few square metal buildings that were probably hangers. A parking lot was scattered with a few cars on the other side of the main building—the actual airport.

This was a small town.

"Is it bad that this is the smallest town I've been to?"

Xander chuckled and unbuckled himself. He stood and stretched. The hem of his sweater rode close to the top of his waistband. I waited for the tantalizing bit of skin to show, but the damn sweater was too long.

I was getting a possessive streak regarding my husband. I'd like a room to ourselves. A bed to ourselves. And the ability to be loud when we had sex. Nothing that was a necessity, but there it was. I might not know what I wanted to be when I grew up, but free to have noisy adult relations with Xander whenever I wanted was essential.

"A few of the villages in Kosovo were smaller," he pointed out.

"We traveled through them. We didn't stay there." He was from here. All of Xander's past was here. I wasn't sure what our future was going to be like after the start we'd gotten, but everything that made him *him* was in this town. Where he'd gone to school, his first kiss, the roads he'd learned to drive on.

I'd never seen him drive. "How are we getting to Dawson's?" Did King's Creek have Uber? Did it even have a bus?

"He and one of his hired guys, Tucker, dropped off a vehicle." He sucked in a breath and peered out the window toward the parking lot. "Hopefully it's not Beckett's old wheels."

"Why?"

He smirked. "You'll see." Lifting his chin toward Shirley, he said, "Great flight as always."

The flight attendant grinned, her expression indulgent, like she'd gotten to fly her kids around the world. "You always take me to the best places."

"Taking off somewhere else after this?"

She shook her head. "Going back to Billings to be on standby. Kendall rescheduled all the meetings for the next couple of weeks. I think we might be picking up Eva and Beckett this weekend."

Xander's jaw tightened. Did his family stress him out that much? I'd be thrilled if I could be with all my sisters again, even pain in the ass, bossy Em. I'd taken for granted how long we'd all lived in proximity to each other. Photos over the phone weren't the same.

My scant luggage was waiting at the bottom of the steps leading out of the jet. Xander hefted both our bags, his backpack slung over his back. I clutched mine for dear life and smelled the fresh mountain air—

And coughed. Exhaust fumes and the smell of hot tarmac weren't fresh mountain air. I scrunched my face up and waved my hand in front of my nose.

Xander grinned. "Living with Hector and Eris spoiled us."

Mentioning our friends sent a pang of longing through me. Their little girl had a head full of dark hair and looked like a miniature Hector. Xander and I had stayed long enough to meet the new arrival. Brady had remained behind, muttering something about helping them through the winter, but he was always watching Rina. I hoped he lasted the winter. Hard work and a woman who didn't put up with his shit agreed with him more than the soul-sucking job hunting he'd been doing.

A man with sparse, graying hair rushed out to meet us. He wore nothing but jeans and a T-shirt and had a set of keys dangling in his hand.

"Hey, Xander. Dawson left these for you."

"Thanks, Rick. I'll apologize ahead of time for the noise."

The man chuckled. "Every time I hear those pipes, I expect to see some teenage

King boys. Now that you're all grown up behind the wheel and obeying the speed limit? It's just odd." He rushed back inside.

Xander led me through the one-room airport and out the front doors.

I soaked up King's Creek. In the distance, mountains were just visible in a haze. The sun was warm, similar to the weather we'd just left.

"Will it get cold here at night too?"

"Probably. You never know. We could get snow next week and then have temps in the sixties all October." He tipped his head toward a large, obnoxious, gas-guzzling pickup in the corner of the lot. "That's our ride."

"Seriously?"

"Not exactly environmentally friendly. It probably gets five miles to the gallon."

I stared at the monstrosity with jacked wheels and a row of extra lights with *KC* printed on each bulb. "Who'd want to drive that?"

He shot me a lopsided grin. "A teenage

cowboy. Beck, to be exact. I think Dawson takes it out muddin' and that's the real reason he won't get rid of it, but I guess Eva's forbidden him from ever selling it."

Eva was Beck's wife. From what Shirley had said, I'd meet her soon. Xander helped me crawl up into the monster truck, then jogged around and swung in like he'd done it a million times. He probably had.

He fired up the engine and I jumped. "Good God, is it really that loud?"

He grinned and pulled out. When we hit the highway that ran to town, he floored it and the pipes rumbled, making my bones vibrate. I laughed, horrified and exhilarated. At least the truck wasn't sitting in a dump somewhere, it was still getting used. That was the only contribution driving it had offered.

The way to his brother's ranch was interesting—and beautiful. We zoomed past a mix of brownish-green pastures dotted with cattle and fields full of dried golden something.

"Corn," Xander answered when I asked. "Some sunflowers." He rambled on about whether the fields might be for a rancher's personal use or to sell on the market. I got a quick education in all things farming and ranching but it hardly skimmed the surface.

I recalled the article he'd been writing and the pictures he'd taken. "How's that similar to the Philippines?"

"Corn's a staple crop there too, but sunflowers aren't the crop there like they are here." He explained more differences and similarities as he pulled into a long drive. At the end was an impressive log cabin. A better description might be mansion. The place was huge with picture windows, a peaked roof, and a porch meant for long nights watching the sunset and drinking lemonade.

A large barn and at least two shops were spread out on the property and surrounded by fences. Cattle grazed in a few pastures and horses in another.

"Wow. This place is huge." Washington,

DC was big. It had huge buildings and large houses. But the sheer amount of land around this one ranch . . . The buildings next to the house were as big as grocery stores. Somehow, at the same time, it had a coziness I hadn't been expecting. This place was a home.

"It's where I grew up."

I could picture a young Xander careening through the lawn and toward the barn, his little cowboy boots kicking up dirt. What would it have been like? This was why I was so into the environment. I'd been so distanced from it, living in the middle of a big city, surrounded by more big cities. Any time we got past the city limits had felt precious. I swore the spaces were getting gobbled up faster than I could blink. What was once a field Pearl and I had flown kites in was now a superstore. A development had gone into the area that Em had used to run cross-country. I'd become passionate, driven—and more city bound.

Kosovo had been a revelation about what I was physically capable of. Montana was enlightening too. I loved my home, but it wasn't my future. I wasn't sure what that was yet, but it wasn't living off my parents or making my home in a place surrounded by concrete.

The house was a testament to modernity, but the land embraced it. They supported each other. The people who lived and worked here did it for themselves, but also for the animals, and the land.

I'd expected a giant feed lot with cattle packed side by side. Instead, black cows, some white, dotted the pastures that stretched for miles. "Talk about grass-fed beef."

Xander saw me eying the grazing cattle. "We supplement too. It's hard not to with the size Dawson has, but yeah, it's pretty damn close to free-range, organic, grass-fed meat." He lifted a shoulder. "Plus Dawson wouldn't feed his animals garbage. It might not be organic, but it's well researched and good for them. The reality behind the beef industry sucks, but Dawson's managing despite it all. A lot of ranchers are."

Some of my classmates had been gunning for the beef industry, but I hadn't been as interested in that as energy. "Sounds like there's a story there."

"Yeah, I guess."

Was this the equivalent of writer's block? Did he have photography block? He hadn't elaborated on our late-night discussion of what he'd like to do with his money—with his life. "I'd love to learn more about it. All I've heard is the bad."

"Sure. Dawson would be happy to talk about it." He parked and slid out. I stared at him for a moment before I got out after him. I wanted him to tell me. Yet I couldn't explain why it was so important that he didn't shrug that off too.

A man as tall as Xander swaggered out of the barn. Cats scattered as soon as he cleared the doorframe, like they were ashamed at having been caught existing near humans. He wore a cowboy hat and a joyful grin. The man that must be Dawson clapped his work gloves together before he gave us a full-armed wave.

"Do I finally get to meet the missus?" He jogged toward us, his gait easy with those long legs.

Xander shoved his hands into his pockets and grinned. "I promised her that you were only an asshole on the weekends."

"And it's Tuesday. We're in luck." His brown eyes sparkled as he removed a glove and stuck his hand out. "I was just playing with some barn cats, so I recommend you wash your hand after you shake mine."

"Okay?" I laughed as he pumped my hand.

"Nice to meet you, Savvy. Or is it Sapphire for those not married to you?" The guy was a flirt, that was obvious, but I felt nothing but brotherly love. He didn't give me any hint that he thought I was only with Xander for the money.

"Actually, only my family calls me Sapphire."

His grin turned sly. "Do you like them?"

"Most days."

"Sapphire it is, seeing as how we're family now. Come on in. The bedroom is the same as you left it." That last remark was aimed at Xander.

He leaned down to my ear. "It's a full bed at least."

I giggled and Dawson looked back at us, his brow quirking. "How was the flight?"

"Long."

"And grueling in the jet, right," Dawson said wryly as he bolted up the steps of the porch. He held the front door open for us. "Xander said that you don't eat much meat, so I went to the farmer's market and scored some butternut squash and a spaghetti squash. I had to fight Mrs. Pemberly for the eggs the McKinley girl was selling, but I got a couple dozen."

"Mrs. Pemberly still hates you for losing every library book you ever checked out."

Dawson's grin was unrepentant. "She's the only lady I haven't won over yet."

"The only?"

Dawson lost his grin. "I said lady. Bristol Cartwright doesn't count."

I played the name through my mind. Xander saw my confusion and clarified, "The neighbor."

"The still-broke neighbor cuz you tolerate Xander." Dawson chortled and led us into a kitchen that was set off from the rest of the main floor by an island and breakfast bar. The open layout inside the house showed off the woodwork and the rustic railing running along the stairs and the second-floor landing. "What's your poison? Coffee? Lemonade? Beer?"

"Water," I croaked. I missed drinking water willy-nilly. Xander had mentioned that he'd never take drinking water for granted after his travels, and I understood why now.

"Mountain spring water, coming right

up." He grabbed a glass from the cupboard and filled it at the faucet.

I wasn't expecting anything more than water, but damn. Cold fluid wicked down my throat without the oily residue that bottled water always seemed to leave behind. "It's good."

"Rural water at its finest. I've tasted some that has a plastic chaser, but not King's Creek water." Dawson's smile was so proud, and realization dawned. King's Creek.

"Is the town named after your family?"

Xander put his hand on my back. "Yes, but both our mom's side and our dad's side have been here forever. The land is from Dad's side and the oil is from Mama's."

I drained my glass and set it on the granite countertop. This cabin was so unlike the ones I'd spent my last few months cleaning.

I sagged at the reminder of how far we'd traveled in a short amount of time.

Xander steered me toward the stairs.

"We're going to have to catch up to mountain time."

"Take all the time you need," said Dawson. "The others are coming later so we'll work cattle this weekend."

Xander didn't reply as he led me upstairs and carried our bags.

"I slept on the plane, but I'm exhausted." I shot him a regretful look. "I'm afraid I might replay my first night in Kosovo." I'd fallen asleep so hard he could barely fit himself into the bed and then I'd slept fifteen hours.

"It's not a problem. You get used to the jet lag and having to adjust in new and unusual places."

How much did I want to get used to it? What kind of career would I have, traveling that much?

Xander stopped at a door midway down the hall, set down the suitcases, and opened it up. His childhood bedroom. Our place for the next . . . I didn't know how long we'd be here, or where we were going next.

This was his life, the way my husband lived. It was the way I was now living. And I'd learned enough about myself during the last six months to know that while I enjoyed traveling, and I appreciated having the ability to go where I wanted, I wanted a place to call my own. And I was afraid to have that talk with Xander.

Xander

THE ROLLING GAIT of Fool's Gold under me was its own therapy. As a teen, I'd taken off on him for hours, sometimes the whole day, after fights with Dad. Today, Dawson was with me, and he hadn't stopped talking. No wonder I always took off alone.

"Beck and Eva are flying down on Friday. It's just them. Her brother's been down a few times. Good guy—I almost talked him into a job."

"Doesn't he develop apps or video games?"

"Yeah, but it can be pretty sedentary. He takes to this stuff like a fish in the stock pond."

"Do you need the extra help?"

Dawson lifted a shoulder. "I'm thinking about bringing a third person on. There's always more work to do."

I nodded and kept riding. I'd gotten up early enough to help Dawson with chores. Savvy had still been sleeping when we'd gotten back for breakfast, so Dawson and I had saddled up the horses. Riding through our land loosened the tension that had built the closer the plane got to King's Creek.

Dawson squinted in the sun and adjusted his cowboy hat. "What about you? What are you doing for work?" At my side-eye, his grin was unrepentant. "Might as well practice your answer. You know everyone's going to ask."

"Everyone" being my other two brothers

and Dad. "Odd jobs here and there while I take some pictures."

"Where's your camera?"

"In my room where it won't get dropped in some pasture."

Dawson tsked. "Didn't realize it was a sensitive subject."

"It's not."

"What odd jobs then?" The wry note in Dawson's voice was enough to set my teeth on edge. He thought my photography was a sensitive subject and maybe it was, but only because no one understood it or what it meant to me.

"I just got done helping a buddy expand his outdoor business—hiking and camping and stuff. Savvy helped clean cabins and I helped build a couple more. Then we both did guided tours."

"How are things . . . with the wife?"

"You mean are we going to stay married for a year so the bastard next door doesn't get the money?"

"Obviously, I want you to be happy." He

adopted another crooked grin, his body swaying with his horse.

I chuckled. "I get it. But the trust wasn't a huge motivation behind my nuptials."

Dawson cocked a brow. "Love at first sight?"

"Something like that. It was convenient for both of us, but at the time, there wasn't much I wouldn't have done to be with her longer. That doesn't change that we're still getting to know each other."

"Just make sure you don't fuck up until after you're thirty."

"Oh, I plan on spending all my Valentine's Days with my wife. But you know this means it's your turn."

Dawson shuddered. "Don't start. Grams is already on me."

That made me grin. Dawson was the baby, destined to be the favored one. He was the youngest, so when Mama had died, while losing her hadn't hurt him any less just because he'd had less time with her, Dad's behavior after had bothered him the least. "Less than a year and you don't even have a girlfriend."

"I don't get out of King's Creek that much. All the single women in town are either married already or single for a reason."

"There's dating apps."

"I use them for sex."

A cough escaped. What else had I expected? I cleared my throat. "You need to get out of King's Creek more often."

"I was kidding about the apps. It's not worth the hassle." He gestured to the cows grazing in the next pasture. "These ladies keep me busy. What can I say?"

We reached the edge of the pasture and gazed across the ravine. Our fence ran along the edge. Our land technically extended past it on the other side, but right in the middle of the trees and the small valley that flooded in hard rains was the border of our land and the Cartwrights'. Old Danny never would've allowed us to fence on his side.

Dawson squinted into the trees at the lowest point of the ravine. "Aw, hell. He lost a cow in that mess."

The bloated body of a cow that was long past dead was slumped in the shadows. Danny never fenced off his side of the damn ravine, and it cost him precious cows. Cows equaled money. Cows were profit. No wonder his ranch was tanking in so many ways.

I slid my gaze to my brother as he glowered at the lost cow. It had probably broken a leg slipping down the side to get some water. "You gonna let Bristol know?"

"Gonna let her know to fucking water her herd better. That stock pond is probably nothing but mud and it's driving them out here." He pulled out his phone. Why Bristol hadn't blocked his number, I didn't know. They probably kept each other's number just so they could text and rub it in when the other fucked up.

I turned my horse around. Dawson sent

off his message. Neither horse needed much guidance to get back home.

As we neared the house, I groaned. A familiar plain black Mercedes sat out front. "Is that Grams's vehicle?"

"Of course. She can get a two-for-one. Make sure you and the wife are going to get along until after Valentine's Day, and pester me about who I'm seeing."

Dawson was never seeing anyone. He had a girlfriend in college but she'd refused to move to rural Montana. After that, he dated, but never anyone for long, claiming it wasn't easy to find a woman who tolerated rancher's hours.

I was glad I didn't have that problem. I just had to hope my wife didn't mind not having a home.

We rode to the barn and swung down.

Dawson jutted his chin toward the house. "Go on, save your wife. I got this."

"Thanks, man." I handed him the lead rope and walked as fast as I could without running. Grams might think something was wrong if I came running up to the house—something wrong between me and Savvy. Grams wasn't an overly nurturing grandparent. Her motto in life was *rub some dirt on it and quit crying.*

I didn't care that I smelled like fresh air and horse sweat. It was as natural to me as breathing, but Savvy might think differently. Maybe I could get her on a horse while we were here.

Savvy was at the dining room table, her hair wild around her shoulders, still blinking sleep out of her eyes. She smiled and nodded at Grams, who sat across from her, but I knew the dazed look well. People often wore it around my grandmother. She was a force and not everyone was ready for her.

"Grams," I greeted warmly. It was nice to see her—and not have to avoid her for the first time in several years.

"Xander!" Grams's voice boomed through the main floor and probably bounced off the doors of the upstairs bedrooms. She rose and straightened her suit coat. Her gray bob was sleek, not a single strand would dare be out of place.

She rounded the table and held her arms out. I met her halfway and was encompassed in a hug unlike any I'd ever gotten.

"I'll be damned, kiddo. Congrats. You did good."

I smiled and hugged her back, but her compliment fell flat on my ears. *I did good?* Grams wasn't the warm, fuzzy kind but she'd never said that to me. Never. To be fair, I'd hadn't done much to earn a "You did good," but she'd seen my pictures, murmured something like *nice*, and moved on to another topic of conversation.

Figuring why it bothered me was easy. "I didn't think you'd say that until after I turned thirty."

Grams clapped my shoulder. "The first hurdle is over and Sapphire seems delightful. Gentry's told me about her father."

Savvy cupped her hands around her water glass. "She says she's not going to hold it against me."

I chuckled and moved toward the kitchen. "You hungry?"

Savvy winced. "I missed breakfast." She glanced at the clock on the oven. "And lunch."

"No problem. I'll make us both something. Dawson's never short of food. He'd be a chef if he wasn't a rancher."

Grams waited until I was back from washing my hands to say, "You've been dragging your wife around the world. Where are you going to settle down?"

I tensed at the fridge. "My work takes me to different places."

"Photographers have homes."

I opened the fridge and dug out eggs and cheese. I could make a simple omelet. Grabbing some ham for my own omelet, I withdrew with my armload and closed the fridge. Photographers with thriving businesses had homes.

"You can't drag Sapphire all over with you." Grams never let a subject die a quick death. "You're newlyweds."

"We're still exploring options," Savvy answered, her tone lacking conviction. I looked at her but her tense smile was aimed at Grams.

Grams nodded. "You'll have a lot more after you're married for a year."

Why did everything have to come down to that damn trust? I wished I could go back in time and ask Mama what she'd been thinking. Had she been terrified that we'd grow up wild men and end up lonely? That we'd end up crusty old ranchers who were more dangerous to themselves and others, like our neighbor? I didn't know, but I couldn't wait until the trust was distributed and all I had to do was sock it away. I had no idea what I was going to do with it, but like I'd told Savvy—I wasn't a planner.

I gave Grams my most indulgent smile. "You'll be one of the first to know where Savvy and I decide to settle, Grams."

A pleased look crossed Grams's face. I liked to think she had more interest in her grandkids than whether or not we could keep the money she'd made off the sale of part of the oil company. No one had to ask whether she regretted gifting the money to Mama for our future. Once she'd learned of the trust's restrictions, she'd been trying to rectify it ever since.

I was cracking eggs when she said, "Your father and Kendall are on their way."

"What? Now?" Shit. They lived in Billings and it was only a couple of hours away. "Aren't we doing cattle this weekend?"

"He wants to visit you." She beamed at Savvy, who sat stiffly in her chair. "He said he didn't have much time to talk with you in Las Vegas."

That wasn't necessarily a bad thing. I exchanged a look with Savvy. Her expression was so hopeful. She thought that if I confessed to Dad, he'd forgive me and it'd be like we had a fresh start to our life together. Dad wasn't obsessed with the past. He wanted me to answer for my present and future. I had to tell him at some point. But later was better than sooner, like *after* I'd paid him back.

The next moment, several people piled through the door and I clenched my hand around the spatula.

Looked like it would be sooner after all.

CHAPTER 17

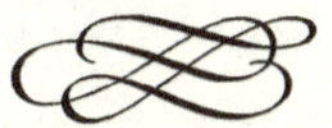

*S*avvy

A FEW MONTHS AGO, I would've been useless. Now, while I might not be ready to kick ass on a horse—or get on one at all—I could stand in the muck, by a fence, and wave my arms around to keep the cattle from backtracking out of the corrals. I hadn't had to scale the fence yet due to an angry cow. Xander had made sure I knew how to though. He'd made me practice.

Xander's family was great. They gave each other crap in an uninhibited way that my family never did and never would, except maybe Pearl and me.

Right after his dad had arrived, Xander had whisked me away for a tour of King's Creek, then an evening horse ride of the Kings' land. As I'd clung to the reins, he'd sat behind me in the saddle and shown me the land they'd sold to their friends, the Cartwrights. But Grams and DB had kept the mineral rights, suspecting that there could be oil. The ink had barely dried on the deed before they'd pursued that oil, inciting the family feud. The drilling had negatively impacted the Cartwrights' ranch, and honestly, I'd have been pissed at Grams and DB too. The money the Cartwrights had gotten as land owners was nothing compared to what Grams and DB had made. The drills were no longer active, but the black abandoned wells were visible in the distance.

The next day, Xander had taken me to

Billings to show me the head office and, I suspected, to stay out of his dad's path.

Kendall drifted toward me. Most of the cattle had been worked. Xander had told me what it would entail and how Dawson chose vaccinations and methods of identification for his business, but all I could see was a bunch of guys straddling corrals and bending over cows. Dawson wandered around with a tablet, updating records or something. Kendall clapped her hands together. Dust particles puffed and glinted in the sunlight. She wore work boots, so different from the stylish knee-high boots she'd arrived in. All I had were athletic shoes. None of the boots Dawson had found fit me but he kept trying despite my assurances that I'd be fine with a little manure on my shoes.

Not something I thought I'd ever have to say.

"What do you think?" Kendall's grin was infectious and her teal eyes glittered in the sun.

"Interesting. I have so many questions but they're all so busy."

"You can ask any of the guys. I mean, Dawson's in charge now and he'll talk your ear off, but he gets tied up during this time of year."

Eva hopped down from the gate she was perched on with Kate and sauntered toward us. The bright pink ends of Eva's hair brushed her chin. When she'd arrived with Beckett, I'd had trouble picturing them as a couple. She was definitely the yin to his yang. He'd been all GQ handsome in a suit and tie and she'd been dressed in ripped leggings, a flirty skirt and a loose, buttoned-up blouse with nothing but ones and zeroes on it. In short, he looked exactly like the tech mogul that Xander had described and Eva looked like she designed video games.

"I heard Dawson evaded Grams yesterday."

Kendall laughed but snuck a glance at Kate and sobered. Xander had speculated that Aiden hadn't told Kate about the stipulations of the trust, but I couldn't imagine why that would be kept from her. She and Aiden had been married more than a year. It shouldn't matter by now. "Grams is a force. It was nice that she stopped by at least."

Eva screwed her nose up, but spoke quieter. "Does she ever stop by when it isn't about money?"

"She's not that type of grandmother," Kendall said, almost fondly. I think she respected Grams as a powerful woman, not so much as a grandmother.

"She seemed nice," I said.

Eva softened her doubt with a smile. "She wouldn't want to scare you away."

Kate ripped her gaze off her husband, who was straddling either side of the chute that a cow was stopped in and giving her an overall exam. His ass could grace a billboard and sell any damn thing he wanted—just like all his brothers' asses, though the only one that got to me was

Xander's, and I'd done my share of peeking while he was swaggering around in his boots and cowboy hat.

Kate hopped down and scurried over to us. I swallowed the shame I'd first experienced when I'd met her and Aiden. When Dawson had answered the door, I'd caught sight of Aiden first as he'd brought their luggage upstairs. Aiden was all sharp angles, precise in every fold and wrinkle of clothing to the point where even Chief would say *damn*, and he exuded a seriousness that naturally made tension bloom in any room.

After seeing him, I'd expected a leggy woman who was catwalk-ready at any moment. So when Kate had stepped inside, chatting with Dawson on the landing as she shrugged out of her coat, shock had stalled me dead. Some might call her plain, but only because her beauty was quiet, understated. She had rounded curves on a frame a few inches shorter than mine. Her soft, bright presence balanced all of Aiden's hard edges. It'd be easy to write her off as a nobody, but as soon as Dawson introduced me to her, my respect for Aiden grew. Intelligence shone in Kate's eyes and when she smiled, I wanted her to be my friend forever. She was the type of woman lesser men would ignore rather than try to be worthy of. She didn't cower like she was meek, but she was either shy or didn't need one second of the spotlight.

My new hobby had become studying Xander's family. They all seemed to accept me as readily as my family had accepted him. The guys acted like Hector—respectful, but willing to put me to work. Their wives were more like Eris than Rina—except for Eva. She might be a little more like Rina once she got to know me.

It was exciting.

I was making friends with people who weren't my family and could decide to have nothing to do with me.

That they all cared about Xander was

obvious. He needed to talk to his dad. He needed to quit avoiding him.

Kendall spoke up. "Listen, Savvy. We thought the guys could have some time tonight to be charming assholes with each other while we steal you and go to the Tap."

"Are you asking me out?"

Kendall grinned and her breath puffed out. "Savvy, would you do me the honor of having a few drinks with me in a dive bar tonight?"

"I'd get down on one knee, but . . ." Eva picked up her boot and grimaced at what was stuck to the bottom. They looked newish, but not fresh out of the box. All the women's clothing and footwear had seen dirt and manure a few times before.

"It's not like an interrogation or anything, is it? You three aren't going to torture me to see if I'm worthy of Xander?"

"Honestly, we don't know Xander well enough to decide that," Kate said quietly, but with a slight smile to take the edge off her little land mine of a statement.

Kendall chuckled and squinted into the sun. "Maybe we should've done that with him when we first met him."

"Full disclosure, I've seen him in his underwear." We all stared at Eva and she put her hands up. "I was using his room when I first came here as Beckett's assistant." She rolled her eyes. "Fake fiancée."

"I've heard the story. The fake fiancée part, not the underwear." Add it to the list of things Xander didn't talk about.

"Anyway," Eva continued, "I was in Xander's room because we didn't even know he was coming, but he showed up in the middle of the night and crawled into what he thought was an empty bed." Her cheeks flushed. "I haven't thanked him for scaring me into Beckett's bed that night."

Kate giggled. "Who scared who more?"

"Since I fell on my ass between the bed and the wall, I think it was me. Xander thought it was hilarious, more so after Beckett came rushing in."

Kendall fiddled with her bun. "I'm going to risk sounding like Grams, but I can't wait to see what scares some girl into Dawson's bed." We all blinked at her. None of the King men had to work hard to get women into their bed. Kendall sputtered when she realized what she'd said. "I mean . . . Lord. You know what I mean."

Laughter broke out between us. Tonight was going to be fun.

Xander

THE GIRLS SPILLED out of the house on a wave of laughter and perfume. The sight of Savvy laughing and joking with all of them wormed its way inside me. How often would Savvy and I come to Montana so I could see her like this?

Dawson set five long-necks on the

counter. "Now that the vegetarian is gone, can we grill?"

I snagged a bottle before my brothers got there. "She's not a strict vegetarian. You'd just get interrogated about where the beef came from before she ate any." Dawson pointed to the pastures and I flipped him off. "*I* know where it came from, jackass."

"Is she afraid she'll end up like the Pioneer Woman?"

"Who the hell's the Pioneer Woman?" I looked at my brothers. Beck was next to me on the other side of the counter from Dawson. He shook his head. So did Aiden from his barstool as he scrolled through his phone. The guy never quit working. Even Dad shook his head, his reading glasses perched on his nose as he caught up with the King's Creek newspaper.

"She's got her own cooking show. Her schtick is that she lives on a ranch." Dawson shook his head when none of us caught on to what he was saying. "She tells the story of how she was a vegetarian before she met her rancher husband. Then he made her some awesome steak or something. Christ, guys. Keep up with the times."

Beck took a drink of his beer. "How did you get through that spiel without making some sort of dirty comment about the guy's meat?"

Dawson picked up a pair of tongs and pointed them at Beck. "I don't mess around when it comes to food, and I'm starving." He hitched up the tray full of seasoned and marinated steaks and went down the hall to the back door.

Beck followed him, and I was about to when Dad spoke. "Sapphire tell you that I hired Abbot Security?"

Aiden glanced up from his phone but went right back to work. I couldn't count on him to be a wall of support. The brother I'd grown up with was different from this guy.

"Yeah. You didn't have to do that."

"I might've anyway. It's hard to say." Dad

took his glasses off and set the paper down. "Walter's approach turned me off at first, but he came so highly recommended. That's why I agreed to meet with him in Vegas."

"But you didn't hire him then."

Dad's smile was sly and sometimes I forgot that he hadn't gotten to where he was today by being crap at his job. "I made him work for it. Seriously, though. I try to keep my business local, but when he said he could help me integrate with Montana companies that don't have the extensive reach and knowledge he does, it was a given. He knows what he's doing."

I nodded and tried edging out the door, but Dad wasn't done. "Sapphire's not working for him anymore, I see."

"No, we decided to travel."

The look Dad shot me asked the question louder than if he'd spoken. *Did you both decide, or did you make the decision for her and she had to chase after you like we've all had to do?* After a beat, he started, "There was a company I was supposed to meet with in Las Vegas."

I wanted to groan. I'd forgotten about the very reason Savvy and I had met in the first place.

"Saving Sunsets," Dad continued. "I was supposed to meet with a Sapphire Abbot and Brady Younger. I thought it was extremely coincidental that Walter Abbot showed up with a daughter that had the same name after my meeting had been canceled, but I couldn't get ahold of the company afterward."

"It folded while Savvy and Brady were there. She said the founder wasn't a good businessman."

"That's a shame. The premise was good. It's disappointing that the follow-through was lacking. I've been looking for a company that provides similar research data and the educational opportunities they advertised. I'm thinking of hiring someone instead."

I turned toward the back hallway that

led to the garage, where Dawson grilled just outside the door to be out of the wind. "Well, Brady's taken. He went to Kosovo too and is doing work there as a hiking guide."

"Too bad," Dad's murmur followed me out. "I was interested in what they had to say."

I made my getaway before the subject turned to me. Yet I'd managed to have a conversation with my father that hadn't left me with the usual sting of inadequacy. Dad might've been talking up Savvy's skills instead of mine, but that was good enough. And it showed me that I would have to work harder to earn my place at her side.

CHAPTER 18

Savvy

MY SIDES HURT from laughing so hard. These girls liked to have fun. The few times I had been able to afford going out with friends from college, there had always been an agenda, and it had often revolved around a guy, or finding a guy. Tonight was nothing more than us getting to know each other. For them, it might be a little vacation. They all had jobs they were getting away from.

Accomplished women. I got why Xander felt inferior around his brothers.

Kendall's smile stretched wide. She was in the middle of a story about running to a parts store in Cheyenne, Wyoming, with Aiden while Gentry was in a meeting. "Then he says, 'Maybe you want to check with your husband,' like I wasn't just pointing in their catalog at the exact car battery we needed. So Aiden turns around, about to chew into the man, and I said, 'Oh, no, he's not my husband, he's my son.'" She smacked the table with her palm as she laughed. "I've been waiting to use that line for *forever*."

I snorted, imagining the salesman's reaction. Aiden and Kendall were the same age.

But there was more. "So he goes, 'Are you kidding me?' I mean, it's none of his business and he's the one that assumed I was dumb, so I say, 'His dad owns an oil company so it made more sense to marry him instead.' Then I blinked all innocent and smiled like the vapid female he thought I was."

Eva's grin glowed with wickedness. "If you ever get to use that line when you're with all four of the brothers, you *have* to video it."

Kendall's head dropped back. "Oh my God, that's on my bucket list. Can you imagine?" Her smile faded. "You think they'd all be cool about it? I wasn't sure how Aiden would take it, but since the guy had been kind of insulting, I took a chance. He didn't flinch, and when I made the oil company comment, he just shrugged and nodded—it was priceless."

"I think Beckett would be a good sport," Eva said. "Dawson would probably call you Mom first."

Kate fiddled with her White Claw can. "Like you said, in the right situation, Aiden would be game."

In unison, they all turned to look at me. I raised my brows.

"What about Xander?" Kendall prodded.

"Um . . ." How would Xander react? He talked about his mom a lot, but he seemed to like Kendall. "I don't know. Maybe as a joke?"

"Most definitely," Kendall agreed. "It would only be to mess with someone. I feel like there should be a name besides stepmom for those of us who are similar in age to our stepkids."

"Isn't it 'trophy wife'?" Kate's eyes flared wide and her cheeks lit red like she was inches from a bonfire. "Oh—"

Kendall sputtered and threw her head back on a laugh. I chuckled with Eva. There'd been no malice in Kate's statement. The joke in her voice had been clear, but I doubted she was ever that honest with people. She'd been reserved the entire night and I didn't think that was unusual.

"I was kidding— I—"

Kendall dabbed at the tears gathering in

the corner of her eyes. "I know, but that was hilarious. I can't believe I didn't think of it myself."

After a few minutes, Eva rose. "I have to pee again. Anyone wanna be my posse?"

"Me," I said, rising.

"We'll need a name," Kate said as we were walking to the back hallway. "King's Queens, or something like that."

Her comment brought the memory of my wedding night. *I am a King and you are my treasure.* My heart warmed at the real meaning behind the words. He was a King, but his family was the treasure. I couldn't imagine spending so much time away from them. It'd been less than a week, but I didn't want to go. I would eventually, but I wouldn't want to go far. I missed my sisters. I even missed my parents. But this helped.

I wanted to travel, but I didn't want to journey all over the world for years on end. So that narrowed down my future aspirations. Being around these women was inspiring. Instead of being intimidated, I was motivated.

Two shadows were tucked deep in the hallway, lit by the exit sign. A slender woman stood tall with worn-jean-clad legs that went on for miles and hair that glowed like the bonfire I'd thought of earlier. The man was older, burly, and standing like an immovable stone.

"I told you to quit selling to him," the woman growled. She had to be close to my age, maybe a year or two older, and a whole lot more badass. She wasn't intimidated by the mountain of a man at all. I was and I'd just turned the corner.

"He's a paying customer. I'm not a bouncer and I have a business to run."

"Dammit, Errol. You're taking advantage of him."

The man snorted. "Ain't no one taking advantage of your daddy, Bristol."

Whoa. How many Bristols could there be in little King's Creek, Montana?

Eva tried to slink into the bathroom,

sensing the conversation was just as awkward as I had, but Bristol spotted us at the same moment. The man saw his chance and darted back into the off-sale portion of the building.

Her gaze landed on Eva and recognition lit. Then it landed on me. "The newest addition to the King herd?"

I'd expected the venom, but there was just as much curiosity. Her arms were crossed, but I took a chance.

Sticking my hand out, I said, "I'm Savvy, Xander's wife."

The word's rolled out, still foreign on my tongue.

She eyed me like she didn't understand a single syllable I'd said. Then she slowly extracted a hand and gave mine a quick shake. "Bristol. The wicked witch of a neighbor that I'm sure you've heard all about."

"You have the hair, but you're not green."

Her lips twitched. "It's the red from the neon lights. Neutralizes my tone."

Eva pulled up next to me. "Hey, Bristol."

"Eva, right?" Eva nodded and Bristol took a step back. "Well, I'd better go before I get you into trouble."

I didn't have a chance to argue—I wanted to get to know this mystery woman—before she shouldered her way out the exit door, her face tucked into the collar of her shirt.

Eva nudged me with an elbow. "She's not harmless and that's why I kind of like her."

"Why do they hate her so much?"

"There's history there I don't understand, but ultimately I think when she didn't show up to the funeral, they felt like she chose her drunk of a dad over their mom, who'd doted on her."

I did the math. "She had to have been a kid."

"Yep. But she backs her dad, every time, no matter what despicable thing he does."

I had no idea what her dad was like, but I'd been afraid to even tell mine I didn't want to work for him. Chief was a lot of things, but I knew without meeting Daniel Cartwright that they were nothing alike.

"There's a lot of history there," I murmured. It seemed easy enough to ask, to talk with Bristol instead of fighting her head-on.

But then I thought of the times I'd asked Xander to talk to his dad. And when I'd taken the job with Chief and Xander had left. Talking wasn't his strong suit and it'd almost broken us up once.

Xander

THE HORSES' nickers carried across the pasture to us. They were tied up on a fence post, grazing on what hadn't turned brown and brittle yet. I'd packed a blanket and food for me and Savvy. Our picnic was spread out, already eaten. I'd packed myself a leftover roast beef sandwich from the four roasts Dawson had cooked last night after we'd worked cattle. For Savvy, I'd made a cucumber and avocado wrap. I shouldn't have been surprised that Dawson knew what avocados were, let alone how to use them. Maybe I should've asked if he had plans for it before I cut it up.

Savvy gathered up all our items and stuffed them into the tote bag. "I can't believe how nice out it is. Is this what the weather is usually like this time of year?"

"Sometimes. Some years, there's snow, but it doesn't stick around long. Most years, it's like this though, and the bluff blocks the wind."

She looked around. We weren't far from the ravine that Dawson and I had ridden out to earlier in the week. It was a high point in this area and rugged enough that the cows didn't like to come out this far. The butte jutted nearly vertical from this patch of level ground, leaving what was like a large landing.

"Mama used to bring us out here for picnics."

Savvy pointed to the ravine that dropped off to the left and the rolling hills that rose from the river valley in front of us. "I thought I recognized this area. This picture is in your room."

"It's one of hers, yes. She taught me how to use her camera here." I ran my fingers along the outer edge of my camera bag. On a whim, I'd actually packed it.

The fact that it was on a whim showed how long it'd been since photography had been the center of my life.

"I can see why you always came here when you were upset. I feel like my mind is a thousand times clearer, and talk about inspiring. It's gorgeous."

The breathlessness of her voice and the way her gaze soaked in the grassy terrain and touched on the glittering blue peeking between the trees were just as she'd said—

inspiring. I unzipped the bag and withdrew my camera.

Savvy glanced over, her small smile encouraging. She framed her hands like a photograph. "That'd be a perfect shot, right?"

I had the perfect shot all lined up, but it wasn't a landscape. She looked over at me and I hit the button. The series of clicks didn't bother the horses or their grazing.

Savvy's cheeks flushed and she glanced away. I took another shot.

"I have plenty of the land," I said and lined up another shot. The sun glowing behind us made her hair several shades lighter and once we'd sat down, she'd let it out of its top bun. She looked relaxed, happy, and free. This was the Savvy that I'd fallen in love with.

"That's the first picture you've taken of me."

I lowered the camera. "I know. Does that bother you?"

"Seems odd. We don't even have a selfie together."

"I'm not a selfie guy. And photography has been . . ." I set the camera aside. "Taking pictures got me through a lot, and then it wasn't enough." *I* wasn't enough. "I didn't want to take random photos of you and have them feel . . . insignificant. Because you're the most important person in my life and I had to be sure I didn't fuck those shots up too." The words I'd been thinking fell out of my mouth. "I love you, Savvy."

We'd been together for most of the year, we'd been through a lot, especially her, and neither of us had said those words.

She sat up, like a prairie mermaid, dressed in an old flannel of mine that Dawson had saved for when I visited. Her jeans had once been pristine, but now they had rips that showed tantalizing, creamy bits of skin.

"Xander . . ." She crept closer until she was kneeling in front of me. Cupping my face, she looked deep into my eyes. "I love you too, and I'm really excited about this life we get to live together."

Our life together. I hadn't thought much beyond what we were doing in King's Creek. Had she?

I gripped her hands in mine. So many questions. So many plans we could talk about, but that would wait. We were alone and while we might be exposed to the big wide world, we had more privacy than we'd had in weeks—months.

Pulling her onto my lap, I claimed her mouth and took my time kissing her, tasting the sweet remnants of the grapes we'd had with lunch.

I rolled her onto her back and stretched over her. She arched into me as I kissed my way down her neck. "Can anyone see us?"

"No." The Cartwrights were more militant about trespassers on their property than we were. Dawson's two hired guys were off after a long day yesterday and my family was lounging around the cabin or in town running errands. "No one will see what's mine."

"You get home and turn possessive?"

"When it comes to you? Yes." I tugged up her shirt and she twined her hands through my hair. I'd never given my hair much thought. It wasn't as close cut as most of my family's. Dawson might not be as strict with his trimmed sides, but it wasn't nearly as messy as mine.

The way Savvy liked to feel it up, I was never going to cut it shorter than it was now.

I unbuttoned her pants and worked my way down. I'd love to strip her down, but we were out in the middle of nowhere. The temperature was fine—with clothing on. So I'd keep her warm instead.

Tugging her pants down her legs, I was reminded of our time behind the camper's cabin in Kosovo. We'd had less privacy and I'd managed to take her without removing a stitch of fabric from either of us. While I didn't want to bare her to the wild, I needed more than a quick fuck in the woods.

I tossed the pants aside and looked my fill of my gorgeous wife. It was a futile attempt. I'd never have enough of this woman. She'd followed me across the world, circumnavigating the globe to land at the base of this butte with me. She'd led strangers through the mountains and kept them safe, she'd worked cattle, and she'd even survived a run-in with our cranky neighbor.

How had I found this treasure?

I hadn't. She'd found me. All of my travels, and my sapphire gem had found me in a random city with a camera in my hand.

It was fate.

I ran my fingers up her calves. She turned her head and her hair shifted, a shining halo spread around her. Splaying my hands over her knees, I pushed her legs wide.

The image before me was searing. A goddess under the sun. I'd never violate her privacy and take a picture of her like this, in all her glory, whether she wanted me to or not. This was between us. This was mine and only mine. I didn't need a picture to remember it forever.

I dipped my head down and raised my hips to keep from strangling the blood supply to my throbbing erection. My zipper pinched in, but I ignored it. My discomfort was nothing when I could finally give Savvy the pleasure I'd been wanting to give her for days—weeks. Months.

I took my time tasting her. She writhed under me, her hips rolling up. With a growl, I gripped her ass and pulled her closer to my face.

Her breath hitched. "Xander."

Since we'd gotten married, we'd never had time like this. I'd had to wait too fucking long to make slow, hard love to my wife.

Her knees hitched up as I adjusted the speed, bringing her close and backing off. I hadn't used more than my tongue, but she vibrated with tension.

"You're such a tease," she gasped.

The strain of coming so close to climax, only to be repeatedly denied, was in her voice. I inserted a finger into her tight, wet heat. Any chill to the day had long since vanished.

She bucked against me and I sped up the pace of my tongue. I didn't need to move my hand. She rode it and she rode me, taking everything I'd been holding back.

"Oh my God!" Her voice echoed over the land as she came hard against my mouth. My head yanked as she twisted her fists in my hair.

Worth every second. And I drew it out for several seconds. She didn't bother being quiet. For once, our only neighbors were cattle and the horses, who couldn't care less about humans fornicating.

Her feet landed on the blanket on each side of my head. She tugged me up her body and I barely had a chance to wipe her release off my face before she smashed my lips down onto hers.

Being cradled between her legs lent its own sense of urgency to the situation. I reached down to undo my buckle, fumbling way more than I cared to during my rush. Each time I'd delayed her gratification was coming back on me tenfold.

I finally freed my demanding erection but she batted my hand away and placed me at her sweltering entrance. I didn't hesitate. As I thrust inside, a groan ripped from my chest.

She broke the kiss to moan and work herself against me. I tipped my forehead to hers and forced us to slow down.

"I'm taking my time with you, sweetheart." I pulled out and inched back in, my body shaking from the strain of holding myself in check.

"We can do slow next time."

"The problem is that I don't know when our next time will be. We're hardly ever alone."

She bit her lower lip, looking deceptively innocent while grinding against my cock. "It can be in a few minutes. Unless . . . we're needed back there."

I grinned, hooking her leg under my arm and increasing the thrust of my hips. "Oh, honey. I'll make sure we have all damn day."

CHAPTER 19

*S*avvy

I STROKED my hand up and down Xander's chest. His flannel was unbuttoned and the T-shirt he'd had on underneath it was lying next to us. Eventually, we'd stripped down to full nudity and continued having sex for another couple of hours.

The sun's rays weren't strong this time of year, but I wasn't going to have a single tan line from today. I grinned.

He pushed my hair away from my face. "Whatcha thinking about?"

"Tan lines."

His deep chuckle reverberated through my cheek. "Tan lines. We won't have any from today."

I sat up and leaned over him. "Exactly what I was thinking." I let my gaze wander over his strong face. We hadn't had much time to lie around since we'd met. "I'd like more of this."

"Wilderness sex? I'm on board."

I pushed his chest. It was unyielding. "No. Well, yes, but not like that. I want time for us." I let my thoughts wander down a more serious path. "We've worked cattle. What are we doing next?"

"What do you want to do?" His *we have no money yet* was implied.

"I want . . ." I glanced around. My life the last year had been unrecognizable from every year before it. I'd been into environmentalism. I'd recycled. I'd shopped discriminately, my intentions to decrease the waste of the action as much as possible. But this Savvy was so much more experienced in the world.

On the hikes, I'd talked with the guests about what they did for a living and what had brought them to Kosovo. I'd met IT people, stock market experts, furniture builders, and social media influencers. But one thing linked us all together: a love for nature and the yearning to preserve what we could, to keep it a place where we could find ourselves living in an untouched environment.

How the hell that translated to a career, I didn't know. Yet. But the seed of an idea was germinating deep in my mind. "I wouldn't mind seeing my family."

"Stay with them until we're flush?" He didn't sound the happiest about the idea, but I was pleased that he'd do it for me.

"No, actually . . . Eva talked to me about what she and Beckett are doing with his trust." Scholarships, donations, program launches. Xander knew all of that, but I doubted he'd ever discussed the nitty-gritty details with Beckett. "How it's a shitload of money, but once you start doing stuff with it, it's like a tub drain is pulled out."

"It goes fast?"

I nodded. "She told me how they're investing it and how they've divvied it up to try and get the most use out of it, but the biggest takeaway was—it goes fast. Even that many millions."

"What do you think we should do?"

I reclined against his shoulder and stared at the sky. The sun was sinking in the west and it wasn't even dinnertime. "I'd like to pay it forward. I'd like to work from the ground up, literally when it comes to the environment. I want to create places where people come to visit and learn and experience and go back home and try to do better. Even if they're avid recyclers, they maybe also try to . . . I dunno, make their own taco seasoning?"

"Taco seasoning?" He laughed and the sound wasn't as pleasant as before.

My face burned and I turned more on my back and fiddled with the ends of my hair. My mother's voice drifted through my mind. *Frizz and split ends never solved a problem, Sapphire. Perhaps you should try talking it out or writing.*

"You know what I mean," I mumbled.

He rolled to his side and propped his head up. His fingertips touched my cheek and he added enough pressure to get me to look at him. "It's not silly. I get what you mean. I know what it's like to know what you want to do, but have no clue how to carry it out."

"But you can do so much more with pictures and words. I just want to grow a few more lavender plants and send guests home with natural sachets."

His lips quirked. "They'd actually get use out of the sachets. My written words suck." He dropped his gaze and let out a long breath. "It's why I haven't finished that article."

"But Xander, your pictures are

gorgeous." I wished he took more. I wished he used that camera and captured the beauty around us and shoved it in people's faces.

"They're all right. But by themselves, and by myself they won't sell a lot."

Admittedly, that sounded boring. The thought of writing long articles and doing all that research propelled me back to college. If I had to do it for a living, it needed to be fun. "Maybe don't sell them at first. Just put them up somewhere with some interesting facts. Gather a following."

He sat up next to me and propped his arms over his raised knees. "A website?"

"You could blog." Ideas that I'd been wanting to ask him about piled into my brain so quickly, I could recite them. "Vlogs, podcasts, YouTube, social media—you could do anything." I twisted onto my knees to face him. "Everything's so visual nowadays. Look at what your photos did for Hector's business. You could pick and choose topics to educate viewers—subscribers—patrons?—whatever.

I could help come up with the topics and do the posts and you could take the pictures."

I'd loved working for Saving Sunsets right out of college, but their reach had been limited. Doing this, Xander could reach all corners of the world. Well, those that had Wi-Fi, but it was a start and appealed to a bigger audience than Saving Sunsets had.

Xander's enthusiasm wasn't growing with mine. His brows were drawn, but at least he was thinking. "The pictures would be used for social media?"

He was so attached to doing something "momentous" with his work that he'd closed himself off from the possibilities.

"You wouldn't have to work to be published. You'd make our own damn publication." A gasp escaped. Excitement piled on top of endless possibilities. "With the money coming, you could reach far and wide. You could lift the voices of others trying to communicate similar topics."

"Make my own publication?" His brows drew further together, but his brown gaze swirled now too.

I waited, squeezing the breath in my lungs, to hear his opinion. We were a couple, but something like this had to be his decision, not just mine. Photography was his passion, one that he wanted to make more than a hobby.

A slow smile spread across his face. "Make my own damn publication."

"Hell, yes. You don't need anyone's approval."

His grin dimmed. "I'm not an old man, but I am turning thirty soon. They didn't really teach us about this in college, and it wouldn't have mattered if I'd stayed."

"I used to listen to some podcasts on the commute to Saving Sunsets' office." Which had been with Davis, our driver. I regretted that time that could have been spent learning my way around the city, being among the hub of people going about their day, and learning what was important to them for survival.

I'd had a fun experience learning public transit with Xander, but no one was dictating my life ever again.

"Brady was into it more. He has friends from school that have YouTube channels, and of course there'll always be a new social media outlet to master. We can call him and brainstorm." I peered into his eyes, the fading sun reflected back at me from the amber depths. "You think it's something you can get into?"

"I think so." He reached over and dug out his camera. "I feel like taking pictures again, so that's a good start."

I eased out of his way, though he would've taken a shot with me in it, and he focused on the sinking sun. Clouds were scattered across it, but the brilliant yellow-orange glow was a stark contrast to the land with its browns and greens.

The evening was silent besides the clicks of his camera. Then he focused on the horses. Their tails swished and swayed as they grazed in the new location Xander had moved them to after we'd finished fooling around.

Xander got lost in taking pictures and I got lost in watching him do it. We'd been married for months, but it felt like our life together was finally beginning.

~

Xander

I WAS ALONE in the house, flipping through the pictures I'd taken the day before. I kept going back to one shot of Savvy with her fingers in the shape of a square frame. Her smile was highlighted, like the sun had peeked out of the clouds at just that moment.

All the other pictures paled in comparison to the ones of her, but this one was downright stunning.

I had my computer set up in Mama's office. Eva and Beckett had flown back to Denver last night. Aiden and Kate had left this morning. And Savvy was out with Dad, Kendall, and Dawson, learning about cattle and ranching. I'd like to be with her, and I wasn't purposely avoiding Dad, but my talk with Savvy after our picnic had kindled a slow burn that was growing.

My fingers itched to comb through my pictures and figure out how to use them. Make my own damn publication. I needed to create a portfolio, an initial one to share with the world—or a few people at a time as I grew a following and figured out how to monetize it.

I glanced up from the screen. Dawson hadn't changed much in the office. He'd moved Mama's things out but left her art on the walls. Her art remained all over the house and in King Oil headquarters. Kate had showcased several of Mama's photos in Billings's library.

We worked hard to remember Mama.

But my brothers and I had a harder time remembering this office as any place other than where we'd found her the night of the attack.

I swallowed hard and went back to my work. That was why I'd chosen to work in here. Other than the normal mother-son relationship, Mama and I had bonded over photography. I'd make new memories in this office in the place the person who'd believed in me had spent so much time in.

I pulled up the pictures I'd taken of Hector and Eris's property. They were good. Damn good. But I could do better. Later next year, I'd have enough money to buy a new camera. I could take better action shots, even video.

The door creaked further open. I expected Savvy, but Dad came in, shutting the door behind him.

I sighed and sat back, closing my laptop. I'd gotten the feeling Dad wanted to talk to me—alone—since we'd arrived. Shame boiled out of the carefully walled-off reservoir I usually kept it in. I should've talked to him before. I should've done what Savvy had been asking me to, and I should've done it without her having to ask.

"Dad."

"Xander."

Dad sat, looking like the man I'd grown up with. His jeans were an older pair he'd worn for years, his boots were scuffed, and his hair was flattened around his head from his cowboy hat. He would go into the office wearing suits when the office used to be in King's Creek, but when he'd come home, he'd change clothes and ranch. My brothers and I had grown up doing chores and living a mostly normal life.

Dad crossed an ankle over his knee, a position I doubted he ever took while in a board room. "How's life been treating you?"

"Good."

"You and Savvy are doing well?"

I kept my mind off our sex fest today. "Yes."

"She's a wonderful girl."

"Yes."

Disappointment flickered in his eyes. I couldn't help it. I'd rather not talk to him at all than lie to him, and since my life revolved around a whopper of a lie, it left little for me to say.

A long exhale left him. "I had an in-person meeting with Walter Abbot a couple of months ago."

I refrained from closing my eyes and pinching the bridge of my nose. More failure welled inside. He knew. He knew and it wasn't because I'd told him.

"And you talked to Lex?" I asked.

"Lexington? Yes. He had a lot to say about you." Dad slapped his knee, his jaw clenching for a moment. "I have to say it was hard to sit and pretend to know what the hell he was talking about." Dad lifted his solemn gaze to mine. "It was also hard to come to the realization that what he said made a lot of sense when I looked back on the years."

My head bobbed. "I dropped out of college."

I thought I'd experience more of a relief to tell him that, but it was ten years too late and he already knew.

Dammit.

"Why?" All Dad's disappointment drained into that one word.

"I knew what I wanted to do, and I knew you wouldn't agree."

"I don't care about the photography—"

"Exactly, Dad. You don't care. You think it's just a fun hobby for me like it was for Mama. You would've pushed me to finish college, then you would've pushed me to find a job, a respectable one, and then whatever I picked wouldn't have been good enough."

Confusion filled his eyes. "What do you mean? Finishing college, yes. I mean, hell, Xander, it was already paid for." He inhaled sharply. "How fast did you spend that money?"

Giving me and my brothers the full

amount for school was supposed to have been the first lesson. Save and use wisely. If you can finish college and pay for it all, then you're on the right track. This was back before we'd all known we had an obscene trust fund waiting for us to say *I do*.

"It's almost gone."

He shook his head like he hadn't heard right. It'd been a lot of money, but not enough for someone to live off of for a decade.

"I worked," I explained. "Wherever I went, I earned my living. I only used it to get me by, or to fly home."

"Then why lie? All these years—"

"Because of this. Because you think I made a bad decision, just like when I wanted to drop out of wrestling."

"You were good."

"I hated it." That was a strong statement. I'd resented it. I'd only been in it for two years. Practice every damn day and tournaments every time I turned around.

By the time I'd hit high school, there had been so much more I'd rather have been doing than running more laps around the gym. "You wanted me to stay in it because you thought it kept me busy."

He raised his brows, challenging me.

"Pictures kept me busy."

Dad scrubbed a hand over his face. "I didn't think you were lazy, if that's what you're saying. I wanted you to follow through on something. You dropped out of wrestling. You quit football before you graduated. Any time someone said something to piss you off, you left. You left whatever you were doing and vanished. I wanted to see you finish something to the end. But I had to hear from a practical stranger that you'd dropped out of college."

"Maybe if you'd let me do what I wanted, then I would've been interested enough to follow through."

"College, Xander. You had your pick of majors."

"Did I?" *What about business*

administration? Maybe something in public relations if you insist on taking that camera everywhere. "Don't worry about the money. I'll pay you back soon enough."

Profound disgust filled his gaze. "I hope that isn't why you married Sapphire."

I threw my hands up. "See? You think the worst. I was too lazy to work for a living so I must've married for the money?" It burned that it looked like that was exactly what I'd done. "Did you pay any attention, at all, to how she and I are together? Do you think I'm still with her, or that she's still with me, for the money?"

Dad's jaw ticked and he wouldn't allow me to drop my gaze. "Fair enough. You two seem to care about each other. But what are you going to do for the next several months? Winter's coming. Do you have enough money to take you both somewhere warm? What are you going to do for living accommodations?" His hands gripped his knees. "Or are you going to couch surf until you're millionaires?"

I hated that his questions cut through my newfound excitement. I hated that I didn't have answers. All I had going for me was that I'd proved I could pinch pennies and get by on little. But Dad's point wasn't lost on me. It wasn't just me anymore.

"It's honestly none of your business." My heart pounded. By now, I'd usually have stormed off, but that had been to avoid telling him the truth. The truth was out there now and I had no reason not to face him.

The unflinching look he gave me stretched out long enough to be uncomfortable. "Isn't it? I believe that's my money you've been living off since you left school."

My pride wilted. Wasn't that the crux of my issue? All this time I'd avoided Dad to keep from having to defend my choices, but all along he was the one fueling them. All along, I'd needed his help in the form of cash and that meant he'd been right about everything. And if he was right about everything, then I couldn't follow through on a damn thing and I was doomed to fail.

I pushed back from the desk, the sound of the wheels on the hardwood stark in the silence. Leaving my computer behind, I rounded the desk to head for the door. "And I told you I'd pay you back."

Dad did nothing more than turn his head to follow my path. "Xander."

He didn't bark my name. It was the even, quiet tone that made me stop.

"You can walk out on me, you can run from your problems, but maybe ask yourself how you're going to deal with life now that you have a wife to think about. Or are you going to walk out on her too?"

My teeth snapped together and I ground my jaw. My hands clenched at my sides and I stormed out. I stomped out of the house, right to the barn, and out the other side to grab my horse. Dawson and Savvy both saw me. Kendall must be hiding, having known her husband planned to confront me.

Savvy lifted a hand and trotted toward

me. She hovered at the edge of the barn while I caught Fool's Gold. I passed her on the way to grab the saddle, my boots crunching in the straw with the horse's hooves.

"I take it you talked to your dad," she said only loud enough to be heard above the creaking of the leather saddle.

"Yep." I methodically strapped the saddle in place. Fool's Gold sensed my mood and shifted. The horse anticipated a long ride, used to the routine.

"The truth is out now. You two can move on from there."

She hadn't seen his disappointment. How unsurprised he was that I'd fucked up everything he'd given me. He probably thought I'd fuck up the trust money too, or worse—do nothing with it but traipse from country to country, only now I'd have the luxury of never needing to work.

My skin itched. I had to get away. I could travel and do something with my life. I'd prove it. "Where should we go?"

Her eyes flew wide. "What?"

"Go. We should get out of here before the snow flies. We don't even have to go far. Head north to Canada, rent a cabin, wait out the winter, make our plans."

"We have plans, Xander."

I shook my head. "I can't think here." I led Fool's Gold outside. Savvy followed on the other side, her top bun bouncing with each step.

"But—"

"We can leave tonight or in the morning. I'll pack when I get back." I swung up and with a twitch of my heel, I was off, leaving Savvy behind, just like Dad had said I would.

CHAPTER 20

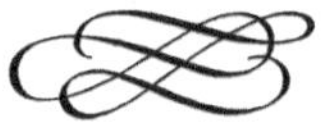

Savvy

I COULDN'T HELP IT. I waited on the porch, staring out at the pastures, hoping to see my husband ride back in. Logically, I knew he was coming back, that he hadn't ridden to town and caught a flight out. That'd be absurd.

Yet anxiety curdled in my gut and I waited.

The door eased open. I expected Kendall. She and Gentry were preparing to head home to Billings. I figured the guys had sent her out to make sure I was doing okay.

It wasn't Kendall. Gentry smiled, his eyes crinkling at the corners. Xander was lankier than his dad, and he probably seemed more like his mother when it came to mannerisms, yet the resemblance was undeniable. When Xander grinned, it was unmuted and full of life. Gentry kept things close to the vest, but both men picked and chose who they shared that side of them with. I had a feeling Xander's mom, Sarah, hadn't been so picky.

Gentry settled on the porch swing next to me. Just like Chief, he oozed power, but unlike Chief, he was subdued about it. He didn't feel the need to make sure everyone around him knew. "I threw a wrench in your weekend."

After Xander had ridden off, barely able to look at me, Gentry had come out the back door of the house, his expression drawn, like he'd kicked his favorite puppy.

"It was bound to happen eventually." I gave Gentry a sad smile. "I just think he wanted it to happen after he paid you back."

He kicked his boots out, making the swing squeak and sway until his heels caught and stopped it. I couldn't believe this guy who'd wrestled a cow three times his size the other day was the same tailored-suit-wearing man I'd met in Vegas. "I think I played it off well enough that Lex didn't get any enjoyment out of informing me. I pretended I already knew. I could've gotten an Oscar for my performance."

I chuffed out a laugh. "That's actually comforting, yes. Chief wanted me to marry him, you know."

"Chief? Oh, your father. He wanted you to marry Lex?"

"He looks better on paper."

"I'm sure he looks good until he opens his mouth. Young and cocky. He'll probably go far. But Xander won you over?"

"I was the one that brought up marrying. He didn't even tell me about the trust until I threatened annulment, and then it was only to get me to stay."

Gentry didn't say anything but nodded thoughtfully.

"He's talented," I said to fill the silence. Chief was never quiet, and I didn't know Gentry well, but his gaze was always sharp. His mind was never idle.

"The photography?"

So many things. "Yes. He helped his buddy out with some travel brochures."

"It'd be nice to hear about it." I didn't miss the wistfulness in his voice. Gentry wanted to connect with his son, but the way he did it with the others wasn't working on Xander.

"He's not like his brothers."

Gentry snorted. "Ain't that the truth. He's his mama's boy."

"And you got along with her." My teasing was gentle, but pointed.

"I did. She was my best friend, but

ranching was her passion and it was right here. Xander's passion is out there." He fell quiet for a moment. "Sarah didn't leave an instruction manual for raising the boys when she died. I only wanted to set Xander up for success, not drive him away."

"I drove him away once too."

Gentry's gaze landed on me but I didn't take my eyes off the pastures spread out before us. "But he came back?"

I frowned. "No. I went running after him. It was my fault he left."

The words fell empty between us. I got why talking to his dad unnerved Xander. The disappointment oozing off Gentry was palpable, and it wasn't aimed at me. I think I could've been a total shit to Xander and Gentry would still expect his boy to stick around and deal with it. Not leave me.

He'd left me once and I blamed myself. But this relationship took two. Now, he'd left again. I was stuck behind, worrying.

And here I'd married him so I wouldn't be alone in the big bad world when my parents disowned me for my big rebellion. That hadn't turned out at all like I'd thought it would. Neither did swinging on the porch all by myself with all these questions about my future.

"Listen, I've heard about your work history."

My gaze flashed to him. What had Chief said? He'd thought Saving Sunsets was a toddler bike in a Harley world. "There's not much there."

"Don't discount it." He gave me a pointed look. "Or let anyone else discount it."

I'd loved my role at Saving Sunsets. There had been less-desirable aspects to that job, but my main responsibility had filled my inner well to the brim. Bernard had been onto something with Saving Sunsets, and the failure of the nonprofit was a loss to the environmental consulting world.

Gentry was right, I did downplay my work history. But after last summer, I had more of it. So maybe Saving Sunsets wasn't my dream, but it'd been a good start. I wouldn't discount my time there again.

"Anyway," he continued, "our investors like to see what we're doing to help lower our carbon footprint, and how other forms of energy compare to oil when it comes to environmental impact. In fact, it's becoming more critical to investors, and King Oil needs to step up its game. You know all that, it was why we were supposed to meet that day in Las Vegas."

The truth of everything was out. "You know about that?"

"I could use a consultant."

"I have some contacts I could get you in touch with. The friend that I worked with is out of the country at the moment . . ."

Gentry stared at me with a bemused smile.

I blinked. "Are you offering me a job?"

He chuckled. "Sorry I didn't make that clear enough."

"It's because I married Xander." He was offering out of guilt.

"King Oil is a family company first. If I forget that, it's harder on everyone and it doesn't matter if we're talking about the work climate or the earth's climate. You're smart, you're passionate, you're well informed, and honestly, family or not, I wouldn't offer if you weren't qualified." His grin was knowing. "It just so happens my family is often the best at what they do."

A job. In a unique position where I could actually make a difference. Being around the Kings the last several days had shown me that they were passionate about what they did. They weren't motivated by money, but by doing the best job possible—and they happened to make loads of money while doing it.

I'd have access to the top in the business. I could make a bigger impact. I'd have to talk to Xander first, yet my gut said this was a good thing. So different from the pity job Chief had offered me.

"I need to think about it and I have to talk to Xander." And convince him not to leave.

"Of course. Let me know by the end of the month."

A deadline. My lips quirked. He was serious and if I declined, or took too long to decide, he'd move on. I respected him more. It made the job offer real.

The door opened and Kendall crept out with a suitcase, wincing as it whacked against the door. "Sorry, did I interrupt? I just wanted to load these, but we don't have to leave, if you wanna . . ."

Gentry rose and crossed the porch to take the bag, only reminding me of how Xander jumped to do the same thing. Xander credited his mother with a lot, but he'd picked up a few things from his dad. "I think perhaps if we take off now, this young lady's wait might not be as long." He turned with a sympathetic but friendly smile. "It was nice seeing you again, Savvy."

"I hope we can do it again soon," Kendall

said, giving me a hug. "You two are always welcome in Billings."

Gentry's expression was probably the same as mine—doubtful that I could ever get Xander to go there and just visit. But it sounded nice.

They loaded up and drove off. Dawson came out to check on me and wandered back inside. The sun sank below the horizon. Anxiety and loss crept up my spine.

How he processed his feelings was up to him, but I'd been left behind, worried and blaming myself. Had he thought of that? Was this what his family went through? Or had they resigned themselves to his long-term disappearances? I'd been through it once. Tonight was no picnic. I worried about him, but this was his home. He knew the horse and the land.

I didn't agree with Xander. I didn't think we should leave and I didn't want to. But as plans clicked into place with my determination, leaving was exactly what was going to happen.

~

Xander

"HEY," I drawled. Savvy's face was drawn and she hugged her arms around herself. Guilt clawed at my throat. I'd needed space. I'd needed time to think. I'd needed to get away from Dad and his opinions. I'd thought Savvy would understand, but tendrils of unease curled through my gut. I tried to keep it light. "It's getting chilly out."

"Maybe if you'd come home earlier, I wouldn't have waited out here so long."

Shit. This was worse than I'd thought. I stopped at the base of the porch steps. "You didn't have to wait outside. I was coming back."

Following the guilt came worry. I'd left her before and hadn't gone back for her.

Could I blame her for being paranoid even if I'd only taken off on a horse?

I propped my hands on my hips but stayed where I was. I was steeped in horse sweat and it wasn't until Fool's Gold and I had been riding for two hours that I'd realized how therapeutic it was. I'd missed it. "I knew you were here, where it was safe. I just needed time, Savvy."

"You've been gone for hours—after announcing that you want to leave the country."

"I'm sorry."

"People worry about you, Xander. When you take off and go radio silent for months, they worry."

We weren't just talking about today anymore. "I know what I'm doing. You don't have to worry about me."

"It's not just me." Her foot rocked the swing, an agitated move that made it appear like she was at leisure, enjoying the night, but there was nothing relaxed about her. "Did you even try to talk to your dad after he confronted you?"

"Yes."

She stopped swinging and studied me, waiting.

I had nothing else to say, but her expression said I'd better come up with something. "Of course I did. That's why I left."

"So when we get into an argument, are you going to take off too?" She left the "again" unsaid, but it rang through the night like a dinner bell.

I took the porch steps two at a time and kneeled next to her. "You know I need my space. Dad doesn't give me space."

"You haven't seen him for months. You didn't get a chance to say goodbye." She tilted her head and her expression went neutral. "He offered me a job."

"*After* I left, he offered you a position at King Oil?" Aiden and Kendall worked for the company. Grams was still involved.

She rolled her lips in and worked her

jaw before she said, "Maybe he thinks I'm a good choice for the position."

"I know you're good at your job, Savvy." I hadn't meant to insult her. Several members of my family worked with the company. It just hadn't occurred to me that Dad would headhunt my wife.

She glanced down at her hands, twisting her fingers together. "He was confident that I'd be good for the position."

Dad had been ready to work with a consulting company earlier. Hadn't he done that yet? "Did he make one up for you?"

Her brows popped. Wrong thing to say—but totally what Dad would do.

She rose and stuffed her hands into the front pocket of her pink hoodie. "All our time together has been about me proving what I could do. Everyone thought I wasn't strong enough, I wasn't worldly enough, I was too sheltered, too spoiled, too inexperienced to live my own life and decide for myself. I even had to prove myself to you. I can't go through a marriage where we're not on the same page."

"I'm not going to leave you."

"But you already have."

The words rocked me back on my heels like she'd smacked me. "I know when I left DC—"

"It's not just DC. Why Kosovo?"

"I told you—"

"About Hector. You didn't go there for your career. He was convenient. You left when it was easy. Leaving Montana would be the same. You haven't committed to a place. You haven't committed to a career. How do I know you're committed to me?"

"Because we're together."

"We weren't today. You left because you can't commit to your family. A conflict arises and you leave."

My mind spun. I should've known there'd be issues when I came back. I should've known that leaving the way I had would bother my wife. I couldn't change what I'd done, but I wasn't prepared for this conversation. I'd ignorantly thought I'd ride back and Savvy would talk about our next adventure.

"Remember why I married you? How afraid I was I would be left alone in this world with no support? You were so knowledgeable and I thought I'd be safe with you." She shook her head, tears glittering in her eyes. "Now I'm the one with knowledge. I know I'll be okay no matter what. I have a family who cares about me and they may not understand me, but they'll support me. They'll be there for me."

"What are you saying?"

"I'm saying . . ." She tilted her head back and stared at the porch ceiling. "I'm stronger than I thought I was. I have a month to think about the job, and I need some space."

"Savvy." She couldn't be serious. She was just pissed that I'd taken off for the day.

"Xander." She pushed her long locks back from her face. "I've been through a lot of changes. I can keep going, doing what we're doing, thinking I need to be better, or I can go back home, visit my family, and use my last name like I did with Saving Sunsets. Bernard was right. It opens doors and I can take advantage of that in a good way.

"But I thought we were . . ." In love. In this together.

"Fifty million is a lot of money, but I met Bristol. I've seen that shack on her farm. I was terrified of living that woman's life." She let out a scornful laugh. "I don't care if she gets the money. I don't know that she won't do more with it than I could, but I know that I have to take charge of my life."

We'd started out wanting to be together. How could she think that had changed? "Savvy, we can talk about this without you leaving."

Her eyes narrowed. "You don't want her getting the trust."

The money itself didn't matter. Who it went to if I lost the trust didn't matter.

Failing my family again did. Facing my dad with a failed marriage after I'd spent my college money and lost the money Mama had put aside just for me would eat away at me for the rest of my life.

I didn't get the words out in time. Savvy huffed. "This time I'll be the one going. I'm going to be the one with so much confidence in leaving, fuck how anyone else feels."

My pulse raced. I didn't like the idea of her going. Would she come back? Would I see her again? Would she ask for a divorce? She had no way of getting to town unless Dawson or I gave her a ride.

Headlights pulled into the drive. Was Dawson expecting someone?

She went around me and opened the door to the house. She grabbed her backpack and suitcase from inside the door.

How the hell had she found a ride? "Where are you going?"

"I'm taking an Uber to Billings."

How the hell . . . "King's Creek doesn't have Uber."

Her smile was sad. "You've just never needed one."

"Chief miraculously found an Uber driver that could take you to Billings after dark?"

She stiffened and faced me. "No, Xander. *I* found a ride. I'm paying for it and my flight home." She started down the stairs.

I jogged after her. My hands twitched to take the bags from her. To take them and throw them back on the porch. "Savvy, tell me what I can do to make this right."

The driver, a woman, which made me feel better and further drove home the point that Savvy wasn't stupid or impulsive, opened the back door and returned to the driver's seat within seconds. I was grateful for the semblance of privacy.

"I don't know, Xander. Only you can decide what you're going to do."

CHAPTER 21

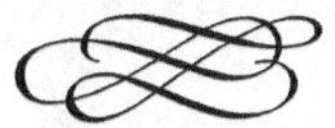

Savvy

I DIDN'T KNOW what I was doing. I dropped my head into my hands. The papers were in front of me, drawn up by a lawyer that Mother had recommended.

Just because she'd recommended one didn't mean she agreed with my decision. Biting back my pride, I'd outlined the reasons why and she'd given me a curt nod and her lawyer's number.

Overall it would be a simple divorce. Simple, but necessary for me to move on.

I had insisted Xander get his shit together, and I hadn't heard from him.

Fine. It was fine. Just because I stayed out of the sitting room and slept in Pearl's room while I was home didn't mean it bothered me.

I'd flown back to DC. I'd unpacked everything from my suitcase except the ring that had been left in it since Kosovo. I should've seen the signs. Neither of us had worn our rings in Montana. We hadn't thought of them. I'd like to think it made sense—we'd each only worn a wedding ring less than two months of our lives. It was better not to look into it too hard.

Instead of crying into my pillow that still smelled like Xander no matter how fresh the sheets were, I made plans. I hadn't hit the ground running, but I'd been crawling.

The flight home had given me time to think. The job with King Oil would be a good one. Gentry had sent the information. The pay had made my eyes bug out. But . . .

I'd changed since meeting him all those months ago. I could do what I wanted to from an office, or I could do it from the front lines.

I'd called some contacts I'd networked with through Saving Sunsets and asked them about the basics of running a nonprofit—and how to do it successfully. Then for the entire two months I'd been home, I'd outlined how I'd run one. Gentry's job deadline had come and gone. I had declined the offer.

Good thing Chief hadn't known about it, and that Gentry hadn't told him.

My return had shocked my parents. Chief had been a tense ball of dread until he'd realized his contract with King Oil wasn't going to be affected by the state of my relationship with Xander. Chief had offered me another assistant job too, and as tempting as it had been to hop into something I could earn money with immediately, I'd refused that one too. It'd swallow me up again if I went back. I'd discussed rent and a timeline for when I'd be ready to move out with both parents. I wasn't making the same mistake I had before, and I wasn't skipping out on critical conversations with my parents anymore.

I'd found seasonal work at a shopping mall—at a stand that wrapped gifts with an environmental twist. While it was fun to find ways to make old newspapers look elegant and festive while they encased a new TV, or a doll, or a processed meat and cheese set, I spent the entire time planning—including when I was commuting. No more personal driver, and no more getting lost . . . after the first few times.

Saving Sunsets had aligned with my goals. That was why I'd stayed on a sinking ship and been stranded in Las Vegas. The benefit to sticking around so long was that I'd gleaned a lot about the right ways to run a nonprofit—and some of the major wrong turns to avoid.

I puffed out a breath. Thankfully, Pearl had a desk in her bedroom, leaving few reasons for me to leave other than work and food. I made sure to get outside each day. The cold nipped my nose and we'd had a dusting of snow already, but I wouldn't let memories of snowmen and snowball fights tarnish my daily dose of sunshine.

I stared at the desktop, my eyes drifting away from my laptop, where I had a business plan nearly complete. My heart tugged at the loss of the job offer with King Oil. I could've made a difference from the top down. That was a position where people would've listened to me.

I straightened, picturing lead being poured down my spine. I could do this. From the ground up. With no money but plenty of connections to fundraise.

My gaze slid over the envelope. The lawyer's office had offered to send the papers for me, but as my heart had clogged my throat, I'd shaken my head and held my hand out. The address was already on it.

Well, Dawson's. Was Xander still there? Was he even in the States?

I doubt he thought I'd divorce him, but I had to. All that money. I pinched the bridge of my nose. I could do so much with it.

But it wasn't mine. I had to have faith in my ability to generate my own. I had to have faith in this endeavor. I had to have faith that if my marriage had been destined to be, it would've worked out.

There was a knock on the door. I ripped my gaze away. My stupid chest grew tight with each knock, only to be smothered by foolishness a moment later. Xander would've shown by now if he'd wanted to work on us.

"Yeah?"

Mother poked her head inside. "I'm going out. Would you like to come along?"

Mother offered each time she ran errands. She worried that I was wasting away in this room with no one to talk to. All I could do was lob messages back and forth with Brady and Rina. I had no idea when I could fly out and see them.

"No. I have . . ." My gaze landed on the papers. I could drop them in our mail. I could go with Mother and mail them. I could continue to be a coward and leave them on my desk.

But it was nearly Christmas. How shitty to get served divorce papers on Christmas. Yet if I was going to go through with it, I should do it well before Valentine's Day. I was running out of time, and waiting any longer meant I didn't really want this divorce. That I hoped we could still work it out. Somehow.

I flattened my hand on the large manila envelope. With today's technology, I was sure there were more expedient ways to do this, but I hadn't asked for them.

I sucked in a sharp breath. "Can you mail this?"

Mother's mouth tightened. I'd told her about the trust and how my relationship had ended. Both pride and disappointment had shone in her eyes. Like she'd told me earlier, she was there for me when I fell, but I could walk through my life on my own.

She gave me a clipped nod and took the envelope. "Are you sure?"

No. "Yes."

Her reassuring smile didn't do anything to make me feel better. She left and I was halfway out of my chair to catch her and rip the envelope away. I gripped the sides of the chair and breathed through my panic.

When I finally relaxed, if that's what I could call the feeling, I tried to go back to the business plan I had on my computer. I sat poised, ready to write, but didn't move for I don't know how long. I stared at the screen. My gaze flicked to the bare spot on the desk where the envelope had been.

I stroked the wood and tears sprang into my eyes.

I was home alone and my faith in myself was crumbling. I tried to return to the laptop but the screen had gone dark. No happy bubbles careening around. No pictures of my privileged life ping-ponging from corner to corner. Nothing. I could change the screen saver from the default, but I didn't. It fit my mood.

I sniffled.

I might as well give into the tears. I wasn't going to accomplish anything else tonight. I just hoped it wasn't the first sign of many failures to come.

Xander

"IT'S A COLD BITCH OUT THERE." Dawson toed his boots off and shuffled across the hardwood floor on his stockinged feet. He tossed a big envelope down. "Something, uh . . . came for you."

He didn't run away, but he backed away slowly.

I scowled and ripped my gaze away from the computer. I'd been here for over two months, soaking up Dawson's Wi-Fi and getting my shit together.

I guess it took a wife leaving me to make me grow the fuck up.

I had a website set up, but I was still learning the damn thing. If I'd waited for a few more months, I could have paid someone else to do all this, but there was a sense of accomplishment that came with watching how-to video after instructional YouTube to build something that was purely mine.

My time was bogged down because I was tying a lot of revenue streams into this website. I had a blog. I hadn't written a damn word for it, but I had my portfolio loaded onto my site. My business wasn't officially live, but it was all under my real name. No hiding. If Savvy could own her wealthy background in a field where it'd be held against her, I could too. I had an account on every social media site and ideas on how to use them. I had yet to post. I had plenty of past pictures and notes to work with, but no plans for the future.

My future was a big, black, gaping hole of unknown.

Savvy had left Montana and according to my past, I should've been gone too. One plane ticket to anywhere was all I needed. But I hadn't left. All those years, I'd taken off, but whenever I'd come back, everyone was still here, in King's Creek.

My brain knew that Savvy wasn't from here. Nothing tied her here other than the great time she'd had before she'd been so pissed and disappointed in me that she'd left and told me to figure shit out.

I'd figured it out. But unlike me, she hadn't come back.

My chest grew tight when I thought that I'd left for fucking years before showing up again. That I'd ignored written messages and voicemails while doing my own thing and . . . hiding from the world.

That was what I'd been doing. Hiding. Not taking responsibility. Blaming everyone else for why my life wasn't working out when I'd tried something different.

Not my wife, though. She'd been stranded in a big city with no way to get home and she'd sucked it up and asked for help. She'd taken a job she didn't like to make ends meet. Then when I'd left her behind, she'd packed it up and found me.

And she'd been right. I hadn't given her credit for any of it. She'd done all the changing and I was still me. Irresponsible.

Dawson disappeared and I frowned. I helped him out in the mornings and evenings, then retreated to the house to get work done. Usually after he came in for supper, he pestered me about what I'd been doing all day on the computer. Talking to him was always easy and he'd had some good ideas for my business plans. But tonight, he'd dropped the envelope and vanished.

My gaze landed on the mystery mail. No one but my family knew I was here, yet it wasn't unusual to receive a parcel of mail every once in a while.

The official return address caught my eye. A legal office. In DC.

I sat back and air eked out of me like a tire with a slow leak. My mind turned into sludge and refused to think. I stared at the address. My name in official letters. *Xander King*. I had no initials, no title. There wasn't "Asshole who fucked up his marriage" behind my name. Just me.

I ripped it open like tugging a Band-Aid off. Now I knew which one hurt more.

The papers were as official as the envelope.

I set them down. Slumping back in my chair, I stared at the far wall. One of Mama's pictures hung next to the fireplace.

She'd be so ashamed of me. The kid who'd never learned to deal with his emotions without hurting someone. The kid who didn't have a fucking job and lived with his brother and had just been served divorce papers.

I don't know how long I sat there, but eventually Dawson emerged from his master bedroom on the first floor.

He took one look at me and stopped at the edge of the short hallway. "You hungry, man?"

"She wants a divorce."

He puffed out a breath and scratched the back of his neck. "I was afraid of that."

"She could have millions and millions of dollars, but she'd rather divorce me."

Dawson crossed to the table, but he didn't say anything. We sat, two bachelors staring at the wood grains running through the surface.

Funny thing was, I didn't feel like going anywhere. I could take Fool's Gold out. I could walk into the airport and pick a flight to board. I could ignore these damn papers until the year mark passed and I got millions.

But the thought that I might not get the money whipped away the blanket of deception I'd been hiding under. A part of

me had thought I'd land on my feet. I
wouldn't be the ultimate disappointment
and let the neighbors get what my
grandparents had worked their asses
off for.

The envelope in front of me upended all
that. I had no plan. Without at least the idea
of that money to cling to, I was nothing. I
was turning thirty soon and had been too
afraid to do a damn thing with my life, and
I'd used my college money and trust funds
as excuses.

Even worse, I'd ruined my marriage in
record time.

I'd known as soon as I'd seen her that
she could be my world. That I wanted her
to be my world. I'd had no idea until now
what a miracle it was that she'd wanted to
be with me too. Sure, we'd had our reasons.
But she would've done what she needed to
do without me. I knew she would've.

Did she want the divorce, or had she
just given up on me?

I could ask. I could fly there and

confront her, show her what I'd been doing. And then what? She'd ask the hard questions. Where were we going to live? What exactly did I have planned for the money? Why was I worth an extra few months of her life?

I didn't want a few measly months. I wanted a damn lifetime with her. She knew that, but she'd already told me that wasn't enough.

I closed my laptop. Dawson was tense, but he didn't say anything, just watched. I slid my computer into its case and loaded it and all my notes in my backpack. My camera was next.

Dawson's head tipped down as I rose. He thought he knew what I was doing. Savvy's words rang through my head. *People worry about you, Xander. When you take off and go radio silent for months, they worry.* There were other people who cared about me and I'd been pretty insensitive when it came to them.

"Can I borrow the truck? I need to go to Billings."

Surprise that I'd said that much rippled across his face. "Sure. Between me and Dad, we'll figure out how to get it back from the airport."

"I'm not going to the airport." I jogged upstairs. He was confused and I wasn't helping. I'd message him when I got to my destination, but it was evening. By the time I got to Billings, it'd be late.

I packed my belongings, seeing my few possessions with new eyes. Talk about a lack of commitment. Only it was *all* relationships I'd resisted committing to, not just my love life. I'd refused to commit to people or a place or even possessions.

I dug the simple gold band out of the side pocket of my backpack. As I flipped the cold metal between my fingers, the word *commitment* echoed through my head. I shoved it back in, zipped up the pocket, and jogged downstairs and out the door.

I hopped into Beck's old pickup and fired up the noisy engine. The gas tank was full, but it would be nearing empty by the time I reached Billings. Savvy wouldn't approve of the waste, but I wasn't waiting for an Uber.

The trip went quickly and I may have pushed the speed limit. I parked in front of my destination and sent a quick note to Dawson so he'd know where I was.

I hopped out and grabbed my belongings. Nerves rattled my insides. I doubted I'd get turned away, but after the way I'd acted, I deserved it.

I rang the doorbell and waited. Anxiety mounted with each second. The porch light shone on me like an interrogator's spotlight.

The door opened. "Xander? Is everything all right?"

I swallowed the lump of panic over the papers burning a hole through my backpack and making it weigh at least fifty pounds more than it should. "Dad, I need to talk to you. I need your advice."

CHAPTER 22

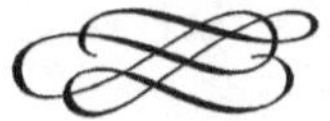

avvy

I WAITED at the top of the stairs, dancing from one foot to another.

Mother walked inside and shook snow off her Max Mara double-breasted camel coat. I froze when I saw the papers in her hand. But there was no familiar manila envelope. As if Xander would've used the same one to return the divorce papers. Still, I could breathe again.

"Did I get anything?"

Mother glanced up, her pleasant expression startled. She shouldn't be. I'd stood in the same spot daily since I'd let her mail the divorce documents off. "No, dear. Sorry."

She said the same thing every day. And each time, it was all I could do to keep from sagging against the railing as relief weakened my legs.

Xander had to have the papers by now. He had plenty of time in the last few weeks to sign them and send them back.

But he hadn't.

I trudged back to my room. Pearl's room.

I looked at my bedroom door. I needed to go back in there. It was one more step to take before I lived on my own. I wasn't ready to afford a place in the city. New Jersey might be a good place to run my business with a cheaper cost of living, but I hadn't looked around yet. That would make this all too real.

With a sigh, I went back to the desk I'd been diligently working at. I was at a stopping point. It was New Year's Eve, and getting ahold of anyone was impossible over the holidays. Anyone I'd tried to call and make connections with was on vacation or not interested in hearing about new projects until after the New Year.

If I couldn't work, I couldn't sit at Pearl's desk and stare at the wall. My bedroom was too much to hang out in before thoughts of Xander sapped my ambition and made me melancholy, but the sitting room had fewer memories. I'd start there.

When I got to the door, I sucked in a breath. I'd avoided my bedroom and the TV room. I had to stop sometime.

I pushed the door open and looked around. The TV hung above the electric fireplace. The couch was in the same spot. Xander hadn't spent as much time in this room as in my bedroom. But I looked for his presence all the same.

Pathetic. I'd sent divorce papers. I had to get over him.

I dug around the cushions for the remote. The doorbell rang. Were we getting company? Pearl had said she wasn't taking leave until January. Em and Carter were going to his family's for the holiday. I was going to ring in another year married, but all by myself.

Thinking about that wasn't going to solve anything. I puffed hair out of my face. My holiday position had dissolved after Christmas, and I'd have to find something else to support me while I got my business going. I could job hunt while I watched a movie.

"Sapphire?" Mother's voice filtered in from the hallway.

Crap. Had a courier sent the papers over? "I'm in here," I called, stuffing my hand as far as I could reach through the seat cushions. Had Pearl lost that damn thing before she'd left and never bothered to tell anyone?

"You have a visitor."

Me? I straightened and pushed a mass of hair off my face. Facing the door, I froze. Air whipped into my lungs and stopped. My face, flushed from being nearly upside down searching for the remote, turned cold. I was stunned. Speechless. Unbelieving of what was in front of my eyes.

Xander stood in the doorway, his hands tucked into a pair of new jeans. A Henley-style shirt I hadn't seen before hugged his muscles and caressed his hard abs. His hair was still on the long side, but it'd been trimmed and was brushed off his face. His backpack was slung over a shoulder.

Damn, he looked fine.

I looked like one hard blow would send dandelion puffs all over the room. The only thing I had going for me was that I'd showered this morning. Otherwise, this college sweatshirt and black leggings had seen better days. I blew hair out of my face. "Hey."

"Hey."

A gentle hand pushed him inside and shut the door behind him. I was locked in with Xander. The dark circles under his eyes did nothing to detract from his handsomeness. I drank him in. Tall. Broad.

His boots dug into the carpet. New ones. Had he bought everything to come see me? Or had it just been time to swap in a new set of clothes for the ones he'd trashed going all over the world?

"I . . . uh, got your papers." His jaw muscles flexed, but he wasn't angry. Determination simmered in his gaze.

"I thought it was for the best. The money isn't mine."

He didn't argue that it wasn't his neighbor's either. He didn't beg me to wait until we'd both filled our bank accounts and our pockets. He just nodded. "How've you been?"

Shitty. Depressed. Bored out of my mind. Caught between wishing I'd never met him and treasuring every second we'd had together. "Good. You?"

He nodded again. "Same. I've been working on my new business."

My brows popped. "Where'd you go?"

He blinked, trying to understand my question, then clenched his jaw. Well, he deserved it. It was a natural question. This was Xander. "I've been staying with Dawson."

We'd had a big argument and he hadn't gone anywhere?

Right, because I'd left.

"Is it what we talked about? Your business?" What we'd talked about doing together?

"Yeah. Want to see?" He lowered his backpack. He was going to dig out his computer, and then to look through everything, I'd have to sit next to him.

"No, thanks."

He froze, then slowly slid his computer back into his bag. "No problem. I'm sure you have your own stuff to do."

"Yep." Words halted on my tongue to describe everything I'd been doing and all my thoughts and how I really hated turning his dad down because that would've been a dream. "It's a start, and it'll take a while." Frustration welled. What the hell were we doing? Prolonging the pain? "What are you doing here, Xander?"

"I came to talk. I haven't been very good at that."

"Look, I know you don't want the divorce, that we're so close to the money—"

"I've been with Dad for the last few weeks."

The words shocked me to silence.

After a moment, he pressed his fingertips together and continued. "I got the papers and realized that maybe a man who's been married twice, pretty successfully, might be able to give me some advice." His smile was wan. "He had a whole ton of advice banked. But we talked. I showed him photos and what I've been setting up. And we talked some more."

It must've been significant enough to bear repeating. "You talked about your mom."

"Mama. Me. Him. Everyone else. I told him about every country I'd been to. He had to take some time off. Kendall arranged it so he could work from home while I finished planning . . ." His gaze turned tortured, yearning gleaming in the brown depths. "Planning where I'd like to live."

"Like a house?" He was going to stay somewhere? Long-term?

"Like a home. But Savvy, every time I think about a home, I think of you. It's going to be just a house without you."

"But I can't . . ." What couldn't I do? Live with the man I'd fallen in love with? The man I married. "What did your dad say?"

"To talk to you. To find out what you wanted and if we could make it work together. Then he said from there, it'd all figure itself out."

"Where would you live?"

"Wherever you want."

That sounded like heaven. "But wouldn't you have to travel for your new business?" Was it the same thing we'd talked about that day we confessed our love to each other and had toe-curling sex under the sun all afternoon?

Heat licked up my body. I'd purposefully avoided thinking about anything physical with Xander. Other than piling pillows behind my back every night, and maybe warming them with a heated blanket so it felt like a semisolid body behind me once in a while—or every damn night—I'd been successful.

Forgetting what Xander felt like and tasted like and how good it could be between us was impossible with him standing right in front of me.

"We could still travel. Or I could, if you weren't able to." My expression must've given him alarm. He rushed on. "But we'd talk about when and where and how long I'd be gone. It wouldn't be long-term. I'd be more than willing to work around your vacations. I have ten years of material to work with."

I blew out a hard breath as my notes and spreadsheets danced through my mind. "I doubt I'd get much for vacations for a while with what I'm doing." The moment I could hire another employee was a long way off.

"Dad said he hasn't been able to find an applicant that fits the position as well as you."

Hope surged. "He's just saying that."

"Not really. You're refined and can behave in a board room and at a conference, but he's also seen you with your boots dirty and your hands full of barn kittens."

They weren't exactly feral. Dawson and the guys who worked for him spoiled those things and they were cuddle monsters.

"He said several applicants want to either scare off environmentalists, thinking they're protecting the company, or secretly take down the company and use it to land an even bigger position. But the way you talked to him about the oil world and wind energy, and how you interviewed Dawson about the beef industry, impressed him."

"I'm not exactly impartial when I'm married to you."

"You see the people on both sides. That's what he wants." Xander shrugged. "No pressure. It's yours whether we stay married or not."

"I have a nonprofit idea in mind."

"You could do both."

I scowled. I didn't feel like I could do even one of them right now.

"You could, Savvy. I'd be around to help."

I'd be around to help.

He hadn't flown around the world to find me, but he had gone across the country. Was that good enough?

More importantly, he'd done the emotional work I'd accused him of avoiding. He'd done it and he didn't want to get divorced and it wasn't about the money. He was thinking about putting down roots, trying to find a way to meld both of our dreams together.

And he was here. In the same room with me. He hadn't rushed off when the papers had arrived at his place. He'd remembered what I'd said and he'd done his due diligence. He'd proved himself.

That left me with only one more question. "Did you sign the papers?"

Xander

MY HEART PLUMMETED. *Did you sign the papers?*

She still wanted the divorce. Dad had warned me this was a possibility and he'd talked me through it. Every time I'd wanted to be the idealistic artist and insist that love was all we needed, he'd talked me off the fanciful ledge.

What are you going to do if she still wants

the divorce? How will it make you feel and how will you deal with it? Be specific.

The good news was that I'd predicted everything I'd feel accurately. Disappointed. Depressed. Like I'd fucked up the most important thing in the world. The bad news was that I wasn't prepared for the devastating strength of those feelings. My chest burned like someone was ripping it open. I wanted to drop to my knees and pound my head against the floor, chanting *dumbass.* I wanted to walk away and keep walking. Not talking to anyone ever again sounded like a great plan.

Tell her what you feel and what you're thinking. In the end, you can only be honest.

"I love you, Savvy. I'm ready to make this work, and I'll understand if you aren't. But I had to come here and tell you in person that I want you, and I want to be with you always and I don't care where in the world we do that." I shoved my hands in my pockets. If someone walked in, it'd look like we were having a stand-off. Her with her arms crossed and me, closed off like always. "I married you so I could be with you. That feeling hasn't gone away."

Her gaze softened, her eyes misty. "Why don't you get those papers out?"

Crestfallen, I did as she asked. My stomach wanted to revolt, acid swirled to work its way up, then everything went numb. I could hurt later.

I should've called her when I'd received them. Should've asked her if she wanted to talk first. Should've told her that I had to mend some fences with Dad because I needed his help to un-fuck everything I'd done. Instead, I'd made her wait. That was unacceptable.

My fingers fumbled on the front zipper of my backpack. "I signed them."

"Let me see them."

Wishing I could delay the inevitable, I handed them over. We were one step closer to divorce. I wanted to shove my hands in my pockets again, but I forced myself to stand still.

She took them. Her expression, determination cemented with resolve, cut through me worse than a butcher knife.

She looked me in the eye, gripped the papers, and ripped them down the middle.

"Wha—" I didn't dare read into the action. Maybe she had more official documents. Maybe she wanted more from me before we divorced. Maybe she wanted me to wait for a month before we were done like I'd made her wait.

"Where would you like to live?" she asked, half of the contract dangling from each hand and a sly smile on her lovely face.

Still too scared to hope that I was hearing her correctly, I thought for a moment. "You seemed to be infatuated with Montana, and I'd be close to home, but we might want to look for land closer to Billings so it's easier for you to travel here. I know that you'd rather not use a private jet. But anywhere. I'll go anywhere with you." I took a step closer. "Does this mean . . ."

"Yes, Xander." She closed the space between us and dropped the papers. They fluttered to the floor as she flattened her hands on my chest and gazed up at me. "I love you too and want to stay married."

My grin barely had a chance to form before I slammed my mouth on hers and lifted her up. I swallowed her giggle and she twined her legs around me.

"God, baby," I managed to get out while devouring her. "I thought I'd lost you. I thought I'd fucked up too bad."

"Me too."

"You didn't—" I couldn't get any more words out. She tightened her legs around me and blood drained from my brain. The message that this woman and I were still on had reached my dick and it pounded behind the fly of my pants.

Now was not the time to maul her. We'd just reconnected. I wasn't going to go farther than kissing when we were in the sitting room of her house.

"On the couch," she gasped.

I turned enough to keep from tripping on my backpack and dropped to my ass. She moved her legs to my sides, straddling me.

The kiss deepened. I did more than taste her, I consumed her. I wanted to run my hands up her sides, but it still felt like too much too soon.

Until she started wiggling that fine butt of hers. Sitting wasn't exactly easy with as strong of an erection as I had, and the pressure of her body grinding against mine only added to the exquisite pain.

"Savvy," I groaned. I couldn't tell her to stop. I didn't want her to, but this was a special sort of hell.

She abruptly pulled back and slid off my lap.

Left bereft, my head spun. "Sorry, did I . . ."

She whipped her shirt over her head and stole my words. Those creamy breasts I'd craved each night were cupped by a light pink bra. The bra hit the ground.

Next, she shucked her pants and underwear off and kicked them to the side. I couldn't look away. My goddess was in front of me.

"I need you now. I've dreamed of this every night and thought I wouldn't have the chance to be with you anymore."

She'd pulled those words from my mind. My gaze strayed to the door. "What about . . ."

Hell with it. We were adults, we were married, and as old-fashioned as her parents seemed, I didn't think they'd mind if Savvy and I messed around in this room. Her mother had practically shoved me in here.

I unzipped my jeans enough to get my dick out, cool air kissing the tip and making it throb harder. I didn't have time to do anything more before she straddled me again. Sliding my hands down her sides, I relished her warm, satiny skin. I kissed my way across her cleavage to capture one nipple in my mouth. As I did that, she positioned herself over me and pushed down.

My head dropped as hot, wet paradise enveloped me. "Savvy . . . You feel so fucking good."

All she did was moan and bite her bottom lip. If she was afraid of making too much noise, I could help with that.

I cupped the back of her neck and drew her close. She rode me with slow, sensuous rolls of her hips. I muffled her moans and she stifled mine. Palming her breasts, I moved as best I could with her.

Her knees dug into the cushions. I thrust up as much as possible. Were the flaps of my jeans digging into her? Would the denim rub her raw? She didn't act like she cared.

I let her ride me until her hands tightened on my shoulders. She needed more. Threading an arm between us, I found her soaked clit.

"Xander," she moaned.

I licked up every syllable as I massaged lazy circles on her bundle of nerves.

Her whole body jerked as her climax hit. Her teeth caught my lip, but I held on to her as she shook in my arms. Just as she was coming down, I flipped her onto her back and spread over her, shoving my pants further down with one hand. Using that same hand, I hitched her knee up and drove into her willing body.

"Savvy." I touched her forehead with mine as I worked in and out of her tight channel. "I don't care where we're at—we're fucking like this any time you want."

"God, yes. And I'm going to scream your name over and over."

My orgasm swelled and I angled my hips just right, just how she liked it, and stroked her enough to give her another climax.

Somehow we managed to keep it down, grunting and moaning through our peaks. I stayed in her for minutes afterward, both of us catching our breath, then I took the throw we'd cuddled under the last time I was here and covered us both.

I maneuvered us onto our sides, and we spooned. No one entered. I didn't know if her mother was even home, but we were left alone. I stroked the skin of her abdomen. I'd never get enough of touching this woman. I'd never get enough of her. The need was stronger now than when we'd met.

"Are you sure about Montana? We can look here."

"I love Montana." She looked over her shoulder, a furrow between her brows. "I really would love that job."

"Dad would love to have you."

"But I've been working on something I'm really excited about."

"I'll show you mine if you show me yours."

I lost track of the hours we spent on the couch. Eventually, we dressed and ordered in food. Then I took my wife upstairs and did everything she begged me to.

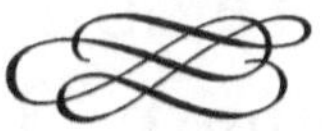

avvy

I JUMPED out of the car and sprinted across the short driveway. Rina caught me and we danced in a circle while we hugged.

"I can't believe you made it back!" Rina laughed.

After squeezing Rina for several more moments and then flinging myself into Eris's arms, Xander and I switched. I gave

Hector a quick squeeze around the baby he held.

Brady was next. He squished me against him and twirled around like I'd done with Rina. When we were done and laughing, he held me at arm's length. "Look at you, pampered princess. All country girl now."

I kicked up my new but broken-in Ariat boots. "I was a ranch hand all winter."

Not really. Dawson had humored me, but since winter was their slow season and I hadn't wanted to take away from the work of his employees, he'd let me follow him and Xander during my break from planning.

"I won't believe it until I see it." He crossed to Rina and threw his arm around her. She playfully scowled at him but cuddled into his side.

Xander chuckled. "You'll see it in several installations that are scheduled to start posting next week."

The launch of his new business, and we weren't going to be in the States for it.

Xander and I had worked hard the last few months, him taking pictures of Dawson and the land, and me getting the nonprofit going from our apartment outside of Billings while our new home was being built. With the trust, we had enough money to use all the best environmentally-friendly methods for building.

I oversaw construction and prepared to open the doors of Savvy Energy Solutions, a nonprofit that provided education on energy consumption and offered scholarships and grants for small companies that worked within the environment. Small companies like Hector's, who'd agreed to let us make him the first recipient. There'd be an application process for the rest, but this benefitted my business and Hector's, and gave us an excellent excuse to fly and visit.

I even had a client ready to work with me once this vacation was over. Gentry had reached out to Savvy Energy, insisting that he could not find anyone to fit the new position and he'd gladly work with the company until he did.

I'd told him it was nepotism. He'd claimed that Brady had refused to move back to the States since he'd gone into partnership with Hector and Eris and I hadn't given him another contact.

My father-in-law was a slick oil man.

Xander crossed to me and hooked his hand through mine. His camera was over his shoulder. He never went anywhere without it anymore. Half his SD card was filled with photos of me. I had a notebook in my backpack for ideas for future content. His passion was my hobby, and a nice distraction from launching a nonprofit.

I pointed at Brady. Rina's hand rested on his abdomen, a familiar move that Brady seemed more than content with. "I didn't believe that until I saw it." They'd started dating before Christmas and it was probably the hardest Brady had ever worked for a girl. That he put out any effort at all meant he was serious.

"She made me work for it," Brady drawled. "I might've bought into this business, but she thinks she's still in charge."

"You got discounted shares because of me." Rina lifted a dark brow. "City boy."

We all laughed and piled inside. It was almost exactly a year since I'd arrived the first time. Xander and I were no longer the broke married couple we'd been when I'd first landed on their doorstep, but we'd only parceled out some of the money for us, for the property near Billings we'd bought, for the travel adventures we'd decided to take once a year—and for our future children. With no stipulations on the trust.

Eris waved us to the table, where she had set out homemade pastries and steaming cups of what everyone had started calling Hector's Tar. "So, tell us all about what's happened this last year."

"Xander refused to divorce me." I didn't

gloss over a thing. Then Xander pulled out his camera and showed everyone the photos we were using for our first series on ranching and the environment. Then we switched to the nonprofit.

"I picked the name and convinced Savvy to use it," Xander said.

I hadn't needed much convincing. Savvy Energy was both a play on words and an excellent way to describe what the company was all about.

"Wait." Brady leaned in to look at the header on the website. "Are you the spokesmodel?"

"Yep," I said. Not only would the company sport my name, but the picture Xander had taken of me framing the sky the afternoon we'd spent together in the pasture was plastered across the website. The *about* page on my website was open and honest about who Xander and I were and where we came from.

We'd most likely get pushback, having grown up wealthy. We'd get doubted. We'd get questioned about what seemed like a conflict of interest working with King Oil, but I wasn't worried. I hooked my fingers through Xander's and exchanged a smile with him.

We'd proved ourselves already.

EPILOGUE

awson

"I CAN'T BELIEVE you showed your smug face here."

I tucked a hand into the pocket of my black jeans. My good ones, the pair that I wore to church and get-togethers where dirt on my boots wasn't allowed. I shouldn't have worn them here.

Danny Cartwright didn't deserve my best, even at his funeral. Technically, this was a viewing or a memorial, not a funeral. He'd died and was being laid to rest within days. I'd almost missed the announcement.

I faced Bristol so she could see that I wasn't smug. I was relieved, dammit. Danny Cartwright had been a raging alcoholic who'd made rash, uneducated decisions that had gotten people hurt and made his cattle sick.

Bristol's pale-green eyes flashed. No one had eyes like her. I didn't have to travel around the world like my globe-trotting brother to know. She looked at me like she was calling my bullshit each time—and she probably was. Polite and demure were not qualities given to her by her piece-of-shit father. God knew her mother hadn't stuck around long enough to impart anything but grief.

Bristol was brash, insensitive, and blunt as fuck. She was a thorn in my side and now she controlled her ranch and land— and might prove more ruthless than her dad.

"Paying my respects, Bristol Jane."

Another spark of fire in those rare gems. She hated when I added her middle name. I used to do it as a kid. Mama used to call her that and I'd continued to do it afterward. Once I realized it irritated her, I never let up.

Bristol put her hands on her trim hips. She wasn't dressed up any more than I was. Well-worn blue jeans that hugged her athletic figure and a black long-sleeved shirt. The girl was burying her father, you'd think she'd wear a dress—but no. I'd never seen Bristol in a dress. Never. But maybe trousers and a nice blouse? Did she even own those? Or did she think her father wasn't even worth a dry cleaning bill?

She lifted her pointed chin. "You didn't respect Pop and you don't respect me. So you can go."

She shifted, and her cowboy boots, the same ones I was sure she'd worn this morning for chores, scraped against the wood floor of the funeral home. Her gaze darted around the empty space. I doubted anyone else was going to arrive. No one had liked Danny. The only person who'd given him their unfailing loyalty—or loyalty of any kind—was his daughter and I couldn't figure out why. Blood ties? Pride? Or was she just like him? She could be mean as hell.

"People pay respects, Bristol Jane, even if they didn't get along."

She tilted her head, her orange hair swaying. "Is that what you call our family feud? Your grandparents stole our mineral rights because they 'didn't get along'? Your family calls the police on mine because we 'didn't get along'? You come to a funeral home like it's a petting zoo because we 'didn't get along'?"

"I don't know. Is that why you didn't come to my mom's funeral?"

She reared her head back like I'd slapped her and I'd never raised a hand to a woman in my life. Even my heifers got spoiled. "I was eight, asshole."

"Swearing in church is never recommended."

She looked at me like I couldn't figure out how to chew bubble gum and walk at the same time. "It's a funeral home."

So it was. "When's the funeral?" Fighting with Bristol used to be something I looked forward to, like a hobby I rarely got to engage in, but lately it was tiring. I only had a couple of months before I had to secure the trust so she didn't get it and then I could forget she'd ever existed.

I could forget that we used to meet where her land bumped up against mine and crawl through the hills like explorers in new territory. I could forget that I'd helped her name their new dog and I'd held her hand when she'd cried after her dad had run that dog over on one of his many drunken trips home from the bar. I could forget how long I'd looked for her at Mom's funeral and how she'd never shown.

"There isn't a funeral." Bitterness laced

her voice and she clenched her jaw. "I didn't even want this—*Pop*. He didn't want this."

That surprised me. I'd ask more, but she wouldn't tell me anyway.

I glanced around. The coffin lid was closed and I wasn't surprised, and yet I was. Danny had looked more and more haggard every time I'd seen him. Yellowish skin without an ounce of fat, bags under his eyes, more missing teeth each time, breath reeking of stale booze, and a body long overdue for a meeting with a bar of soap. His clothes hadn't been in much better shape.

Bristol was right and I'd never tell her. I'd come partly to make sure the boogeyman was dead. I could blame curiosity too. I had wondered how Bristol was taking her dad's death. The obituary hadn't said how he'd died, but we all knew. A liver could only take so much. Any living thing around Danny Cartwright could only take so much.

Bristol glared at me, her arms not quite crossed, but more hugging herself.

A tendril of concern snaked through my gut. Was she doing okay?

I shook my head and she narrowed her eyes, her lips lifting in a half sneer. Mean as always. What the fuck was I still doing here?

"I'll see you around then." I tipped my head, stuffed my cowboy hat on my head, and walked outside without looking back. I didn't have to in order to feel the lick of her hot gaze between my shoulder blades, likely wishing she had her rifle sighted on that spot instead.

The bitter wind kicked around my body, picking up loose snow. Each footstep sent up a flurry. This winter had been a hard one and it didn't look like it was stopping anytime soon.

I shivered and tucked my face into my Carhartt coat. Mama had always joked that she hoped the snow was melted by my birthday.

My summer birthday. My *twenty-ninth* birthday.

I didn't have much time. Bristol would get every cent of my trust if I didn't marry by then. Mama had told me that Bristol was like a daughter to her and if she could ever find a way to raise her instead of Danny, she would. But after she'd died, after the way Bristol had acted, like my mother had never existed?

I wouldn't let her get a damn cent.

ABOUT THE AUTHOR

Marie Johnston writes paranormal and contemporary romance and has collected several awards in both genres. Before she was a writer, she was a microbiologist. Depending on the situation, she can be oddly unconcerned about germs or weirdly phobic. She's also a licensed medical technician and has worked as a public health microbiologist and as a lab tech in hospital and clinic labs. Marie's been a volunteer EMT, a college instructor, a security guard, a phlebotomist, a hotel clerk, and a coffee pourer in a bingo hall. All fodder for a writer!! She has four kids, an old cat, and a puppy that's bigger than half her kids.

mariejohnstonwriter.com

Follow me: